RIVER OF BONES

A WOLF LAKE THRILLER

DAN PADAVONA

GET A FREE BOOK!

I'm a pretty nice guy once you look past the grisly images in my head. Most of all, I love connecting with awesome readers like you.

Join my VIP Reader Group and get a FREE serial killer thriller for your Kindle.

Get My Free Book

www.danpadavona.com/thriller-readers-vip-group/

1

SUNDAY, AUGUST 9TH 9:20 P.M.

The headlamps of Thomas Shepherd's F-150 illuminated the sign welcoming guests to Wolf Lake State Park. He pulled onto the shoulder beside a scenic overlook and descended the gorge trail. A flashlight pierced the darkness. The man in the gorge was state park ranger Darren Holt, his friend and neighbor. The ranger's blue Silverado parked a hundred feet down the dirt access road from Thomas's truck.

"Down here, Sheriff," Darren called from the gorge.

Thomas was still getting used to the sheriff moniker. Technically, he was interim sheriff of Nightshade County, a collection of sleepy villages around the Finger Lakes in upstate New York. Less than a month ago, his mentor, Stewart Gray, stepped down as sheriff at sixty. Thomas once served as an intern under Gray for the County Sheriff's Department during high school.

He pushed aside a tangle of brush and squeezed between the trees, his own flashlight cutting through the gloom. Night sounds sang to the starlit sky as his boots slogged across soggy ground. Brushing the unruly, sand-colored hair out of his eyes, he felt out of sorts. The evening before a day shift, he always finished working around the house before eight, settled down with a book for ninety minutes, then climbed into bed at precisely nine-thirty. Breaking the pattern made him skittish, a trait common to people with Asperger's.

The phone call had pulled Thomas away from the new Rachel Caine novel at eight-fifty. Someone discovered human bones on state park land. The park butted up against Thomas's lakeside property.

The falls roared to his left, though he couldn't see the water through the trees. He leaped over an embankment and landed beside the water. Spray from the waterfall soaked his face and chilled his flesh, despite the humid summer night.

Darren Holt stood a head taller than Thomas. A former Syracuse police officer, the dark-haired ranger had retired from the daily grind and accepted the state park position. Darren lived on state park grounds in a log cabin, a fifteen-minute hike from the A-Frame Thomas owned.

"It looks like I pulled you out of bed," said Darren.

"Not quite. An hour later, and I'd have fallen asleep."

"No rest for the weary when you're the big cheese."

"So I'm the big cheese now? Coming from the lord emperor of state parks, that's saying something."

"How's the sheriff life treating you?"

Thomas glanced at Darren from the corner of his eye.

"*Interim* sheriff."

After Sheriff Gray put in a good word for Thomas, the county commissioner had appointed Thomas as interim sheriff to fill the vacant position.

"As if you won't win the election."

"Never count your chickens before they hatch."

"The election is in November, and you're running unopposed."

"So far. Anyhow, where are these human remains?"

The ranger scratched at day-old scruff and pointed toward the creek bed, the stars dancing across the water.

"A hiker descended the gorge trail and followed the creek bed for a quarter-mile," Darren said, swatting a mosquito with his baseball cap. "Hikers aren't allowed this far off the trail, because the creek floods after we get a heavy rain."

"It thundered like hell Friday night."

"The water came up fast and flooded the gorge, and the flow strengthened enough to scour the creek bed. Forty-eight hours later, our hiker got the bright idea to check out the damage and came across bones embedded in the mud."

"You're certain they're human?"

"They're human, all right. There's a skull buried in the dirt about fifty feet from where he found the bone."

Two more flashlights cut down the trail.

"That must be Virgil."

Virgil Harbough was the Nightshade County Medical Examiner. At sixty-two, the frail and grayed medical examiner had become a familiar face in Thomas's life. It seemed a dead body surfaced every month, as if part of some strange ritual. Virgil struggled through the brush. Supporting Virgil by the elbow was a russet-haired woman fresh out of medical school. Claire Brookins had joined the coroner's office three weeks ago.

"Sheriff," Virgil said, shrugging Claire off his elbow. "Good evening, Ranger Holt."

"Thanks for coming out, Virgil."

"We need to stop meeting under these circumstances." Virgil caught his breath. "You said something about human remains."

"Over here," Darren said, motioning them forward.

Thomas settled his light on the pale bone jutting out of the earth as Virgil knelt down for closer inspection. Claire pulled a brush out of her kit before Virgil stopped her.

"Don't touch anything. Let's get an idea of what we're dealing with first."

"It's human, right?" Darren asked.

"Oh, it's definitely human." Virgil rose on rickety legs and surveyed the land. "The question is, how long has this bone been here. Sometimes people find skeletal remains because they're standing on an abandoned cemetery. It's amazing how many forgotten people are buried under our feet. But nobody in their right mind would dig a graveyard along the river." He made a sweeping gesture with his arm. "This whole area is a flood plain. In rainy seasons, the river expands to the base of the ridge. That's why trees can't get a foothold until you move up the hill."

"And that explains why nobody found the bones until now," Thomas said. "The water dug them out. Any way to determine how long they've been here?"

"I know someone who can," Claire said, drawing their attention. With everyone staring at her, she fidgeted and cleared her throat. "Doctor Stone, from SUNY Oswego."

"Never heard of him," said Virgil.

"Well, he's a she, to begin with." Virgil clamped his mouth shut. "Dr. Astrid Stone is a forensic anthropologist with a doctorate from Mercyhurst. She teaches as an adjunct professor at Oswego. If you want answers about this skeleton and how long it's been in the ground, she'll give them to you."

Thomas moved closer to Claire.

"How soon can we get Dr. Stone to Wolf Lake?"

"I'll make a call," Claire said, glancing at Virgil for approval. He nodded. "If she's in Oswego for the summer, we can have her here by morning."

While Virgil and Claire photographed the remains, Thomas set evidence markers along the creek. The water rushed a few steps away. If another storm came through, the creek would swallow the shallow grave. He stopped beside the skull and glanced over Virgil's shoulder. It was a partial skull, half the head sticking out of the dirt as though the person died screaming. Bits of fractured bone gleamed under the flashlight. He could tell from the size and shape this wasn't a child. But whether the skull belonged to a male or female, teenager or senior, he didn't know. Studying skeletal structure in a lab or textbook was one thing. Identifying victims in the field was quite another.

Thomas noticed Darren staring at him from the trail. While Virgil and Claire worked, Thomas climbed the embankment.

"What's on your mind?"

Darren folded his arms.

"Remember last spring when I told you the Harmon Kings were using the state park to transport drugs?"

"You pinned the trafficking on LeVar."

Darren had blamed LeVar Hopkins, the former enforcer for the Harmon Kings gang, for murdering a teenage prostitute. After Darren asked out LeVar's sister, Raven, Darren and LeVar became friends. Now LeVar lived in the lakeside guest house behind Thomas's A-Frame. Raven worked as a private investigator in the village.

"And I still feel guilty about accusing LeVar. But I was right about the Kings moving drugs through the state park. I'm positive they use the lake and the trails after dark."

"You think the Kings had something to do with these bones?"

"The creek bed and lake are great places to dump bodies. Had it not been for the storm and the hiker moving off trail, we wouldn't have found the remains."

Thomas glanced at Virgil and Claire. They hunched over the unearthed grave, the bones scattered along the creek bed where the flood swept them downstream. Thomas had already dealt with two serial killers since returning from Los Angeles. He'd worked as a detective with the LAPD before a gunshot sidelined him. The idea of another murderer stalking Nightshade County twisted his insides into a knot. Since spring, everyone in the village locked their doors and windows at night, the residents walking on a razor's edge of panic. It seemed inconceivable ghastly events like these occurred inside the idyllic lake community. Thomas removed his hat, wondering if he'd ever get used to wearing the sheriff's badge. He cleared the sweat from his eyes.

"What do you intend to do?"

"I was poking around on the internet last night and found those automatic cameras hunters and scientists use to photograph wildlife. If I place them on the trails, maybe I'll figure out who keeps sneaking around the park after dark."

Thomas hoped Darren's plan would work. Nightshade County couldn't stomach another killer.

But a more troubling thought floated inside his head. He was good with numbers and committed significant dates to memory. Since he returned from Los Angeles to join the Nightshade County Sheriff's Department, he'd memorized the missing persons database for the entire county, going back ten years. Six years ago, seventeen-year-old Skye Feron vanished during the summer before her senior year at Wolf Lake High. Her parents never gave up the search. Every year, the local newspaper wrote a story about the missing girl and fished for answers to the six-year mystery.

Did these bones belong to Skye Feron?

2

MONDAY, AUGUST 9TH 6:45 A.M.

The red sky bled through the canopy like a silent warning. Thomas sipped coffee from his thermos and watched a large-boned woman with slate-gray hair and a strong chin lead a team of graduate students into the creek bed. He hadn't met Dr. Astrid Stone yet, and by the way she barked orders at her students, he felt it was wise to give the crew space and stay out of her way.

Deeper in the gorge, Darren searched the trail with the careful precision of a former police officer. Deputy Tristan Lambert, who stood a hair taller than Darren, watched Stone's crew from beside the creek. Lambert grew up in Minnesota and joined the army before accepting the deputy's position in Nightshade County. In Thomas's opinion, Lambert had all the makings of a fine sheriff. But the deputy showed no interest in running.

The doctor's team fanned out around the bones, Stone's scoff loud enough to travel halfway up the ridge as she assessed the myriad of footprints moving through the gorge.

"Someone already disturbed the scene," she said, shooting a glare at Lambert. "It's as if a shrewdness of apes trampled through. If a single bone is broken because some fat-footed oaf didn't bother to look where he was stepping, I'll have his hide."

Lambert glanced up the ridge at Thomas. The sheriff shrugged back at his deputy. A door slammed from the access road when Virgil and Claire returned. Virgil led the way until he observed Stone snapping at her subordinates. Then he fell in behind Claire. Stone's face softened when she recognized Virgil's assistant.

"Ah, Ms. Brookins. Finally, someone who understands how important it is to preserve a dig site."

"Dr. Stone," Claire said, high-stepping over the branch of a pricker bush. "I worried you wouldn't remember my name."

"Nonsense. I remember all my students. At least the ones who show up for class on time."

Stone shot a withering glare at a male graduate student with thick glasses and a bucket hat pulled over his head. The boy's face reddened.

Dr. Stone divided her crew into specific tasks. The pudgy female assisting Stone worked on the remains with a brush, while the two boys carefully dug into the earth and sifted the dirt through a screen. Once the work was underway, Stone's demeanor lost its edge, though Thomas believed she'd explode if anyone crossed her. Straightening his shoulders, Thomas trudged across the muddy bank and approached the doctor, careful to remain outside her work radius.

"Thank you for coming on short notice, Dr. Stone. I'm Sheriff Shepherd."

Stone sniffed.

"You may run the county, Sheriff. But I'm judge, jury, and executioner at a dig site. Your team disturbed the evidence. I'll ask you once to stand aside and let my students work."

"I wouldn't dream of interfering."

Lambert huffed.

"We're working together. What makes her think she's important? We're capable of digging through the mud on our own."

Stone set her shovel aside and rose.

"Deputy, there are 700,000 active law enforcement officers in the

United States and only one-hundred forensic anthropologists. I would never tell you how to do your job. But one of us here is replaceable, and one isn't. Do the math."

Lambert opened his mouth, and Thomas shook his head at him. Thomas shuffled closer and knelt for a better look as Stone used a brush to remove dirt from the skull.

"What can you tell me anything about this person?"

"I'll reconstruct the skull inside the lab. But this appears to be a female."

Thomas felt his stomach drop. A part of him wished it was male so he could rule out Skye Feron.

"How can you tell?"

"Females have smoother skulls than males. We're not as hard headed." She knocked her knuckles against her forehead. "Until I collect the fragments and piece the puzzle together, I won't know for sure." She ran the brush along the brow line. "Males have a more pronounced brow than this specimen displays. I'm missing too much of the jaw to make a determination. But male jaws jut more than female jaws. The female homo sapiens evolved. Which is to say males are closer to apes." Stone narrowed her brow. "And that explains why my dig site looks trampled. Now, if I may draw your attention to the pelvis my assistants removed from the mud, so your heavy booted deputy wouldn't crush it, you'll note this pelvis offers space for the birth canal. Again, preliminary signs point to a female. Have you lost any women in the last several years, Sheriff?"

Thomas shuffled his feet.

"One."

"For her family's sake, let's hope this isn't her."

"Any idea how she died?"

"Not yet. She could have fallen into the gorge, drowned in the creek, or electrocuted herself in a storm. There's no way to make that determination from scattered bones. Please, Sheriff. Allow my team to work. I'll give you answers after we get her back to the lab. Ms. Brookins? Dr. Harbough? If you'll kindly lend your assistance."

Claire and Virgil gave each other a cautious glance and moved to aid the team. Thomas spoke into his radio and raised Deputy Veronica Aguilar at the station. Aguilar was a diminutive, short-haired deputy with a bodybuilder's physique. Last April, Aguilar accompanied Thomas to the Magnolia Dance, Wolf Lake's annual spring festival. Before then, Thomas had never seen Aguilar in a dress. He was accustomed to her concocting protein smoothies and making crude jokes, the office blender whirring inside the kitchen.

"Aguilar here."

"Aguilar, it's Thomas."

"How are things at the state park, Sheriff?"

Thomas wished she'd call him by his first name as she had before the county commissioner tagged him as interim sheriff. Since he claimed Gray's position, Aguilar had become distant. She didn't fire humorous jabs at him all day like she used to.

"It looks like we'll be here a while. Preliminary indications are we're dealing with a female."

"Age?"

"No determination made yet. I want you to go through the missing persons database. Expand your search to surrounding counties. Give me a list of women who disappeared in the last ten years."

"Roger that."

After the radio call ended, Lambert strolled to Thomas and glared at the workers, his strong forearms folded over his chest.

"That one has an attitude bigger than Texas," Lambert said, lifting his chin at Dr. Stone.

"Give them space. If she bites your head off, remember how important she is to this investigation."

"You think it's that girl who went missing several years back? The one whose parents swear she's still out there?"

"Skye Feron."

"That's her."

Thomas moved his eyes across the woods. The shadows deepened inside the forest, blotting out the sun. A shiver rolled through his body when he pictured the seventeen-year-old girl fleeing an unseen attacker toward the creek. Maybe she stumbled over the rocks in the dark, allowing the killer to close in.

"I hope this isn't Skye Feron. But Dr. Stone seems certain the skull belongs to a female." Thomas searched the woods for Darren. The forest ranger had circled up to the ridge trail. "Darren believes the Harmon Kings are running drugs through the park. This is a good place to make somebody disappear. Could be we're dealing with a gang hit. Darren wants cameras inside the park, ones that will trigger if someone walks by."

"Trail cameras," Lambert said, nodding. "I'll talk to him. You don't want to go cheap with a trail camera. The good ones have night vision and fast triggers. Anything wanders by—a bear, raccoon, or Bigfoot—and the camera will capture it."

A branch snapped inside the forest, pulling their gazes. It might have been an early morning hiker.

But sometimes a killer returned to the scene of his crime.

3

Chelsey Byrd lowered the windows on her green Honda Civic and invited the musty, humid morning into the car. The new car smell still clung to the interior, and this Civic replaced the car she'd wrecked chasing Mark Benson last month after Benson kidnapped Chelsey's partner, Raven Hopkins. Same model, same color. She was a creature of habit.

Half the home improvement store's parking lot sat under water. Though storms Friday night brought flooding rains, poor drainage was to blame here. Barricades cordoned off the left side of the lot, forcing vehicles to crowd together on the right. That was an advantage for Chelsey, as the tightly packed vehicles allowed her to blend in. But people kept walking past her Civic, forcing her to set the binoculars and camera aside.

She peered through the binoculars and swept the storefront for Herb Reid. The overweight dirt bag was suing Middleton Construction after he hurt his back on the job. His boss, Carl Middleton, hired Wolf Lake Consulting to investigate Reid for worker's compensation fraud. She hated defending a creep like Carl Middleton. The owner of Middleton Construction became a suspect in last month's murders before Thomas determined Thea Barlow, Father Fowler's assistant at St. Mary's Church, had killed Lincoln Ramsey and Cecilia Bond.

Thinking of Thomas caused Chelsey's chest to clench. She'd dated Thomas through high school before major depression crippled her. After she'd pushed away everyone she cared about, Chelsey traveled from one failed relationship to the next, never staying in the same town for longer than six months. Her circular life brought her back to Wolf Lake, where she founded the private investigation firm. When Thomas returned to the village, she avoided him, worried she'd relapse into depression if their relationship rekindled. After she found the courage to try again with Thomas, she saw him embracing his neighbor, Naomi Mourning, beside the lake. So she gave up and ended the day with too much wine.

Setting the binoculars aside, she studied her reflection in the mirror. The circles under her eyes darkened each day. She couldn't recall the last time she exercised, nor could she explain why she appeared soft and fat in the mirror despite her drawn cheeks. Instead of brushing out her hair, she'd thrown a baseball cap on her head this morning after waking up late. Her palm ached from slamming the snooze button too many times.

A bearded, rotund man shuffled between the automatic doors with a cart stuffed with tools. Chelsey raised the camera and zoomed in on her quarry. False alarm. It wasn't Herb Reid. This was her sixth day attempting to pin fraud on Reid. It was funny how the man hobbled like a ninety-five-year-old after knee replacement surgery whenever he emerged from the doctor's office, yet had an easy bounce to his step when nobody else was looking. That he was at the home improvement store sounded an alarm in Chelsey's head. People with ruined backs didn't rush to Home Depot to complete a major repair project.

The heat built inside the car and turned the interior into a kiln. She considered raising the windows and turning on the AC, but didn't want to waste gas. The needle sat a tick above empty. Not that she couldn't afford fuel. Chelsey procrastinated about everything, even simple tasks like filling the gas tank. She never went out. Even Raven gave up asking

Chelsey to join her at Hattie's on the weekend. She reached for the Coke bottle and took a swig. The carbonation hit her nose and made her cough, causing her to spit cola down her shirt. God, she was a mess. After the coughing fit, she guzzled the remnants and tossed the empty bottle into the backseat. She groped for another bottle. Soft drinks weren't healthy. Hell, she wasn't even thirsty. She just needed some way to pass the time. Next, she dug into a bag of barbecue potato chips and found only crumbs. She scooped the residue into her palm and shoveled it into her mouth. When your world fell apart, you clung to familiar comforts.

In the row across from hers, a woman in a sun hat loaded mums into a Jeep. The open trunk blocked Chelsey's sight line to the store. Cursing under her breath, Chelsey tapped her foot as the woman rearranged the potted flowers. The pots were all the same. Why did the order matter? Chelsey's hand poised over the horn, prepared to blast the incompetent lady with an angry honk, when she finally closed the trunk and backed out of the parking space.

Chelsey spotted Herb Reid pushing a cart with a wonky front wheel through the parking lot. The bad wheel kept pulling the cart to the right, forcing him to overcompensate with his back and legs. Guess the back wasn't bothering him. A boxed lawn mower shifted on the cart. The push mower had a cutting width of twenty inches and enough horsepower to chew through a forest. How was the injured man going to lift the box into his pickup truck? Chelsey shot a dozen photographs in rapid succession as Reid weaved the cart between two vans and emerged behind his rusted, beaten Chevy.

Chelsey set the camera aside and recorded video with her phone. The supposedly injured man hoisted the box without bending his knees, shrugged it into the bed, and abandoned the cart in an empty parking space. Oh, this was good. She had all the photographs and video she needed to prove fraud. It didn't make her happy knowing Carl Middleton would benefit. But the law was the law, and Herb Reid wanted to fleece the system.

Reid jammed the key into the lock and paused. His head swung to Chelsey's Civic as she raised the windows. The man's mouth twisted into an angry rictus before he stomped in her direction. Dammit. He spotted her.

Chelsey slipped the phone inside her purse and pretended to check her makeup in the mirror. Not that she wore makeup this morning. As she fiddled with her hair, he kept coming. A meaty fist pounded against her window. She raised her palms as if she had no idea what Reid wanted.

"Lower the window, honey. I know what you're up to."

After she refused to comply, he pounded harder.

"Hey, I've seen you following me all week. Did Middleton put you up to this? Lower the goddamn window, or I'll drag you out of the car."

Chelsey pressed the button on her side console. Humid air poured inside the car as Reid leaned his forearms on the sill. She looked at him over her sunglasses.

"Mr. Reid, I'm warning you to step away from my car."

"Or what?"

Good question. She knew how to handle a gun, and she wasn't afraid to take down a female suspect. But she wasn't a rugged fighter like Raven. Reid would squash Chelsey like a grape if she challenged him.

"Or I'll press charges. You're harassing me."

He leaned his head back and laughed.

"That's a good one. You follow me around town, taking your little pictures, and I'm harassing you?" He pointed at the DSLR camera on the passenger seat. "Give me the camera."

"I don't think so."

"Lady, if you don't give me the camera, I'll take it and smash it against the blacktop.

"I'd like to see you try."

Mistake. Never test a man with nothing to lose.

Reid reached inside the car. She clutched his forearm and prevented him from snatching the camera. The man was even stronger than he looked. It was all she could do to keep hold of his arm as he tugged and shoved, squashing her between the seat and the steering wheel.

"You bitch. I want the pictures, and I want them now."

As she wrestled him, her head struck the steering wheel. The car interior spun, and her vision blurred. She felt her heart spin out of control, and suddenly she couldn't catch her breath. The car seemed to fill with water, Chelsey drowning beneath the current as they fought. She grabbed her chest and peered in the mirror. Her face turned purple, and her heart smashed against her chest at an alarming rate.

He backed away and glared.

"What the hell is wrong with you?"

She opened her mouth. The words refused to come. Panicked, she pointed at her chest and glanced at him with imploring eyes. This was it. She was going to die in a sunbaked car, surveilling a fraudulent loser. Reid swung his head left and right.

"I didn't do shit to you," he said. "You can't blame me if you have a heart attack."

Was she having a heart attack? He searched for witnesses. Seeing none, he sprinted for his truck, gunned the motor, and squealed out of the parking lot.

Chelsey opened the door and stumbled out of the car. Her hands and knees landed upon the scalding blacktop as she sucked air into her lungs. Chelsey's chest heaved, and the soda and potato chips spewed from her mouth. She collapsed and curled into a ball, the unforgiving sun torching her. Footsteps approached as a woman yelled for help.

Chelsey wiped her lips and cried.

Raven Hopkins tied her braids into a ponytail and adjusted the cap atop her head. She'd spent too much time in the gym working her upper body and ignoring her legs, and now her hamstrings protested as she climbed the Wolf Lake State Park ridge trail. Darren glanced over his shoulder and grinned, clearly enjoying that she was out of breath and struggling to keep pace. Usually, it was the other way around. If he accompanied Raven to the gym or ran beside her, he was the one out of breath. But she didn't care. She was happy to spend the day with the ranger and relieved to see him smile. He'd been a fitful mess since the hiker discovered human bones hidden in his park.

"Can't keep up, hotshot?"

"Don't slow down and let me catch you," she said, glaring at him in warning.

She thanked the gods when he paused atop a steep hill and lifted himself onto a boulder. He scooted over to give her room and helped her climb up. Their legs dangled over the side, the cooling breeze replenishing her energy reserves. Tall pines loomed over the trail while dappled sunlight poured through the needles and painted textured patterns over the earth. Everything here smelled green and perfect, like Christmas with humidity.

"Happy you took the day off?"

"I am," she said, propping an elbow on her knee.

Raven had three weeks of vacation time to burn before winter and didn't want to waste it. More so, she needed time away from Chelsey. She loved her boss and friend. But Chelsey was impossible to be around and had been since last month. Surly and forever glowering, Chelsey made work miserable.

Habit tempted Raven to call work and check into the Herb Reid investigation. She forced herself not to. Today was Raven's day with Darren, and she didn't wish to be anywhere else. Though she'd known the ranger in passing since last year, they'd only started dating recently. Now she couldn't imagine life without Darren. He made her laugh, and the only time she felt safe and content was when she was around him. Ever since Mark Benson and Damian Ramos kidnapped Raven, she'd become anxious whenever she was alone, always sensing someone watching from the shadows. The worst times were when she was at the office, a converted two-bedroom, single-story house that creaked and groaned whenever the wind blew.

"I still can't believe it," Darren said, peering west through the trees. He was talking about the skeleton. She'd hoped to keep him distracted with exercise and small talk. "How do I reconcile this in my head? It's my responsibility to keep people safe once they set foot in my park."

"This isn't on you. That body predated your arrival by several years."

"God, I hope a kid didn't see those bones."

"Did they identify the victim?"

"Last I heard, the forensic anthropologist brought the remains to the medical examiner's office. They're reconstructing the skull first, then the rest of the skeleton. Even then, I can't imagine how they'll identify the victim." A shiver rolled through his shoulders. "All this time, I walked these trails and lived on state park grounds, and a dead person lay beneath the mud beside Lucifer Falls. The falls get thousands of visitors every year."

"Kids party in the gorge."

"I'm aware. I've cleaned up after them."

"Perhaps some kid got drunk and fell in."

Darren scrunched his face up.

"That's a comforting thought."

"I'm just saying we can't jump to conclusions about gang hits and murderers in the forest."

"I hear you. But I still want to speak to LeVar."

Raven removed the cap and brushed the hair from her eyes.

"LeVar left the Kings in April. He had nothing to do with this."

"But he'll know if the Kings trafficked drugs through the park, or dumped bodies."

"LeVar never killed anyone. That darkness isn't inside my brother."

Darren hopped down from the boulder and offered his hand. She studied him for a moment before accepting his aid. Her thighs screamed now that she was on her feet again.

"I believe in LeVar. But he spent time around some bad guys."

"Don't remind me."

He rubbed his neck.

"Ready to call it a day?"

"I have another two miles in me, Ranger Holt."

"Sure you do."

"I mean it. Don't slow down on my account."

He draped an arm over her shoulder.

"How about we walk back to my cabin and pull the curtains over the windows?"

Heat flickered through her body.

"That's my kind of exercise. Lead the way."

Darren led Raven off trail and through the woods, taking a shortcut back to the cabin. Dried leaves crunched underfoot, and chipmunks scurried in their wake. Ten minutes later, Raven recognized where they were. A line of cabins poked out of the trees, where families enjoyed the forest on a pristine summer day. The ranger's cabin sat at the end of the row, a stone's throw from the welcome center. As their hiking shoes scuffed through the grass, a perturbed voice called from behind.

"Ranger, if I may have a word with you."

Darren swung around. The man waddling past the charcoal grills was on the wrong side of two-hundred pounds. The wide-brimmed hat covering his bald head hadn't prevented his face from turning pink beneath the sun. He wore tacky shorts covered with an explosion of plaid.

"Who's that?" Raven whispered.

"Paul Phipps," Darren said from the corner of his mouth. "He rented cabin six with his wife. They both have a lot of *Karen* in them."

"They always wish to speak with the manager?"

"And I'm the manager." Darren cleared his throat as Phipps strode to them. "Mr. Phipps. Everything satisfactory with cabin six?"

"I should think not. My wife had two-hundred dollars stolen from her wallet. What sort of establishment do you run here?"

Darren flashed a look of concern.

"You keep your cabin locked while you're away, I hope."

"Of course I keep it locked. Did someone paint *buffoon* on my face?"

Raven coughed into her hand so Phipps wouldn't see her laughing.

"You're certain she didn't misplace the money?"

Phipps drew in an exasperated breath.

"The cash never left her wallet until now."

"When did this happen?"

Phipps yanked the hat from his head and slapped it against his leg.

"How should I know? It could have happened while we were asleep, or while we sat beside the lake. Don't you have security cameras?"

"We don't have issues with thievery inside the state park."

"You could have fooled me." Phipps placed his hands on his hips.

"I suggest you stop wasting time and phone the police. Every minute wasted makes it easier for the thief to get away."

Raven shared a glance with Darren. If someone stole money from the wife's wallet—and Raven wasn't convinced Phipps's wife hadn't misplaced the cash—the thief wouldn't stick around. Before Darren replied, a sheriff's department cruiser pulled in front of the welcome center. Phipps gave Darren a confused look.

"They're working on another case in the park," Darren explained.

"Well, this is the last time my wife and I visit Wolf Lake State Park. Seems the park is nothing but a criminal activity playground."

Deputy Lambert, frazzled and sheepish, crossed the lot to where Darren and Raven stood.

"How was your morning with the dragon lady?" Darren asked.

Lambert shook his head, as if clearing cobwebs.

"I'm glad it's over. They cleaned up the dig site and brought the evidence back to the lab." The deputy's eyes fell upon Phipps. "Is there a problem?"

Phipps threw up his hands, ready to boil over before Darren cut in and told Lambert about the stolen money.

"And we need to investigate now, while the crime scene is still fresh," said Phipps, drawing an eye roll from Darren.

Raven thought Phipps watched too many crime scene investigation television shows.

Lambert interviewed Phipps's wife and checked the lock on the door. With Phipps hanging over his shoulder, Lambert scrutinized the windows, searching for signs someone broke inside. He found none. When Lambert asked Phipps to fill out a report, the camper's face turned beet red.

"That's all you can do? Why should I waste my time filling out a report, if you can't find the thief who stole my wife's money? Cops." He sniffed. "We'd be better off with a private investigator."

"Or Matlock," Darren said under his breath.

Raven snorted.

"Raven is a private investigator," Lambert said, eager to push Phipps off on someone else.

Oh, great.

"Consider yourself hired," Phipps said, extending his hand.

Raven accepted it with trepidation.

"You want a private investigator to find your money?"

"And to catch the guilty party."

"You understand our rate is fifty dollars per hour?"

"I'll pay whatever it takes. I want this rapscallion caught."

"Rapscallion?"

"Burglar. Thief."

"Mr. Phipps, a day's worth of investigating will cost more than the money lost."

"That's not the point. We can't let thieves run rampant in a civilized society. If the sheriff can't catch him, it's up to you to uphold justice."

Raven sighed.

"All right, Mr. Phipps. Let's get started."

THE AIR POURING through the blower chilled Chelsey's skin inside the doctor's office. Her gown stopped above her knees, and despite her efforts, she'd buttoned the back crooked, causing the gown to hang off one shoulder. A stack of magazines sat on a corner table—People, Time, Sports Illustrated, and something about parenting. Pamphlets on the wall promised to help her cope with heart disease, stroke, and various forms of cancer. She looked away when her pulse thrummed.

A knock on the door caused her to flinch. She tugged at the gown hem as it rode up her thighs. The doctor was in his thirties with short, sallow hair and glasses with designer frames.

"Ms. Byrd," he said, staring at his clipboard. "How are you feeling now?"

"A little better."

"Heartbeat normal?"

"It speeds up sometimes."

"Chest pains."

"No."

He clasped his hands at his waist.

"Tell me how it feels when your heart speeds up."

Chelsey fiddled with the gown and moved her eyes around the room.

"My skin turns clammy, and it's hard to concentrate."

"Nausea?"

"Yes, and chills."

"I see. You could have a touch of the flu. There's a summer strain running through the community this year. That would explain the nausea and chills."

"But not the rapid heart rate."

He removed the stethoscope from around his neck and placed it against her heart.

"Breathe normally," he said, sliding the chest piece across her flesh. "Everything sounds normal." He moved the chest piece to her back. "Take a deep breath and let it out. Excellent."

He slipped the stethoscope around his neck and scanned her results.

"So you're not having a heart attack. The electrocardiogram showed a normal heart rhythm. No murmurs, nothing to be concerned about."

"But my pulse rate had to be over 150 when I collapsed."

"According to your notes, you're a private investigator."

"That's right."

"And you had a run in with a...suspect of some sort."

"The person I was investigating, yes."

"Were you injured?"

"No."

"Moments of extreme stress can cause your heart to race. You work in a stressful profession. If I had to guess, anxiety caused your episode."

"How can you be sure?"

"The ECG shows your heart is functioning well. Blood pressure is a tad high compared to your last exam. But that's because of your stressful morning. Has anything like this happened before?"

Chelsey rubbed her eyes.

"No."

"Any history of depression." Cold rippled through her body. "Ms. Byrd?"

"That was a long time ago."

"How long ago?"

"When I was eighteen."

The doctor's eyes flashed concern.

"Did you take medication for your depression?"

"Yes."

"When was the last time a doctor prescribed you antidepressants?"

Shrugging, Chelsey glanced at the clock. With Raven taking a vacation day, no one been at the office since morning.

"Twelve, thirteen years ago."

He prompted her for past medications and scribbled notes.

"I'd like to start you on a low dose of an antidepressant."

"No."

"I believe an antidepressant would benefit you."

"I'm not depressed." She said it loud enough for the words to reverberate inside the office. "I didn't mean to raise my voice. But my episode wasn't anything like depression. I couldn't slow my heart."

The doctor paused in thought.

"I'm willing to outfit you with a monitor. You'll wear it for twenty-four hours, and the monitor will record your heart rhythm. Should you have another episode, we'll see what's happening."

"Is it uncomfortable?"

"It's cumbersome. But peace of mind is important."

She picked at her nails.

"Okay."

"All right. You can get dressed. I'll have someone bring your paperwork, and we'll set you up with a monitor."

The door closed, and the sudden quiet shocked her. Somewhere down the hall, voices murmured. Another door opened and closed, and a female doctor greeted a patient.

As Chelsey pulled her clothes on, she was tempted to run from the clinic. Forget the stupid heart monitor. These doctors were incompetent. Maybe she needed a cardiologist, someone who knew what a heart attack looked like. Before she could decide, the physician's assistant entered the room with her papers.

Chelsey chewed her lip. She couldn't face depression again.

5

"Y*ou went through a traumatic experience, Thomas. Give yourself time to heal."*

The temperature feels ten degrees too cold inside Dr. Mandal's office today. As if she turned the air conditioning down to freezing. He rubs the chill off his arms and glares at the clock. Still twenty minutes to go before the appointment ends. The doctor folds her hands in her lap. Her affable demeanor usually relaxes Thomas. It isn't working today. Thomas is a rat pacing a cage.

"Tell me what you see when you close your eyes," Mandal says.

Thomas chews his thumbnail.

"It's dark, and I'm inside my parents' bedroom."

"Are you alone?"

"No, my partner is with me. Deputy Aguilar."

"You speak of her often."

"She's the finest officer I've ever worked with."

"What do you see inside the bedroom?"

Thomas clenches his eyes shut. In the quiet office, his imagination draws him in. And he's there, the drapes an azure tone from the moonlight, the shadows long and razor-edged.

"*Deputy Aguilar has her gun out. There's a noise inside the closet, a moaning sound.*"

"*Good, Thomas. What else?*"

His mind's eye swings around the room. Stops on the two lumps beneath the blankets. The closest is his father. The person beside him should be his mother. But he knows better.

"*My father opens his eyes. He's surprised and angry. Why am I in his bedroom?*"

"*How do you respond?*" *Mandal asks.*

Nothing can thaw the chill running through his blood.

"*I reason with Father. He won't listen.*"

"*Because he's angry you broke into his home.*"

"*Yes. He's trying to wake my mother. The person beside him doesn't respond when he calls my mother's name.*"

The nightmare shifts as he remembers what happened on that horrific night. It's as if a demon raises its bloody claw and snatches reality, twisting it into a grotesque pulp. The gun shakes at the end of his outstretched arms. His father yells at him to get out, cries for his mother to wake up.

The covers move. Slowly peel back to reveal the devil beneath the sheets.

Thomas aims the gun. The sheet stretches and takes a human form... expanding as though it will burst at any second. In the background, Dr. Mandal's voice calls to him. He can't answer. She's drifting away.

"*Get off the bed, Father!*"

He won't listen.

"*Run!*"

Thomas grabs his father's forearm. The brittle bones snap in his grip. The elderly, cancer-stricken man screams out as blood slithers down his arm. Thomas wants to yank his father from the bed and cover him before the evil strikes. He's frozen to the floor, unable to move as the sheet grows toward the ceiling.

The fabric tears.

Thomas opens fire before the monster reveals itself. The gunshots slam the beast into the headboard, splashing blood against the walls. But when the sheet falls away, he doesn't see a mutated version of Thea Barlow.

He sees himself with the knife.

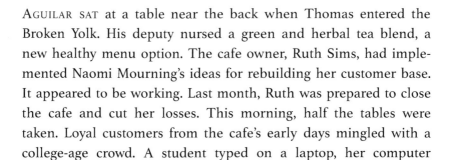

AGUILAR SAT at a table near the back when Thomas entered the Broken Yolk. His deputy nursed a green and herbal tea blend, a new healthy menu option. The cafe owner, Ruth Sims, had implemented Naomi Mourning's ideas for rebuilding her customer base. It appeared to be working. Last month, Ruth was prepared to close the cafe and cut her losses. This morning, half the tables were taken. Loyal customers from the cafe's early days mingled with a college-age crowd. A student typed on a laptop, her computer connected to the internet through the Broken Yolk's new Wi-Fi system.

"Hey, Deputy Dog," LeVar called from behind the counter. Raven's brother had worked for Ruth Sims since late spring. "I've got a fresh glazed donut with your name written on it."

"I'll take a coffee too."

"One step ahead of you. Wait, I can't call you Deputy Dog now that you're sheriff."

"I'm sure you'll think of something, LeVar."

LeVar tapped a finger against his head.

"Trust me, I will."

Thomas carried the donut and coffee to Aguilar's table and took the chair across from hers. She cocked a disappointed eyebrow at his breakfast. Aguilar's mission was to convince Thomas to make better food choices. She wiped the disappointment from her face and smiled.

"Good morning, Sheriff."

"How are you, Aguilar?"

"Why did you want to meet here?"

Thomas scooted the chair forward and set his elbows on the table.

"We don't talk anymore."

"Well, we've been on opposite shifts the last month."

"That's not what I mean." Thomas set his hat down. "Since I filled Sheriff Gray's position, you've barely spoken a word to me."

"I doubt that's true."

Thomas smiled.

"Aguilar, just because I'm interim sheriff doesn't mean you can't break my balls."

"So you want me to make fun of you. That wouldn't be appropriate."

Thomas sat back and took a breath.

"Okay, let's start over. We'll talk about work. What did you find when you searched the missing persons database?"

"A half-dozen women, depending on how many counties we choose to include. I left the list on your desk."

"Thank you. I'll get on it this afternoon." He drummed his fingers on the table as an uncomfortable silence fell between them. Aguilar kept glancing around the room. "So I'm still in therapy with Dr. Mandal."

She sipped her tea.

"How is that going?"

"Better. Since the Thea Barlow shooting, I haven't slept right." Last month, Thomas shot Thea Barlow after the serial killer broke inside his parents' house. Every time he closed his eyes at night, he pictured Barlow's leering grin when she sat up in the bed. Had he not fired his weapon, the psychopath would have stabbed his father. "If Sheriff Gray was in charge, he would have kept me out of the field until Dr. Mandal cleared me. Now I need to self-police."

"I'm sure you'll make the right call."

"I'll appreciate it if you keep me in line. If you think I'm not myself, it's important you tell me."

"I will, but your doctor should make that determination."

"She doesn't see me in the field every day. You do."

She gave an obedient nod. He wished she'd level him with a joke and throw him off his game.

"Anyhow," Thomas said, continuing. "I might be out of the office more than I prefer over the next three months. My father's cancer

progressed, and he's spiraled downward since the attempted murder."
When Aguilar didn't respond, he rapped his knuckles on the table.
"That's where you come in. When I'm out of the office, you're in
charge."

"Me? Why not Lambert?"

"He doesn't want the responsibility. You could run the county,
Aguilar. If you entered the sheriff's race, I'd drop out and vote for
you."

Her cheeks reddened.

"I'm not much of a leader."

"You are in my book."

Aguilar squirmed in her seat.

"I enjoy being a deputy. What's the latest on the unknown
skeleton?"

"Dr. Stone was busy reconstructing the remains at the medical
examiner's office. I expect we'll hear from her soon."

Thomas ran a hand through his hair.

"Something is worrying you," said Aguilar, setting her tea aside.

"I'm afraid we found that missing teenage girl."

"Skye Feron."

"All these years, Skye's parents hoped to find her alive. I can't
imagine how much it will crush them, if we determine the bones
belong to Skye."

"What makes you think it's her?"

"Except for the doctor's preliminary determination that it's a
female skull, not much. Just a sick feeling."

"You know," Aguilar said, nodding at Thomas. "Sheriff Gray
investigated Skye's disappearance."

"I studied his case notes."

"The case predates my arrival. But after working alongside Sheriff
Gray, I can tell you he doesn't put all his thoughts into his case notes."

"What do you mean?"

"If Gray found a piece of evidence suspicious, he might not
include it in his notes unless he had a sound reason to question the
evidence."

"So I should talk to Sheriff Gray."

"That's my recommendation."

Thomas's phone hummed inside his pocket. His eyebrows lifted as he read the message.

"Virgil sent me a text. Dr. Stone reconstructed the skull. It's time to find out if Jane Doe is Skye Feron."

6

TUESDAY, AUGUST 10TH 10:00 A.M.

Sitting at her desk inside Wolf Lake Consulting, Raven tapped a pen against her palm and read over her notes. Yesterday, she'd interviewed a dozen campers about the stolen money. One woman reported a suspicious man pawing around the campgrounds. The suspect turned out to be a maintenance worker fixing a plumbing issue in cabin four. A nine-year-old boy with a face covered with chocolate swore he saw a black man in the forest. Given the boy's father flew a confederate flag on his muscle car, Raven had reason to doubt the child. Still, she noted the sighting. After the interviews, she photographed footprints trailing around the cabins. The prints could have belonged to anyone, and Raven didn't understand how she'd catch the thief. The man was probably long gone by now.

Behind her, the floor groaned. She swung her head around. Her edginess made her feel foolish. What if the courts released Mark Benson and Damian Ramos over a technicality? Would the two men come after Raven?

Scrubbing a hand down her face, she glared at the empty desk beside her. Chelsey should have arrived at nine. Her boss had never been late before last month. Now it was commonplace for Chelsey to wander in at ten or eleven, bleary-eyed and vacant looking. Raven picked up the phone, intent on calling Chelsey, when another noise sent goosebumps down her arms. A scratching sound, like someone dragging fingernails down the window.

She crept into the hallway with her gun on her hip. Stared down the corridor toward the front door where an overgrown branch scraped the siding. She leaned against the wall and clenched her eyes shut. Why was she making herself crazy? Mark Benson and Damian Ramos were behind bars.

In the kitchen, she heated the kettle for a calming tea and pawed through the refrigerator. The three slices of pepperoni pizza were four-days old, and Raven couldn't stomach junk food this early. Behind the soda cans, she found a mixed berry Greek yogurt. She fell into the chair beside the table and spooned the yogurt into her mouth. Her head ached from lack of sleep. Last night, she tossed and turned while her mother snored down the hallway. Raven would never admit to Darren that she'd slept with a night light since the kidnapping. Though the light splashed illumination across the floor, it cast deformed shadows up the wall, morphing every object in the bedroom into a killer with a knife.

After she rinsed the yogurt cup and tossed it into the recycling bin, Raven padded down the hallway and pushed the bedroom door open. Blackout curtains covered the windows, casting the room in perpetual night. This was where Raven or Chelsey slept if work kept them up too late, or one of them needed rest after a long day. A flower print DelValle comforter draped over the bed. Despite the darkness, the bedroom felt homey to Raven. Her boss was a caring person who went the extra mile to ensure neither Raven nor Chelsey suffered because of the long hours. Last December, Raven had crashed in the bedroom after a winter storm iced the roads. Twelve hours later, she'd opened her eyes to Chelsey arriving for work. She hadn't recalled sleeping so soundly in years. On rare occasions, Chelsey brought her tabby, Tigger, to roam the halls and curl up on the bed. The office once felt like a second home to Raven. Now it was a reminder of how far she and Chelsey had drifted apart.

She edged the door shut and returned to the office, hurrying when the phone rang. She answered on the fourth ring and was surprised by Scout Mourning's voice on the other line. Scout had lost her ability to walk after a car accident. The girl and her mother, Naomi, lived on the lake road next door to Thomas Shepherd.

"Hey, Scout. I haven't talked to you in a while."

"Hi, Raven. I was wondering if you talked to Mr. Shepherd about tomorrow's cookout. He's supposed to host with LeVar at the guest house. But since the news broke about that dead person in the state park, I figured he would cancel the cookout."

Last month, Thomas and Darren started a new tradition. They gathered their friends for a barbecue once per week, alternating between the state park and the sheriff's spacious lakeside yard. It was funny how much Raven looked forward to burgers, steaks, and macaroni salad on a summer afternoon.

"It's still on, as far as I know."

"My mom is heading to the store this afternoon and wants to bake a pie. But it won't be as tasty as the ones your mom makes."

"Thanks, Scout. I'll tell my mother how much you enjoy her baking. That will make her day. I haven't spoken to Thomas today. But I'm eating dinner with Ranger Holt after work. He'll know if the cookout is on."

"Okay, great."

A pause.

"Scout, is there something else you wanted to ask?"

"I've been talking to LeVar about the bones the sheriff found. Since LeVar is enrolling in a criminal justice course at the community college this fall, he wants me to show him how I catch criminals on the internet."

Raven covered her mouth to keep from laughing. She couldn't picture her eighteen-year-old brother, four months removed from running the streets with the Harmon Kings, playing Scooby Doo with the wheelchair-bound girl next door. Raven gave Scout her due. The teenager belonged to an amateur sleuthing website called Virtual Searchers, and her research helped catch Jeremy Hyde in April. The girl had a future in law enforcement, possibly as an FBI profiler.

"You know Sheriff Shepherd doesn't approve of you researching murder cases without your mother's permission."

"I understand. That's why I'm calling. I figure LeVar and I can share our research, and if you think it's worthwhile, you can bring it to the sheriff's department."

Raven tapped her nails against the desk. They were pearl-blue this month, the color of fairytale moonlight.

"Tell you what. Talk to your mother and get permission first. Then we'll discuss combining forces on this investigation of yours."

"Okay."

"Promise me you won't do anything before you talk to your mother."

"I promise."

"All right, Scout. After I speak with Darren, we'll let you know about the cookout."

She wondered what she'd gotten herself into. Collaborating with Scout and LeVar? As humorous as it sounded, it would be a welcome change from the daily stress of investigative work and dealing with Chelsey.

Which reminded her.

Before she talked herself out of it, Raven picked up the phone and dialed Chelsey's number. Raven convinced herself her boss wouldn't answer. As she lowered the phone, Chelsey's groggy voice came through the speaker.

"Chelsey, is everything all right? It's after ten."

Chelsey mumbled something indecipherable. It sounded like she was still asleep.

"Hey, Chelsey. Do you need me to come get you?"

"No...no...I'm just a little sick this morning. I hate to do this to you, but you'll have to run the office today."

Sick again. This was the third time this month her best friend blew off work.

"I'm worried about you."

"Don't, it's nothing. Whatever it is, I'll get over it."

"Do you have a cold or something?"

Raven could hear Chelsey forming a lie.

"I'm pretty sure it was something I ate. My stomach is a mess, and my head is killing me."

Checking the time, Raven grabbed her keys off the desk.

"I'm coming over to check on you."

"No!" Chelsey snapped awake, the grogginess replaced by anger and desperation. "You don't need to parent me. I ate something I shouldn't have, and I'll deal with it."

"Just like you're dealing with Wolf Lake Consulting? This is your business, Chelsey. Your desk is overflowing with cases, you're never here, and you still haven't hired a third investigator."

"Just give me twenty-four hours to kick this sickness. I'll take care of everything, I swear."

Raven buried her face in her hand. She hadn't meant to corner Chelsey. But the pressure kept building. Either Chelsey turned away clients, or she showed up for work and stopped dropping the load on Raven's shoulders.

"Maybe you should see a doctor."

"For what? So he can tell me to buy Tylenol and Pepto Bismol? I'm better off resting at home."

"I picked up another client at the state park yesterday. If I don't hear from you tomorrow, I won't have any choice but to turn away new clients."

"That won't be necessary. I'll be in at nine."

"Okay, Chelsey. Please call me if you need help. And swear to me you'll visit the doctor if your sickness worsens."

"I will."

Raven didn't believe her.

7

Thomas hadn't prepared for the circus that awaited him outside the coroner's office. The moment he stopped the cruiser along the curb, three reporters flanked by men with broadcast video cameras on their shoulders rushed across the sidewalk. He lowered his head and made a beeline for the entrance doors. But they ran beside him and blocked his path, shoving microphones in front of his face. A middle-aged man with gleaming, white teeth and a thick mustache jostled his way to the front.

"What do you know about the body found in the state park? Is it Skye Feron?"

A woman in high heels shouldered the man aside.

"Is there another serial killer in Wolf Lake? Should people be afraid?"

They fired questions as he pushed toward the doors. Once inside, they wouldn't be allowed to follow. When he lowered his head, a baritone-voiced reporter yelled from behind.

"Are you fit to serve as interim Sheriff? How can someone on the autism spectrum protect Nightshade County?"

The question stung. He wanted to wheel around and shout the man down. But that's what the reporter wanted—the new sheriff's face plastered on every television screen in the county, screaming like a lunatic.

He released his breath when the doors closed behind him. Their fists pounded the glass. The yelling blended together into an indecipherable cacophony.

Virgil and Claire waited outside the examination room. The medical examiner raised a hand and motioned Thomas to follow. Shiny metal tables stood in neat rows. Dr. Stone was here with her female graduate assistant.

"So glad you joined us this morning," Dr. Stone said.

Thomas caught the impatience in her voice.

"What can you tell me about the victim?"

Dr. Stone swept her arm over the table. Together with her team, she'd cleaned the bones and rebuilt the skeleton. Thomas was impressed.

"After reconstructing the skull from seventy pieces, I can say with certainty the victim is female. Note the smooth skull and wide pelvis, also the jaw structure."

"Age?"

"Molar eruption suggests late teens to middle twenties."

Thomas groaned. This had to be Skye Feron.

"Do we know how she died, or how long she was in the ground?"

"Bones decay slower beneath the soil than organic material. Judging by the amount of degradation, I'd guess this woman died between five and ten years ago. We're fortunate animals didn't compromise the remains."

Virgil stepped forward and noted a hole cutting through the skull. At first glance, Thomas mistook the hole as missing bone fragments. Closer inspection told him this was an entry wound.

"The victim received a sharp blow to the head, indicating perimortem injury. It punctured the skull and killed her."

"So a bullet wound."

Virgil glanced at Claire and Dr. Stone. The doctor shook her head.

"A bullet would have caused further damage to the skull. This was a sharp object capable of puncturing bone."

Thomas scratched his chin.

"What kind of weapon am I looking for?"

The doctor's mouth pulled tight as she reached into the bag of field tools.

"Something like this."

Stone held up a pickax.

DARREN PROPPED his feet on an ottoman and relaxed on the couch. Through the windows outside his cabin, the trees swayed as the wind gusted off the hills. An hour ago, the campgrounds had been alive with the voices of children and parents eager to hike the many trails weaving through Wolf Lake State Park. Now it was tranquil, and Darren felt thankful for the opportunity to relax.

He twisted the cap off his water bottle as he chewed on the peanut butter protein bar—Raven's personal recipe for building muscle and cutting fat. It was better than he expected, and he craved a second bar with lunch. A horn honked as a camper pulled out of the lot, leaving him alone with his thoughts. Soon the busy season would end. He'd be lucky to host a camper once the snow flew in November.

Darren had spent the morning trimming brush along the ridge trail. Since the forensic anthropologist left, he'd avoided Lucifer Falls and the creek. The scenic terrain was tainted now, and would remain so until they caught the killer. He set the water aside. With Raven working at Wolf Lake Consulting today, his schedule was open until she left work. He looked forward to spending the rest of the day with her—dinner with Serena at Raven's house, then back to the cabin for a little private time. Glancing around the cabin, he realized the interior could use cleaning.

As he straightened the couch cover, footsteps stopped outside his window. Years spent as a beat cop in Syracuse heightened his senses.

This didn't sound like a mischievous kid peeking inside the ranger's cabin. The footsteps were too heavy for a child, and the person lingered along the wall, spying on Darren. Quietly, he shifted his body along the wall and pushed the curtain back. Nothing but green grass stretched back to the trees.

A shadow rushed across cabin two. He swung in front of the window and spotted a male figure. The stranger plunged into the forest and raced down the hill, cutting between the trails. Darren grabbed his keys and ran after the man. He'd only glimpsed the fleeing figure and couldn't say if the man was young or middle age. Whoever the man was, he ran like the wind. The figure was a hundred yards ahead of the ranger and pulling away as Darren pushed through a knot of branches.

The forest flew past in a blur. His chest tightened as he sucked air into his lungs. Halfway to the lake trail, he stopped and leaned over with his hands on his knees, chest heaving. Stopping amid the gloomy forest, he listened for footsteps. He'd lost the man.

Was this the thief who pilfered two-hundred dollars from Paul Phipps's wife?

Or had he glimpsed the Lucifer Falls killer?

8

TUESDAY, AUGUST 10TH 12:30 P.M.

Thomas peeled the wrapper open and stared at the soggy sandwich. Meat and onions spilled out between the bread, and there was more dressing on the wrapper than on the sandwich. He groaned. This was the last time he'd buy lunch from the new sandwich shop in the village center. He took one bite, chewed, and twisted his mouth. The rest of lunch ended up in the trash.

Wiping his hands clean, he pored over his case notes and located Sheriff Gray's number. He hadn't spoken to his mentor since the abrupt retirement two weeks ago, after Gray derided himself for suspecting Father Josiah Fowler in the angel of mercy killings.

"Sheriff Shepherd," Gray said with a grin in his voice. Thomas smiled. Gray hadn't sounded this chipper in years. "How's my office treating you?"

"Terrific. I trust you're enjoying retirement."

"I'm loving every minute. Last week, I walked along the river for three hours, and I haven't set my alarm since my last day at the department."

"We'd love to see you again."

"Bah, you don't want me puttering around the office, offering suggestions and making a nuisance of myself."

"Just a heads up. A group of us get together for dinner every week. Right now, it's me and Darren Holt running the show. I can't convince Aguilar to come. She's been weird since...well, you know."

"Since you became sheriff."

"Right."

"Let me tell you about Deputy Aguilar. She'll roast the hell out of her fellow deputies. But she respects authority, and you're the new sheriff in town, so to speak. Give her time to grow comfortable with the changes."

Gray's words rang true. Maybe Thomas was pressing Aguilar. He couldn't force his deputy to let her guard down and act as if nothing had changed.

"I'll keep that in mind. The gang would love to have you over for dinner. It's no big deal, just a small gathering and barbecue on the grill."

"Now you're talking. Give me the time and place, and I'll be there."

"How about tomorrow at five-thirty? You know where my uncle's old place is."

Thomas had purchased his Uncle Truman's old A-Frame after he moved from Los Angeles to Wolf Lake.

"I'll be there, and I'll bring the porterhouse."

"That's unnecessary. You're our guest."

"No, I insist. Now, why don't you tell me the real reason you called?"

Thomas snickered.

"Is it that obvious?"

"I worked in that department longer than you've been alive, Thomas. I'm pretty good at reading people."

"You've probably read about the bones by now."

"Yes."

"I'm worried we found Skye Feron."

Gray turned silent for a second.

"I was afraid of that. Are you sure it's her?"

"It's a female in her late teens or early twenties. We brought a forensic anthropologist in to excavate the bones and help Virgil make a determination. Until she spends more time studying the bones, we won't be able to say with certainty it's Skye. What do you remember about the investigation?"

"Everything," Gray said, the tenor of his voice sinking. "Sometimes it feels like the investigation happened yesterday. You weren't around during those years, Thomas. The case tore the village apart. We'd lost one of our own, and a popular girl at that. Skye Feron ran varsity track for Wolf Lake High, she sang in the church choir, and she volunteered at the humane shelter."

"Sounds a little too perfect."

"Everyone hides a skeleton in the closet. Sorry, poor choice of words. From what I recall, Skye hung out with two cheerleaders— Paige Sutton and Justine Adkins. I interviewed them after Skye disappeared. Skye was supposed to meet Paige and Justine the night she vanished."

"Did she have a boyfriend?"

"A boy named Benny Pritchard. We checked him out. Benny was in Bangor with his parents that week. He's clean."

"Did Skye cancel the meeting or act like something was wrong?"

"Not according to the girls. But I didn't trust the two friends, especially Paige Sutton. They were hiding something, and I never figured out what, despite grilling them in front of their parents. All Justine did was cry, and Paige went stoic, as if nothing was wrong. Paige acted like Skye would show her face in a few days. That never happened."

"What makes you believe Justine and Paige were holding back on you?"

"They were evasive. Wouldn't meet my eye when I questioned them. Whatever happened, it had to do with school. I'm positive of that."

"Did they make an enemy, someone who'd hurt Skye?"

"That was my guess. But why protect someone who posed danger to them?"

"Could be a broken friendship."

Gray grunted.

"Cliques have been around forever. But I've never seen a clique lead to murder. My advice? Start with the friends. Paige Sutton is still in Wolf Lake. I'm not sure what became of Justine Adkins. By now, the girls must have heard about the bones. That might be enough to get them talking. Thomas, how's your father doing?"

Thomas dropped his eyes as if Gray was lecturing him from across the table. He called his parents every few nights. But Mason always wanted to discuss the business instead of his health. Thomas played along, shielding himself from the sadness.

"Time is short, Sheriff."

"Make amends while there's time. Take it from me. There are so many things I wish I'd said to Lana, and now I can't."

"I understand."

"Go to your father. Don't live with regret."

9

TUESDAY, AUGUST 10TH 5:40 P.M.

"You're becoming quite the chef, LeVar."

Thomas stabbed his fork into the last bite of salmon, swallowed, and gave a contented sigh. LeVar had pan-fried the salmon in lemon and garlic, garnished the entrée with herbs, and plated it with whole grain rice. LeVar broke off a chunk and tossed it to Jack, the lost dog Thomas had found in the state park last month. Thomas theorized Jack was a Siberian Husky. But the dog seemed too large for a puppy. Jack snapped the fish out of the air and swallowed the treat in one gulp. His tail thumped as he moved his head between LeVar and Thomas, hoping for another handout.

When LeVar grabbed Thomas's plate, Thomas raised a hand.

"I'll clean up, LeVar. You did all the cooking."

"I don't mind. You let me use the kitchen and hang out in the house. Helping is the least I can do."

"You've been invaluable. The remodeling project on the guest house is almost finished. You helped me put on a new roof, and you're ten times the cook I'll ever be."

"*Aight*, dawg. Don't say I didn't ask."

"Why don't you take Jack outside and let him run off some steam. He's been locked inside all day."

"I got you covered. Come on, Jack."

LeVar opened the sliding glass door, and Jack followed him across the deck as Thomas filled the sink with dishwater. Since he'd found Jack, the dog hadn't needed a leash, unless Thomas took the dog to the veterinarian for a checkup. Remembering caused the corner of his mouth to quirk into a smile. The veterinary technician, a young woman with caramel hair wrapped in a bun, had taken one look at Jack and covered her chest.

"You found this dog in the wild?" she'd asked as she led Jack to the examination room.

"A half-mile from my house."

"I don't think this is a Siberian Husky."

"He has to be. Look at the coat."

The technician shook her head.

"He's a crossbreed of some sort. If it didn't sound crazy, I'd say this dog is a..."

She stopped when the doctor entered the room.

Outside, LeVar tossed a tennis ball across the property. The ball bounced into the Mourning family's yard, where Jack snapped the ball between his massive jaws and sprinted back to LeVar. As Thomas rinsed the dishes, a knock on the deck door brought his head around. Naomi Mourning waited at the glass. Thomas waved her inside. Last month, Thomas agreed to take over the family business, a project management and collaboration firm that specialized in turning around the fortunes of small businesses. Thomas's first order of business at Shepherd Systems was hiring Naomi to run daily operations. Before the job offer, Naomi had bounced between part-time jobs, struggling to pay Scout's medical bills.

"Jack is full of it this afternoon," Naomi said as she waved to LeVar.

"I should pay someone to walk him while I'm at work. The problem is, I doubt I'll find anyone willing to take the job."

"Jack's a handful."

"He's gentle. But nobody would believe it at first glance."

Naomi rubbed her arm and cast a cautionary glance at the yard.

"May I talk to you about something?"

Thomas hung the dishrag over the faucet and dried his hands on the towel.

"Sure. Have a seat."

At forty-one, Naomi had the complexion of a woman twenty years younger. Her brunette hair dangled in a ponytail, and she wore red running shorts and a gray tank top that accentuated her fit body.

"Before I say anything, thank you again for offering me the job at Shepherd Systems."

Thomas swallowed.

"You aren't leaving, are you?"

"No, I love it there. The people are wonderful, and your mother is warming up to me. Not to mention your generosity saved us from bankruptcy."

Thomas had worried over his mother accepting Naomi. His parents, Mason and Lindsey Shepherd, had battled Thomas since he returned to Wolf Lake, pressuring him to quit the sheriff's department and take over the business. Mason's lung cancer progressed each month, and Thomas accepted his father wouldn't be around a year from now. The reality pierced his heart.

"So what's the problem? If you need more time to care for Scout, I'll see to it."

Naomi straightened her shirt and set her palms on the table.

"Thomas, there's a rumor at the office that we're..." She chewed the corner of her mouth. "Together."

Thomas coughed. Since his failed reunion with Chelsey, he'd spent more time with Naomi and Scout.

"That we're dating?"

"Yes. I'm afraid people will get the wrong impression." Naomi twirled her hair around her finger. "Don't get me wrong. You're a terrific person, and under different circumstances..."

"It's okay, you don't have to say it. If anyone mentions the rumor to me, I'll squash the idea. Is everything else all right? You seem distracted."

Naomi tilted her head.

"I'm talking to Glen again."

Glen was Naomi's husband. They'd separated after the collision that left Scout crippled. According to Naomi, Glen blamed himself for the accident, though a tractor trailer had struck their vehicle from behind. Thomas hadn't met Glen, who worked in Ithaca for the local electric and gas company. He wondered why a father would turn his back on his wife and daughter, no matter how guilty he felt.

"That's encouraging. Does Scout know?"

"Not yet. I don't want to get her hopes up. I wanted you to know in case Glen stops by, and you're worried about the stranger knocking on our door."

Thomas smiled.

"So you don't want me to don my sheriff's hat and grill him."

Naomi's shoulders shook with laughter.

"That might be amusing. I just need time to figure things out and see where Glen's head is at. Until I'm certain he's ready to be a father again, I don't want him around Scout. She's experienced too much disappointment in her life."

"I understand." Thomas glanced at the refrigerator. "You want anything to eat or drink? We have a leftover salmon fillet. Another LeVar masterpiece."

Naomi rubbed her belly.

"I would, except I ate a bowl of pasta. That reminds me. Are you holding the cookout after work tomorrow?"

"Sure. You'll be there, I hope."

"We wouldn't miss it for the world. I worried you'd be too busy with the investigation."

"So you read about the state park."

Naomi cast a worried glance over her shoulder. The park loomed over the ridge, the distant falls hidden behind the trees.

"Should we be worried, Thomas?"

He shook his head.

"The bones were in the park for several years. Whatever happened, it was a long time ago."

"And you think it's that teenager who disappeared six years ago?"

"I hope not. But if it is Skye Feron, I need to prove it. Her parents deserve closure."

Jack padded across the deck and waited at the deck door as LeVar jogged up the steps. LeVar slid the door open and leaned in the entryway, out of breath.

"Jack running you ragged?" Thomas asked.

"I need you to follow me," LeVar said. "Someone broke into the guest house."

THOMAS KNELT inside the entryway and ran his finger along the frame.

"You're certain you didn't leave the door open?"

LeVar shook his head, swinging his dreadlocks back and forth.

"Naw, I always lock the place. Just like you told me."

"There's a warp in the frame. That could be from the heat and humidity." He stood and twisted the knob, then he shone a flashlight over the lock, searching for signs someone picked the locking mechanism. He shrugged his shoulders. "Let's walk through the house. Tell me if anything is missing or out of place."

Thomas followed LeVar down the hall. The teenager opened the bathroom door and poked his head inside. Then he pulled the closet door open and ensured none of his clothes were missing. As LeVar went through his belongings, Thomas squeezed past and wandered to the sitting room where an expansive window offered a picturesque view of Wolf Lake. This was his favorite place to sit when he stayed with his aunt and uncle. Sometimes, he'd forgo his bed and rest in the chair so he could fall asleep to the boats crossing the lake and the stars reflecting off the water. He checked the floor, searching for dirt the thief might have tracked in. If there was a thief. Maybe LeVar forgot to lock the house, or the wind blew the door open.

He'd convinced himself LeVar had made a mistake before he found the muddy shoe print on the floor.

10

Justine Adkins couldn't stop trembling. Over her latte, she watched the door as faces she didn't recognize judged her from across the coffee shop. Sitting in the back, she'd hoped to avoid attention. But a solitary woman shaking as if the ground rolled beneath her feet drew attention. Her face reflected in the polished table. Curly auburn hair hung past her shoulders, and a pair of dark sunglasses perched atop her head.

Where was Paige? Justine glanced at the time and gave her former friend until nine-thirty before she left. Coming here was a mistake. Wolf Lake wasn't home and hadn't been for seven years, a full year before Skye disappeared.

Justine snatched an artificial sweetener off the table and read the packet. Then she tapped the corner of the packet against the table and eyed a couple strolling past the window. Three more minutes. That's all Paige deserved.

Closing her eyes, she drained the latte and wiped her face. She tossed the napkin into the trash container, checked the clock again, and gave up. Fate warned Justine to leave while she had a chance. In fifteen minutes, she'd be on the highway with Wolf Lake and all its unwanted memories in the rear-view mirror.

As she rose from the chair, a blonde woman with hair past her shoulders hurried across the sidewalk. Too late. Justine should have fled after Paige failed to show at nine. The bell rang, and every guy in the cafe swung their gazes at Paige. Though Justine hadn't seen her old friend since high school graduation, she would have recognized the woman anywhere. High cheekbones, a button nose, and sea-green eyes that commanded attention. Paige had put on several pounds since school. Yet she still possessed the long, sleek legs of a cheerleader. Paige stopped in the doorway and scanned the room.

Please don't recognize me, Justine thought. Justine's heart lurched when Paige's eyes locked on her.

"Oh, my God," Paige said, pulling Justine into an embrace. Justine patted Paige's back, unsure what to do with her hands. "I'm so sorry I'm late. Traffic was terrible this morning. I got behind one of those buses for old people. Some biddy took three minutes to climb down the steps. I was ready to scream. I mean, if you're that old, you shouldn't go out anymore. Were you here long?"

"Since nine."

Paige fell into the chair opposite Justine's and tossed her hair over her shoulders.

"Why didn't you call? I would have come sooner."

"Because you said you'd meet me at nine."

"Did I? I thought I said nine-thirty." Paige waved a hand through the air. "It doesn't matter. The important thing is you're here. It's been so long."

Again Paige rounded the table and hugged Justine, burying Justine in her hair. Paige's perfume made Justine's eyes water.

"Where are you staying?"

Justine fiddled with the sweetener packet and stared at the table.

"At a bed-and-breakfast outside Kane Grove."

"Why not in Wolf Lake? The resort hotels are gorgeous."

"I got a better deal out of town."

Paige set her hands on the table, and Justine couldn't prevent her eyes from searching for a ring. Though the blonde had just turned twenty-three last month, Justine half-expected to see a shiny diamond on Paige's finger. Paige struck Justine as someone who'd marry a rich guy after college and live off her husband's income.

"So, I haven't seen or heard from you in years. Where have you been hiding yourself?"

Paige had Justine's phone number, but Justine blocked Paige on social media. Nothing personal, but she'd blocked every name she recognized from Wolf Lake. She didn't want the memories.

"I'm still outside Rochester."

"You're only ninety minutes away. Why don't you ever visit?"

The girl behind the counter glared at Justine as though she were an outsider in hostile territory. And perhaps she was. Justine looked at her phone.

"Work keeps me busy. If you don't mind, I'm supposed to meet my cousin at ten-thirty."

That was a lie. Though Justine's parents still lived in Wolf Lake, most of her family had scattered over the years.

"You just got here, and you're already running off."

"Paige, we're here for one reason. Are we going to talk about it?"

Paige pulled her lips tight and drummed her nails against the table. After a moment, she sniffled and wiped her eyes on her sleeve.

"I don't know what to make of the newspaper article. What if it's her?"

Justine set her chin on her fist.

"Maybe it's not Skye."

"The newspaper said it's a female in her teens or early twenties. We were eighteen when Skye vanished."

Justine stared into her empty mug, wishing she had another latte. Not because she was thirsty. She needed something to distract her, ground her, convince Justine the world wasn't spinning too fast for her to hang on.

"All the police said is they found a girl's remains. For all we know, Skye might have left Wolf Lake. She didn't like it here."

Paige widened her eyes and fell back in her chair.

"Didn't like it here? Skye was the most popular girl in high school."

"No, Paige. *You* were the most popular girl at Wolf Lake High. And Skye wasn't happy. She told me many times she couldn't wait for college, that she'd leave and never come back."

"Are you sure that's not *you* you're talking about? You graduated high school and fell off the face of the earth. And anyway, why would Skye want to leave?"

Justine glared at Paige through the tops of her eyes.

"You know why."

Paige scrunched her brow.

"Wait, are you talking about Dawn?"

"Shh," Justine said, leaning over the table. Everyone was staring at them now. "Keep your voice down."

Paige's jaw dropped.

"I can't believe you still think we had something to do with that. It's terrible what happened. But Dawn Samson was crazy, Justine. C-R-A-Z-Y."

Justine turned away.

"Only because we made her that way."

"You can't *make* someone kill herself." Justine winced at Paige's words, wishing her friend would lower her voice. "Suicide is a selfish act. Killing yourself only hurts the ones around you. It shouldn't have surprised anyone. Dawn was such a bitch."

Justine's blood boiled. Suddenly, she was a teenager in high school again, angry and scared. She wanted to reach across the table and slap the taste out of Paige's mouth.

"You made Dawn's life a living hell."

Paige's brow creased.

"That's a bit melodramatic, Justine. The girl couldn't take a joke."

"When does joking cross the line to bullying?"

"Everybody gets bullied, dear. It's part of growing up. Either you fight back, or you learn to laugh it off. We were just having fun."

If only that were true. Justine cringed at unwanted memories. The notes Paige stuffed into Dawn's locker, calling her ugly and fat, threatening she'd beat up Dawn after school. During their sophomore years, Paige and half the cheer team cornered Dawn beside the tennis court. Justine hated herself for not intervening. Outnumbered, she couldn't have prevented the beating. But she only had herself to blame for not speaking up and snitching on her friends. Had Skye been there, she would have stood up for Dawn and made things right.

"Fight back," Paige kept saying, each time she slapped Dawn across the face.

The slaps left red welts on the girl's face and drew tears. Had Dawn fought back and held her own, the other girls would have jumped in. Dawn never stood a chance. The bullying began years before and worsened as the girls grew older. To this day, Justine couldn't remember how it started, or why Paige targeted Dawn. Was it a perceived slight? Or was it predatory—the pack identifying a weaker, injured member and eating their own?

"You were terrible to her," Justine said. "If I'd stepped in, none of this would have happened."

Paige's face froze in shock. A thousand pounds fell off Justine's shoulders, and her heart hammered, as if she'd just run a marathon. She'd waited too many years to tell Paige she'd been wrong. Coming here today, she never believed the words would leave her lips.

"None of *what* would have happened?"

"Dawn killing herself, Skye disappearing."

Paige slapped her hand against the table. Justine flinched. Until now, she'd forgotten how Paige controlled conversations. Even with a master's degree and a high-paying job, Justine still felt beneath Paige. Yet she cared about the woman and had since Skye, Paige, and Justine became inseparable friends during grade school.

"Dawn's suicide has nothing to do with Skye vanishing. And it's like you said. The bones probably aren't Skye's."

Drawing in a breath, Justine said, "If we didn't believe there was a chance it's Skye, neither of us would be here. We have to face this, Paige."

Quiet fell between the women, each lost in their own memories. After a long time, Paige shook her head.

"I can't accept it's Skye." A tear rolled down the woman's cheek, evidence she still had a heart. "After we lost her, I convinced myself she ran away after a fight with her parents. Or something happened with that loser she dated."

"You mean Benny Pritchard?"

Paige scoffed.

"Total loser. We should have recognized the signs that something was wrong when she dated that guy."

An argument poised behind Justine's lips. She swallowed it for now.

"I tell myself every day that Skye is still alive, that there's a logical explanation for what happened. I can't face the alternative."

Paige removed a tissue from her purse and dabbed her eyes. Somehow, the woman's eyeliner didn't run. A giggle escaped Paige's chest.

"I still wear it, you know?"

"Wear what?" Justine asked, though she knew Paige referred to the bracelet.

The blonde woman peeled her sleeve back and revealed the beaded friendship bracelet around her wrist. Justine's heart dropped. She hadn't worn hers since high school. Yet she kept the bracelet on her nightstand. How many times had she determined to toss the friendship bracelet in the trash and sever the last tie holding her to Wolf Lake? Each time she tried, she pictured Skye. Tossing the bracelet away was akin to giving up on Skye, admitting her best friend was dead. Justine sobbed into her hand.

"I still have mine too," Justine admitted.

Paige reached across the table and set a hand on Justine's.

"The police didn't mention a bracelet. That's a good sign, right?"

"It's possible Skye didn't wear hers the night she disappeared."

"Of course, she did. Skye never took the bracelet off. She was a loyal friend." Loyalty. Even today, Paige pitted Skye against Justine, comparing the two friends as if this was a contest. Justine grabbed her bag. "Where are you going?"

"I told you I'm meeting my cousin."

Paige huffed.

"At least call me before you blow out of town. Sometimes, I get the impression we were never friends."

Justine pulled her sunglasses over her eyes.

"If we weren't friends, I wouldn't be here. Call me if anything changes."

11

R aven knelt before the cabinet and filed two investigation folders. Three cases lay stacked upon her desk, and she hadn't completed the paperwork on the stolen money at the state park campgrounds. She blew the hair from her eyes. Chelsey was somewhere down the hall, most likely in the kitchen, pouring herself another coffee. Her boss arrived ten minutes late this morning, complaining of a splitting headache as she blew through the entryway. Glass clinked from the kitchen.

"Can you bring me a cup?" Raven called.

"A cup of what?"

Raven rolled her eyes.

"Coffee?"

"Uh, sure."

Raven preferred tea. But the paperwork grew by the second, and Chelsey refused to lend a hand. Raven needed energy. She slammed the drawer shut, hoping her anger carried to the kitchen and reached Chelsey's ears. Five minutes later, she was knee-deep in case files, and Chelsey hadn't returned with the coffees. Screw it. Raven marched down the hallway to get the coffee herself when someone knocked.

She turned to find LeVar propping the door open with his leg while he pushed Scout Mourning through the entryway.

"Let me get that," Raven said, holding the door.

The firm's handicap accessible ramp was narrow and outdated. Levar must have struggled to maneuver the wheelchair to the door.

"'Sup, Sis?" LeVar planted a kiss on Raven's cheek.

Raven hugged her brother and set a hand on Scout's shoulder.

"What are you two troublemakers doing here?"

"LeVar has the day off," said Scout.

"So you visited me at work? There must be a thousand more interesting things to do on an August morning."

"We want to discuss our ideas on the state park case."

Raven cast a worried glance over her shoulder. She hadn't told Chelsey. Given her boss's mood, now wasn't the time to suggest they combine forces with Scout and LeVar. Raven placed a finger against her lips.

"Not so loud. Chelsey has a headache this morning."

LeVar gave Raven a knowing look.

"Again?"

"Yeah, I hear you. She needs a good talking-to. Come on in." Giving LeVar a break, Raven wheeled Scout into the office and set the girl beside her desk. Raven gestured at the paperwork. "As you can see, every day at Wolf Lake Consulting overflows with excitement and mystery."

Scout giggled. The spitting image of Naomi, Scout wore her brunette hair in a ponytail. She adjusted her glasses as she peered around the room.

"So this is where you catch the bad guys."

"And the bad girls. We get a few of them too."

"Pretty soon, we'll have another investigator in Wolf Lake," Scout said, glancing up at LeVar. Raven swore her brother blushed. "LeVar declared his major this morning."

Raven raised her brow.

"Criminal justice?"

"Yeah," LeVar said, shuffling his feet. "Do ya need to stare at me like that, all googly-eyed and—"

Raven held up a hand.

"No name calling around Scout."

"What? This girl's got a mouth like a sailor. She makes the Harmon Kings seem like choir boys."

"So I came up with a great idea," Scout said.

Raven sank into her chair.

"What's that?"

"Since LeVar is studying criminal justice, and you're shorthanded, why not hire LeVar as your third investigator?"

The surprise on LeVar's face told Raven this was news to him. Raven listened for Chelsey. Her boss was still in the kitchen, doing God knows what. Probably avoiding company. Chelsey had become the ultimate introvert since things fell apart between her and Thomas Shepherd. Raven still hadn't heard the details. What went wrong? One day, Chelsey determined to try again with Thomas. The next, she refused to speak the man's name.

"I'm not sure what to say," Raven said, glancing between LeVar and Scout. She held her brother's eyes. "A private investigator job. Is this what you want?"

LeVar scratched behind his ear.

"I guess so. I hadn't given it much thought...or any thought, to be honest."

Raven blew out a breath.

"I'd be lying if I said we didn't need the help. But you haven't taken your first class yet, and Chelsey makes the hiring decisions."

Glass shattered in the kitchen, followed by an angry curse.

"I'd better check on her," Raven said, pinching the bridge of her nose. "Let's table this discussion for now and pick it up when Chelsey is...reasonable. Sound good?"

Scout raised her eyes to LeVar, who nodded.

"Great," Raven said. "In the meantime, if you find anything interesting on the state park skeleton, send me the information." Raven rubbed her hands together. She had to admit, the prospect of working with LeVar and Scout excited her. Months had passed since the last time she enjoyed investigative work. "I can't wait to get started."

LeVar kissed her again. That was another welcome change. Since LeVar left the Kings, he'd opened up and become a family man.

"See you at the barbecue," he said, grabbing Scout's chair.

"Right, I almost forgot about the cookout. We'll talk then. Just be careful what you say around the sheriff."

"*Aight*, Sis. We'll keep it on the down low."

Raven walked them out and held the door, while LeVar squeezed the wheelchair through the opening. As she watched her brother drive off with Scout in the backseat, she felt her heart sink. A part of her wished Chelsey had called in sick again. She could have spent the day with LeVar and Scout, playing their silly mystery-solving game. Anything would have been better than catching the campground thief, or listening to Chelsey whine about her headache.

Deflated, Raven turned back to the kitchen, Chelsey was on her hands and knees, sopping up spilled coffee with paper towels. She'd pulled the garbage can from beneath the sink and set it beside the mess. Two broken mugs lay inside the can.

"What happened?"

Chelsey gave Raven a death stare.

"What does it look like? I dropped the mugs, and now I'm cleaning up messes while you chitchat."

Raven bit her tongue.

"LeVar drove Scout home. You could have come out and said hello."

"If your head was inside a vise, you wouldn't be in the mood for conversation."

Stooping to help, Raven snagged the broken fragments and tossed them into the container. From the closet, she removed a broom and dust pan and swept the smaller pieces. As she worked, she tested the water with Chelsey.

"You know, things would be a lot easier around here if we hired a third investigator."

Chelsey tossed the wet towels into the trash.

"That was the last of the brew," Chelsey said, ignoring Raven's suggestion. "I'll start another pot."

"You do that. I guess I'll work on the cases."

As Chelsey bent to lift the garbage can, her shirt dipped off her neck, revealing a silver necklace with a dolphin pendant. Raven caught her breath. Cuts covered Chelsey's chest from just below the neck line to the tops of her breasts. The woman looked as if she'd been attacked by an animal with razors for claws. Raven pulled her eyes away when Chelsey looked up.

"What?"

"Nothing," Raven said, clearing her throat. "Call me if you need help with the coffee."

What the hell was happening? As Raven hurried back to the office, she couldn't shake the image of Chelsey's lacerated chest.

12

"Could you pass the sweet potato pie?" Thomas asked.

Raven snickered as the table erupted in laughter. It was a running joke that had begun during the group's first cookout. Who would be the first to ask for a second piece of pie? Eventually, someone always did. Serena's sweet potato pie was to die for, and now Naomi Mourning had baked a mouthwatering blackberry pie that had the table raving.

"All right, Fat Albert," Darren said, passing Thomas the dish.

Thomas saluted Darren with his fork and scooped a slice onto his plate.

"Who is Fat Albert?" Scout asked, drawing more laughter. "What? Is he a famous fat guy or something?"

They'd torn through baby back ribs and half a porterhouse steak. Surrounded by family and friends, it was the happiest Raven had felt all day. She'd even convinced herself the lacerations on Chelsey's chest were nothing to worry about, that a logical explanation existed. Darren caught her grinning and held her hand below the table.

"What's gotten into you?"

"I'm just happy," she said.

He questioned Raven with his eyes, then he put an arm around her shoulder and gave her a squeeze. Across the table, Serena and Naomi discussed recipes and conspired to bake together next time. Raven didn't recall Serena smiling before last April. Rehab had done wonders for her mother, and Serena drew her strength from the love surrounding the table. She had real friends now, an extended family who supported her.

Beside Serena, LeVar cut another slice of porterhouse while he joked with Scout. The girl's face lit in understanding when LeVar explained Fat Albert and Bill Cosby. After dessert, the group broke into smaller groups and scattered around the backyard. Darren convened with LeVar and Scout beside the guest house, and Naomi and Serena wandered back to Naomi's place, ostensibly to sift through kitchen supplies and plan their first collaboration. Searching for company, Raven noticed Thomas and Gray standing away from the others and holding a secretive conversation beside the deck. Raven crept along the deck, remaining out of sight as their voices increased.

"Mark my words, Thomas. Paige Sutton and Justine Adkins knew more than they let on after Skye went missing."

"You think they abducted her? A friendship gone bad?"

Gray chewed on the idea.

"I don't believe so. More likely, the girls got involved in something dangerous, and Skye paid the price."

"If they suspected someone took Skye, why didn't they come forward?"

"I wish I had answers for you, Thomas. Start your investigation with Paige and Justine. They're the key to figuring out what happened to Skye. By the way, a little bird told me Justine Adkins is in Wolf Lake."

"When did she return?"

"Probably the day the story broke. If you ask me, that's proof Justine is involved."

Thomas folded his arms.

"Perhaps she came back because Skye was her friend, and she needs closure."

"Or she knows who the killer is and has reason to protect him."

Raven crept away. It wasn't right to eavesdrop on her friends. But learning the old sheriff suspected two girls named Paige and Justine put a jump in Raven's step. She searched the yard and located Scout and LeVar. It was time to investigate Skye Feron's disappearance.

PAIGE SUTTON LIVED in a classic Tudor with a brick-faced peak along the front and a hedge-lined yard. It was more house than she could afford. But she deserved the best, even if the mortgage payments would last forever. She strode barefoot into the remodeled kitchen and poured a glass of wine, which she carried out to the private stone patio. Eight o'clock, and the sun was almost down. How quickly summer drifted away.

Setting her feet on the chair opposite hers, she sipped the wine and listened to the first cricket chirping. This was her sanctuary, Paige's escape when the memories threatened to cripple her. She closed her eyes and reveled in the night songs. As she let the stress pour off her bones, her hand crept to the bracelet on her left wrist. Her fingers played with the beads, rolling them around as exhaustion crept up on her. She pictured Skye as she'd last seen her—a strong, athletic body and natural beauty Paige couldn't compete with. Skye had been so happy then and couldn't wait to attend Colby on a full scholarship. Then she was gone. Skye's disappearance left Paige with too many questions. Had someone hurt her friend? Or did Skye harbor a secret, something that drove her from Wolf Lake?

The hedges rustled, snapping Paige's eyes open. She set the wine down and glanced toward the sound, expecting an animal to scurry out of the underbrush. Shadows lengthened as the sun died in a bloody inferno. She stood and wandered into the yard. While she scanned the hedges, her arms prickled with goosebumps. Someone was watching her.

Paige snatched the glass and rushed inside the house. She locked the patio door and drew the curtains, feeling stupid for giving in to paranoia.

The converted attic offered the best view of the backyard. If someone was outside the house, she'd see them. She took the stairs two at a time, not stopping until she climbed into the attic. Paige slipped toward the window and stood in the shadows, still sensing eyes on her. The hedges blocked her view of the neighbor's yard. For once, she wished the hedges weren't there and she could see the house next door. She plunged a hand into her pocket and came up empty. The damn phone was downstairs on the kitchen table.

Paige waited five minutes. She unfroze her body and stepped away from the window. Maybe it had been an animal in the hedges. But as she descended the stairs, the night breeze touched her flesh. She paused on the lower landing and stared at the front door. It was open.

Her eyes flashed between the living room and upper landing for somewhere to flee. If someone was in the house, she needed to choose wisely.

A light shone in the kitchen. Had she left the light on?

Paige stepped to the threshold and placed her back against the wall. Listened. Silence bled out of the kitchen.

She needed her phone.

Mustering her courage, she clenched her teeth and spun around the wall. The kitchen lay empty.

Except for the friendship bracelet on the kitchen counter.

DEPUTY LAMBERT'S cruiser pulled to the curb at the same time Thomas arrived in his truck. Still dressed in shorts and a t-shirt, Thomas wished he'd had time to change into his uniform. When dispatch mentioned Paige Sutton's name, Thomas had snapped to attention. Earlier Sheriff Gray discussed Paige and Justine Adkins, Skye Feron's friends from high school. It wasn't a coincidence someone broke into Paige's house after her missing friend's name surfaced.

Paige Sutton waited in the entryway. The blonde wore torn jean shorts and a halter top.

"Ms. Sutton?" Thomas asked as they approached the stoop. "I'm Sheriff Shepherd, and this is Deputy Lambert."

"Thank you for coming so quickly."

"Are you certain someone was inside your home?"

Paige bobbed her head.

"Please follow me. I need to show you something."

Lambert shared a glance with Thomas. As they climbed the stoop, Thomas ran his eyes over the thick hedges surrounding the property. Lots of privacy. Too many places for an intruder to hide. Lambert noticed too. He lifted his chin at Thomas.

"I'll check the yard while you interview Sutton."

Thomas watched Lambert disappear around the corner before he followed Paige inside. The interior was immaculate. High ceilings and hardwood floors. The living room opened to the dining room, where a table for eight stretched across the floor. The house smelled of overkill. What was a twenty-three-year-old single doing in a house like this? The Sutton family fell into the upper half of middle class. Comfortable, but not rich enough to bequeath their daughter a three-hundred-thousand dollar home.

"In the kitchen, Sheriff," Paige said, breaking Thomas out of his stupor.

The remodeled kitchen featured an island in the center with pots and pans hanging from the ceiling. Paige stood at the kitchen counter with her hands cupping her elbows. She kept glancing at the windows, painted black by the night.

"The bracelet," Paige croaked, pointing to the beaded bracelet on the counter.

Thomas locked his eyes on the matching bracelet around Paige's wrist.

"This isn't yours?"

"It isn't mine. Why do you think I called you?"

"Do you know who the bracelet belongs to?"

Paige dragged a tissue beneath her nose and paced between the island and counter.

"There were only three of them. They belonged to me, Justine, and Skye."

Thomas raised his eyes.

"Skye Feron?"

"Yes."

"How do you know this bracelet belongs to Skye?"

"Because Justine left her bracelet at home. She's in Wolf Lake, visiting."

"Is Justine in town because of the news?"

Paige sobbed and nodded. Thomas rested his back against the counter, wondering what Paige was hiding.

"Start at the beginning. Tell me what happened tonight."

The woman recounted hearing someone in the yard while she sat on the patio, then finding the front door open after she descended the stairs.

"And that's when I found the bracelet on the counter."

"Is anything missing from the house?"

"I don't believe so."

This didn't sound like a typical break in. Thomas donned gloves and plucked the bracelet off the counter.

"May I?"

"Yes."

Thomas examined the bracelet under the light, searching for a stray hair or something to identify the person who touched it last. After he slipped it into an evidence bag, he turned to Paige. The blonde woman eyed the evidence bag as though she stared at a ghost.

"No offense, but the bracelet doesn't appear expensive. There must be thousands available for purchase."

Paige swung her head back and forth.

"No. We made them when we were twelve. The beads are identical and placed in the same order. You won't find these bracelets for sale."

"I understand."

Thomas glanced up when Deputy Lambert strode into the room. Paige flinched, not hearing the tall deputy enter.

"The backyard is clear," Lambert said. "The grass is thick back to the hedges, so I couldn't find a footprint."

"Dust the door for prints and see if you can determine how our intruder broke inside the house."

"I'm on it."

After Lambert left, Thomas swung his attention back to Paige. The woman fidgeted like a frightened zoo animal on display for the first time.

"What do you do for a living?"

"I'm a sales rep for Pelletier Apparel."

"Never heard of it."

She dragged her eyes down Thomas's cookout clothes and scoffed.

"I'm not surprised. Pelletier is the hottest fashion company in Paris. They expanded into the United States two years ago."

"They must pay well," he said, gesturing around the spacious kitchen.

Thomas doubted they paid well enough to support Paige Sutton's lifestyle.

"It's important to keep up appearances."

"How often are you on the road?"

"Two, three days a week. Why?"

"In your travels, have you ever encountered anyone who might want to hurt you?"

"No."

"Ms. Sutton, has anything like this ever happened before?"

"Never."

"No strange phone calls in the middle of the night, nobody following or harassing you."

"No."

Thomas blew out a breath.

"I need you to be honest with me. Is this Skye Feron's bracelet?"

Paige stared at the ceiling and blinked away tears.

"I think so."

"Why would someone leave the bracelet in your house?"

"If I knew the answer, I wouldn't need your help."

Thomas scratched his chin.

"Since Skye disappeared, has she ever contacted you?"

"Of course not." Fire flared in the woman's eyes. "I've spent the last six years mourning my friend, not knowing what happened to her. If I'd heard from Skye, I damn well would have told someone."

"Who wanted to hurt Skye Feron?"

Paige's lips quivered. She looked toward the backyard.

"Nobody. Everyone loved Skye. There wasn't a nicer girl at Wolf Lake High."

"Did she have trouble with a boyfriend?"

"Not that I recall."

"She would have told you if she did, right?"

"Skye told me everything. Nobody was closer to Skye than me."

"Not even Justine Adkins?"

Paige wandered across the kitchen and stared through the patio doors.

"Not even Justine."

"I'd like to speak with Justine. Can you tell me where she's staying?"

The woman lifted a shoulder.

"Some bed-and-breakfast outside Kane Grove. I'm not sure which one."

That was interesting. If the three women were inseparable, why did Justine choose a room outside Wolf Lake and not give Paige the address? As he pondered the question, Lambert returned from the doorway.

"The intruder used a lock pick on the front door." The deputy gestured at Paige. "If I were you, I'd change the lock set. Get something modern and harder to pick. I'd also install bolts on all the doors, including the patio."

Paige nodded and turned back to the yard. Thomas and Lambert questioned the woman for another five minutes. They weren't getting anywhere. Paige didn't have enemies or stalkers, and everyone loved Skye during high school. Someone was lying.

"All right," Thomas said, removing a card from his wallet. "We'll finish the paperwork back at the station."

"That's it? You're going already?"

"I'll leave my card on the counter. If you think of anything that will help with the investigation, call me."

Paige picked up the card and stared at it. After a long time, she raised her eyes to Thomas.

"Sheriff, did you find Skye beside the river?"

Thomas chewed the inside of his cheek.

"We haven't identified the victim. Lock your doors, Ms. Sutton. And make sure your neighbors know what happened tonight."

13

Raven checked the clock on Darren's stove and sighed. She needed to wake up early for work. But she didn't want to leave before Darren returned from checking the trails.

Reclining on the couch, she breathed in the scents of pine and campfire smoke and admired the diamond mine of stars through the open window. If she had her way, she'd move in with Darren permanently. A simple life, living in a rustic cabin in the middle of a beautiful state park. Except that was folly. She'd only dated the ranger a short time, and someone needed to care for Serena.

Raven closed her eyes and began to drift away. Until a branch rustled in the woods across the clearing. Probably just an animal pawing around in the dark. But it kicked her wide awake and surged her adrenaline. That's when it hit her. She was alone again. Anything could happen in the dark, especially when two convicted kidnappers wanted her dead.

The doorknob turned.

Raven shot off the couch and reached for her bag, where she concealed the handgun.

The lock rattled. Someone was trying to break in.

Her legs locked. Ice traveled through her veins as she watched...
waited...until the door opened, and Darren stepped inside.

"I need to fix that lock," Darren said. "Either that, or my key is
jacked up."

Raven touched her heart and closed her eyes. She'd hoped
spending time with Darren would ground her. But her anxiety grew
each day, a creeping, paralyzing fear that Damian Ramos and Mark
Benson would escape prison and track her down. The bones below
Lucifer Falls reminded her evil lurked in the shadows.

She checked her pulse and measured a hundred beats per minute
as Darren hung his jacket on the rack. He turned for the kitchen and
noticed her from the corner of his eye.

"Oh, damn. I didn't mean to frighten you."

She brushed the braids out of her eyes and wandered to the
window, checking the forest again.

"No need to apologize. I'm a bundle of nerves tonight."

He took her hand in his.

"Your hands are freezing. Are you sure you're all right?"

"I just need to settle down," she said, releasing his hand and
crossing the room to the kitchen.

She rummaged inside the refrigerator and removed a bottled
water, twisted the cap off and took a long drink. Darren drew a chair
from the table and sat, his gaze never leaving her.

"Maybe you should stay the night."

Raven rubbed the chill off her arms, despite the cabin holding the
day's heat. The thought of driving home in the dark scared the hell
out of her.

"I'd love to. But I can't leave my mother alone all night."

"She's doing great, Raven. At some point, you need to remove the
training wheels and let her ride on her own."

"I know. But she overdosed four months ago. She needs more
time."

He pulled the refrigerator open and rubbed his chin.

"I'm making a sandwich with the leftover porterhouse. You want
one?"

"I guess so."

Darren grabbed the bread out of the cupboard and sliced the steak on a cutting board. He possessed a firm jaw that matched his rugged shoulders, and his jeans fit his body in all the right places.

"Lettuce and onion?"

"Hold the onion."

He plated her sandwich and cut it in half, setting it on the table in front of her. She took a bite and remembered this afternoon's cookout. Surrounded by people she loved, she'd felt safe. Darren set his plate opposite hers and fell into the chair with a groan. He'd spent the day chopping firewood and walking the trails. Darren wiped his forehead and pried the cap off a bottled soda. He occupied himself with the food and drink as he talked, yet his attention never left her.

"How are you holding up?"

She wasn't sure how to answer. Since the abduction, she'd awoken to nightmares and a sensation of someone inside the room with her. The night terrors prompted her to install the night light. It wasn't helping. She'd convinced herself she just needed time to process the kidnapping.

Darren set the sandwich down and rested his forearms on the table. His forehead creased with concern over her non-answer.

"Are you sure you want to spend this much time with a basket case?" she asked.

"What's that supposed to mean? Raven, you experienced a traumatic event, and it will take time to make sense of what happened. Tell me what you're feeling."

She picked her nails and sat back in the chair.

"The nightmares keep getting worse. Sometimes, I dream about Ellie Fisher." Ellie Fisher was the woman Damian Ramos and Mark Benson kidnapped before they grabbed Raven. "I wake up in the farmhouse, and I hear Ellie screaming from another room. Damian tosses me inside the room with Ellie. But something is wrong. She's not yelling anymore. There's blood covering the walls. They slit her throat, and I'm next."

"It's a dream. In real life, you escaped."

"I didn't escape. You saved me."

"Chelsey and Deputy Lambert saved you. I just came along for the ride."

Raven dropped her face into her hands and rubbed her eyes.

"It happens during the day too. I go to work, and Chelsey's sick half the time, so I'm alone in the office. Every little sound makes me jump, and I always worry someone is following me."

"It will get better with time."

"Will it? One month later, and I'm getting worse."

Darren set his ankle on his knee. He bit into his sandwich, considering his words as he chewed.

"Have you considered visiting a therapist?"

"A shrink?"

"Would it be so bad? Thomas sees Dr. Mandal, and you keep saying Chelsey should seek counseling."

"I suppose you're right. Something has to change. I can't live like this another month."

"Don't rush the process. I'm here for you."

"And I appreciate you more than words can express. All this anxiety is in my head. As long as I'm around other people, I'm fine. Like this afternoon at the cookout, we were all together, laughing and talking, and my anxiety disappeared. Heck, I didn't even think about the abduction."

He tapped his hand on the table.

"There you go. Spend time around people. You're always welcome here, and you can call me whenever Chelsey no-shows at work."

"It would be nice to get over this. I used to love being alone." She spied the hurt on his face and covered her mouth. "That came out wrong. I far prefer your company to being alone. But there was something relaxing about a long run in the early morning, or curling up with a book after Mom fell asleep. Now I leap at every noise."

"I understand what you meant about being alone. Why do you think I live here?" He gestured around the cabin. "No horns honking outside my window day and night, no traffic jams or crowded sidewalks. Sometimes, it's nice to be on your own. But it's better if you spend time with friends and family until you get your sea legs back."

As she sipped her water, she stared at him over the bottle.

"I regret something I did after the cookout."

He straightened in his chair.

"This doesn't sound good."

She pressed her lips together and lowered her eyes.

"I kinda eavesdropped on Thomas and Gray while they discussed the Jane Doe."

"Define eavesdropped. Like you overheard them while you chatted with LeVar?"

"I hid beside the house while they talked on the deck."

Darren glared at her through the tops of his eyes.

"Raven."

"Yeah, that was lousy of me."

"Why would you do such a thing?"

Elbow on the table, she rested her cheek on her palm and toyed with the napkin.

"Scout Mourning and LeVar visited me this morning and offered to research the state park case. They have this crazy idea of collaborating with me."

"So they're solving the mystery."

"Right."

"Raven, this isn't a game. Those bones belong to somebody's daughter."

"I'm not minimizing the girl's death, and anything we discover we'll share with the sheriff's department. It's just that working with LeVar and Scout gave me a boost. It made me excited to be an investigator again."

Darren pushed his plate aside. A playful grin appeared on his face.

"Well, did you learn anything important?"

"Why? Do you want in on this investigation?"

"The bones were in my state park."

"Good point."

"Tell me what you overheard."

"Sheriff Gray believes Skye Feron's friends, Justine Adkins and Paige Sutton, lied to him during the investigation six years ago. They're involved somehow."

"That's not much to go on."

"No, but Paige Sutton still lives in Wolf Lake, and Justine Adkins arrived in town a few days ago."

"She came after the story broke about the bones. That's curious."

Raven finished her water and set the bottle aside.

"Could be Justine believes the dead girl is Skye and wants to say goodbye."

"Or Justine and Paige had something to do with Skye's death."

Raven eyed Darren.

"You *do* want in on the investigation."

He smirked.

"It's been a while since I got to play cops and killers."

14

Thomas dialed the Orange Tulip bed-and-breakfast outside Kane Grove. After the front desk forwarded his call to Justine Adkins, the phone rang seven times and dumped to a recorded message, as it had the two previous times he'd called. Either Justine had gone out for the night, or she wasn't accepting phone calls. That made Thomas wonder if she was avoiding Paige Sutton, for the same unknown reason Justine hadn't told her old friend where she was staying.

Sitting at the kitchen table with Jack at his feet, Thomas yawned into his hand and wiped his eyes. He should have been asleep by now. But this case wouldn't let him rest, and he sensed something important happening behind the scenes between Justine, Paige Sutton, and the missing Skye Feron. He massaged Jack's neck. The dog sat up and lolled his tongue, panting up at Thomas.

"What should we do, Jack?" The dog grinned at him. "Paige Sutton lied to me tonight, but I don't know why."

He peered through the deck door. Night hid the lake from his vision, the darkness pressing against the glass like a living thing. A light shone inside the guest house. LeVar was still awake. Thomas wanted to knock on the teenager's door and talk about anything except murdered girls and skeletons in the mud.

On his memo pad, he'd scribbled notes about the case. The girls wore friendship bracelets, and one bracelet ended up on Paige Sutton's counter after someone picked the lock on her front door. If Thomas bought Paige's story, and he wasn't sure he did, Justine's bracelet was at home. Which meant this new bracelet belonged to Skye Feron. Or someone who knew about the bracelets had designed a replica.

Did someone murder Skye, bury her beside the river, and emerge six years later to haunt Paige?

His inability to contact Justine Adkins didn't sit right with him. The woman wasn't a suspect, but Thomas sensed her involvement in Skye's disappearance. He rolled his phone around in his hand, undecided. Then he called Aguilar, remembering his deputy was working the swing shift until midnight.

"I need you to do me a favor. Drive over to Kane Grove. There's a bed-and-breakfast on the outskirts of the city called the Orange Tulip."

"I'm familiar with the place."

"Justine Adkins is staying on property. Check for her Acura, and if there's a light on in her room, bang on the door and ensure she's all right."

"And if there isn't a light on?"

"No reason to wake her. But scope the place out. Someone is playing a dangerous game with Paige Sutton. He might go after Justine next."

"Roger. I'll radio you when I get there."

"Thank you, Aguilar."

Thomas set the phone down and sat back. He hoped he'd acted fast enough to protect Justine Adkins.

~

BEYOND THE FLOOD that had unearthed the teenage girl's skeleton, the Lucifer Falls creek snaked through the state park, wound along a county route, and passed sleepy farmhouses on its way to meeting its mother. The creek fed into the Nightshade River and continued south toward Kane Grove before it cut into the next county. Along its many bends and choke points, water converged during torrential rains and overflowed its banks, scouring away the land. Tonight, the water meandered in quietude, though it coughed up the thick boughs it had swallowed during this week's storms.

Fog crept off the river like a silent, stalking beast, spreading across the flood plains as it bled into Kane Grove. The fog consumed all, including the supermarket on the city's south side, the mist thickening until it was impossible to see the corralled shopping carts.

Justine Adkins encountered the fog when she exited the supermarket, pushing a cart. She'd bought just enough to feed herself for two more nights, if she didn't leave sooner. Going out to a restaurant wasn't an option, if she wanted to keep a low profile and avoid anyone from her past recognizing her. One hand held the car keys between her palm and the shopping cart handle, the keys digging into her flesh and pressing against bone. She couldn't see her car yet, only the ocean of mist wetting her skin.

A silhouette emerged as someone grunted and cried out. A van sat in a parking space catty-corner to her car. Behind the van, a man in a wheelchair struggled to lift grocery bags through the side doors. He held the bag under one arm as he steadied himself with the other by gripping the open door. The man made a pitiful sound as he wrestled with the shopping bag.

"May I help you, sir?"

"Thank you, but I think I can do it."

Justine stopped the shopping cart behind her Acura and clicked the key fob. The car beeped twice and flashed its lights, pulling the man into greater detail. His feet rested on the foot plates, one leg encased in a plaster cast from the knee down. The poor man was injured, not crippled.

"I can't carry bags or push a cart on crutches, you understand. Gotta use the wheelchair until I load everything into the van."

Justine nodded in reply.

The casters squealed like frightened kittens and kept shifting as he hoisted the bag. She flinched every time the chair rolled backward. It was akin to watching a man on his last legs stumble toward the finish line during a marathon. The battle appeared lost.

"Are you sure I can't help? It wouldn't be any trouble."

"You're very kind. But I have to learn on my own. It's only been a month since the accident, you see."

Justine placed her groceries in the trunk. Casting another glance over her shoulder, she rounded the car and set the purse inside. Though he'd refused her help, she couldn't leave him like this.

The bottom of the bag ripped. He cursed as food cans smacked the macadam and rolled across the lot toward her feet. She bent to retrieve the belongings as he sobbed.

"It's okay. I'll help you load your groceries."

"They should reinforce the bottoms of these bags," he muttered.

The lights caught his profile from the side. For a moment, she was certain she knew him from somewhere, though the fog played tricks on her eyes and distorted his face. With the cans clutched between her arms, she shuffled to the van.

"You're too kind," he kept saying.

"Where do you want me to set these?"

"Anywhere inside is fine. Just push them in a bit so they don't roll out the door after I get home."

"Sure."

She wondered how he'd get the wheelchair into the van and lift himself into the seat. A crutch lay in the back, and candy bar wrappers and food particles littered the floor. As she stacked the cans away, crumbs soiled her hands. She wiped off her palms, gritting her teeth as she eyed the filth staining her hands.

"Could you be a doll and grab the crutch for me?"

"I'd be happy to. Are you all right to fold the chair yourself and lift it into the van?"

"Yes, ma'am. Just need that crutch, if you would be so kind."

The crutch lay beyond her reach. She couldn't grab it without crawling inside the van, something she wasn't comfortable doing. His gaze burned into her back.

"Can't you reach it?"

"I'm trying," she winced, stretching her arms out.

Justine had no choice. She placed one knee on the floor. Knew the grit would ruin her slacks. As her hand closed over the crutch, she heard the metallic shriek of the man lifting himself out of the chair.

Something thundered down and struck her head. At first, she thought she'd whacked her skull on the sliding door. Reaching behind, she touched her head as her eyes wobbled. Blood covered her palm. More blows rained down, each more frenzied than the last. His spittle wet her neck as he breathed against her flesh.

The inside of the van spun and undulated before her vision failed.

15

Raven's shoulders slumped after lying to Chelsey. She'd told her boss she was driving to the state park to speak with Paul Phipps about the missing money, and that much was true. But Raven hadn't told Chelsey about stopping at Thomas Shepherd's guest house to meet with Scout, LeVar, and Darren. Today was their first day working on the state park skeleton case. Technically, she was doing investigative work, though she hadn't started a case file at Wolf Lake Consulting to make it official.

She parked on the shoulder. The sheriff was at work this morning, and she didn't feel right blocking his driveway. Swishing through the soft grass, the sun warm on her face, Raven wished every work day was like this. Pulling open the door, she heard their voices from the front of the guest house. LeVar had set up a card table beside the window. Scout sat at one end in her wheelchair, the morning light painting soft highlights through her hair. Darren conferred with LeVar and Scout, the ranger's arms propped on the windowsill.

That's when she realized this wasn't a game for them. They were serious about this investigation—Darren wanted answers so he could keep the park safe, while LeVar and Scout determined to catch a killer and take him off the street. Whatever guilt Raven harbored vanished in that moment. This was vital work, far more important than catching the campgrounds thief, or nailing a disgruntled spouse in an infidelity case.

"I hope you didn't start without me," she said, tossing a pen and pad on the card table.

"We already figured it out, Sis," LeVar said, grinning. "You snooze, you lose."

Darren squeezed her hand and kissed her cheek. She met his eyes and felt her heart melt.

"Since you already solved a six-year-old mystery, brief me while I stare at the lake." She pulled out a chair and motioned for LeVar and Darren to take their places around the table. "I take it this will be our official headquarters?"

"Why not?" LeVar rocked back in his chair. "I've got the space, Scout lives next door, and Darren is a short walk from the cabin."

Darren nodded and said, "It's discreet and perfect. But we don't want Thomas catching us before we're ready to share our findings."

"We'll store our data and notes on my computer," Scout said, gesturing at the PC in the corner. "LeVar carried it from my room."

"That's generous," Raven said. "You don't mind living without your computer for a few weeks?"

"It's not optimal. But Mom watches me like a hawk and doesn't want me on the Virtual Searchers site without her supervision. So I'm not missing out on much." Scout held up her phone. "Plus, I can research anything on my phone. I store all my links in the cloud."

"Speaking of Scout's mother," Darren said, clasping his hands on the table. "Naomi needs to be in the loop. Regardless of Scout's value to this investigation, we can't hide anything from Naomi. She deserves to know what her fourteen-year-old daughter is up to."

They all turned to Scout, who pouted her lips. The girl threw up her hands.

"She won't be happy. But if that's what the group wants, I guess I don't have a choice."

"All right," Raven said. "We'll use Scout's PC until I locate an alternate option. Chelsey stores old, unused computers in a closet at the firm. I'll sweet talk her into donating a PC...once I break it to her that we're investigating the state park case." Raven clicked her pen. "What's first on the agenda?"

"We need security cameras on the guest house."

"Isn't that overkill?"

"Someone broke inside three days ago."

"Oh?" Raven turned to LeVar. "I wasn't aware of this?"

LeVar shrugged.

"Nothin' stolen. Shep Dawg found a shoe print near the window."

"What happened to Deputy Dog?"

"He ain't a deputy anymore. But he's still a dawg."

Raven scrunched her brow. Her brother owned little, but the intruder must have seen something worth stealing.

"Hey, Darren. I wonder if this break-in is related to the stolen money."

"Paul Phipps's wife?" Darren rubbed his chin. "I hadn't considered the possibility. Wouldn't that be something if it's the same guy?"

"We can't have people breaking in," said Scout, shifting her chair. "Not with sensitive information on the computer. I say we place two security cameras outside and send the feeds to our phones. That way we can monitor the guest house from anywhere. Better safe than sorry."

"Doesn't Thomas have cameras aiming into his backyard? He installed them after the Jeremy Hyde murders."

"He has 'em," LeVar said. "Problem is, they don't cover the guest house."

"So we need a monitoring system. I'll place an order this afternoon. We should get them within seven days."

Raven shook her head.

"That's too long to wait, since LeVar already had a break-in. There's a place in Syracuse that stocks everything we need. I'll swing past after work." She turned her head to Darren. "You mentioned monitoring the trails at Wolf Lake State Park. What's the status on that?"

"My shipment of trail cameras will arrive this afternoon. I want two cameras covering the trails in and out of the gorge, in case our killer returns to the burial site. I'll stick a third camera between the campgrounds and the trail leading toward our...headquarters."

"Ain't nobody getting past me, anyway," LeVar said, puffing out his chest. "Now that we got a monitoring system, let's catch a killer. What about these two women Skye Feron went to school with?"

"Justine Adkins and Paige Sutton," Raven said. "According to Sheriff Gray, the three girls were close friends during high school. Something happened that placed Skye in danger. It's conceivable her friends are hiding evidence."

"What do we know about Justine and Paige?" asked Darren.

"Paige Sutton lives in Wolf Lake. She'll be easy to track down. Justine Adkins moved outside Rochester, but she returned to Wolf Lake earlier this week to visit. We need to figure out where she's staying."

"Didn't someone break into Paige's house Wednesday night?" Scout asked. "That's the rumor on the village message boards."

"I heard the same rumor. No way I can ask Thomas without tipping him off."

"The break-in has to be related to our investigation. Was anything stolen? Is the killer warning Paige that she's next?"

Darren held up a hand.

"Wait. We're assuming a lot here. Our skeleton is a Jane Doe. The bones might not belong to Skye Feron."

"But if they do," said Raven. "We can catch the killer by determining his motivation. What happened between the three girls that put Skye in danger?"

"We should start with their backgrounds. Dig into their pasts."

"That's where I come in," said Scout, swiveling her chair around and wheeling herself to the computer. She called up a browser and clicked a link. "Wolf Lake High alumni members maintain an unofficial message board. It doesn't have the bells and whistles of Facebook or Instagram. But graduates use the message board to chat about the past and plan reunions."

Raven rose from her chair and leaned over Scout's shoulder.

"I wasn't aware of the website. Then again, I grew up in Harmon. How far back do the messages go?"

"A decade."

"Damn. Those are a lot of messages. But if the message boards hint at what happened to Skye, the sheriff's department already knows."

"We're not searching for messages about Skye. We'll target messages which mention Paige and Justine by name, since they may be the keys to this investigation."

"All right. LeVar and Scout, the ball is in your court. Scour the forum and learn everything you can about Skye's friends. Focus on significant events that preceded Skye's disappearance."

Scout glanced at LeVar, who gave the girl a high five.

"What do you want me to do?" Darren asked.

"Set up those trail cameras and figure out who's moving through the state park. While you work on that, I'll purchase more cameras and aim them at the guest house."

Darren folded his arms.

"Hey, LeVar. Do the Harmon Kings use the state park trails to move drugs through the village?"

"Nah, bro. Not saying Rev doesn't push drugs or have contacts in Wolf Lake. But they don't use the state park."

"Are you sure? The forest around Lucifer Falls is a great place to hide a body."

"That's not how Rev operates. If Rev puts a bullet in your head, he damn well wants the world to know. He's all about sending messages, making sure his enemies don't cross him."

Raven opened her mouth to respond when LeVar's phone rang. The teenager's brow lifted when he glanced at the screen.

"I gotta take this. Y'all work out the details. I'll be back in a second."

The door closed. Scout, Raven, and Darren glanced at each other.

"Anybody know what that was about?" Raven asked.

Scout lifted a shoulder, and Darren shook his head. Raven muttered a curse under her breath. She'd become protective of LeVar since he left the Kings. He had a steady job with Ruth Sims at the Broken Yolk, and he'd declared a college major. A year ago, she couldn't have pictured LeVar attaining his GED or enrolling in college. The truth was, she'd believed he'd die before his twenty-first birthday, if he didn't leave the Kings.

A minute later, LeVar returned. His calm expression appeared painted on, and his fingers clawed at his blue jeans.

"Everything okay?"

"Yeah. Why do you ask?"

Darren stood up from his chair and circled the table.

"What are you hiding, LeVar?" Darren asked.

"Nothing."

Darren gestured at Scout.

"The Mourning family lives next door. If you're in trouble, you need to consider the people around you."

LeVar's jaw worked back and forth.

"I ain't in trouble. Told y'all. I gave up the Kings and put gang life behind me."

Raven softened her eyes and touched his shoulder.

"Then who called?"

LeVar stared at Scout, then lowered his eyes.

"That was Anthony."

"Anthony Fisher?"

"Yeah."

Anthony Fisher was the youngest member of the Harmon Kings. When LeVar ran with the gang, he protected Anthony from Rev, the notorious leader of the Kings.

"What did he want?"

LeVar pushed his hands into his pockets.

"Anthony wants out of the Kings. He figures, if I could do it, he can too."

"I can't imagine Rev will take kindly to Anthony leaving."

"Nope."

"LeVar, stay out of it. You're not the kid's father."

LeVar folded his arms over his chest.

"Anthony doesn't have a father, so I'm as good as he's got." LeVar shuffled his feet. "He wants to meet in Harmon."

"Hell, no. Tell Anthony to come to Wolf Lake if he wants guidance. Or call the sheriff's department. Thomas will protect him like he protected you."

"That'll raise suspicion. If Anthony plans to jump ship, you can bet Rev already knows. Anthony traveling to Wolf Lake will draw Rev, and you don't want the leader of the Harmon Kings in our village."

"I'm worried Rev will target you and Anthony."

LeVar's eyes hardened.

"He'll get what's coming to him if he does."

"It's not safe for you to return to Harmon."

"I gotta help my boy. Who else he got?"

Raven looked to Darren. If they didn't stop LeVar from driving to Harmon, Rev would kill him.

16

"Last session, we spoke about your father. You planned to visit your parents before you returned today. How did that go?"

Thomas glances everywhere but at Dr. Mandal.

"I've been busy with two new cases."

"I read about the skeleton below the fall, and the kidnapped woman."

"Crime never sleeps."

"And yet you still had time to get together with your friends."

Thomas drums his legs. He knows Dr. Mandal is right. But he doesn't appreciate the woman playing parent with him.

"I'll go tomorrow."

"You don't need to promise me, Thomas. This isn't about me. This is about you and your father."

"He doesn't want to talk about the lung cancer."

She presses her lips together and leans forward with her hands clasped over her knee.

"Not many people living on borrowed time wish to discuss their projected funeral dates. This was never about you and your father discussing his cancer. You need each other, because you are father and son."

"We've never had a father-son relationship."

"And yet you are. You can't change the past, Thomas, and you can't *change your father. But you can be there for him, as his child, during his time of need."*

THOMAS HUNG up the phone and scrunched his brow. He didn't like this at all. Paige Sutton had just called because she hadn't heard from Justine Adkins.

Lambert rapped his knuckles on the office door and brought Thomas out of his thoughts.

"Everything all right, Sheriff?"

Thomas let out a breath and rocked back in his chair, his hands clasped over his belly. If he added a few inches to his height and fifty pounds around his gut, he'd be the spitting image of Sheriff Gray in twenty years.

"That was Paige Sutton. She can't locate Justine Adkins."

Lambert frowned and lowered himself into a chair.

"Perhaps she blew out of town and drove home. You said you sensed a riff between the women."

"I did. But Aguilar pawed around the bed-and-breakfast last evening. Justine's car wasn't in the lot, yet the owner claimed she hadn't checked out."

"She had a room in Kane Grove, right?"

"At a place called the Orange Tulip."

"I'll make a few calls and check with Kane Grove PD."

"Thank you, Deputy."

Lambert exited the room and left Thomas alone with his fears. He felt the investigation spinning out of control, as the Thea Barlow case had a month ago. He drummed a pen against his desk as he considered his next move. Then he lifted the receiver, called the Orange Tulip, and waited while the clerk transferred him to Justine's room. No answer. Next, he phoned the front desk at the Orange Tulip. The manager sounded harried and too busy to talk after confirming the woman hadn't checked out this morning.

"Is her car in the parking lot? She drives a red Acura."

The manager gave Thomas an exaggerated sigh.

"Hold one moment." Acoustic guitar played over the phone while Thomas waited. "I don't see a red Acura, Sheriff. If you locate Ms. Adkins, she needs to tell me if she intends to keep the room past tomorrow morning. I have many guests clamoring for the room, and I can't wait any longer."

The manager ended the call before Thomas could reply.

Rising from his chair, Thomas wandered into the operations center and rested his back against the wall. He watched Lambert across the room, the deputy's head bobbing as he jotted notes on a sheet of paper. Lambert hung up the phone and turned his chair around.

"We found her car."

"Justine Adkins's Acura?"

"I put a call into Kane Grove PD. Turns out they received a complaint about an abandoned vehicle at the KG Shopping Market. The owner assumed somebody's car broke down. But when nobody showed up to tow it away, he called the police."

Thomas grabbed his hat.

"Call Kane Grove PD and have them meet me at the grocery store."

"Will do."

Thomas hopped into his cruiser and gunned the engine. He sensed time was running out on Justine Adkins, as if someone set an hourglass on its head. As he turned onto the highway, he radioed Lambert and had him run a check on Justine's credit cards. Lambert confirmed she'd used her credit card at the KG Shopping Market after ten o'clock last evening, around the time Aguilar had searched for Adkins at the Orange Tulip.

The detective awaiting Thomas was a lanky woman in a dark blue pants suit and heels, her almond colored hair cut in a shaggy, angled bob.

"Thanks for coming over, Sheriff. I'm Detective Presley."

"Thomas Shepherd," he said, offering his hand.

"We're fortunate your deputy called when he did. The manager wanted the Acura towed. Any idea what happened to the owner?"

Thomas gave Detective Presley the background surrounding Justine Adkins and her two friends.

"So this might be related to a missing persons case from six years ago?" she asked.

"It might very well be. This must be the car."

Thomas followed Presley to the red Acura. The tires straddled the line, suggesting the missing woman struggled to park the car in the fog. With gloves on his hands, Thomas grabbed the handle. The unlocked door opened.

Presley turned away and plugged her nose. The interior smelled like roadkill, and he almost expected to find Justine's dead body tucked between the seats.

Thomas nodded at the bag on the passenger seat. Justine's wallet sat atop a folded sweatshirt. Snatching the wallet, he opened it and found a hundred dollars in cash and two credit cards.

"This wasn't a robbery. If someone took her, he left her bag with the wallet inside."

Presley popped the trunk.

"I found where the smell is coming from. I guess cold cuts don't last long inside a hot car. I'll radio the station and have the crime techs check the car for evidence. But it appears someone snatched her out of the parking lot and drove off."

"I take it the shopping market has security cameras."

"They do, but it was foggy last night. Not sure how much we'll see."

Presley followed Thomas inside. The store manager led them to a gloomy room in the back and copied the security camera footage. Thomas gave the video a quick scan and came to the same conclusion as Presley. Too foggy. Between the poor camera quality and the dense mist, he couldn't spot the Acura, though he caught Adkins pushing a shopping cart through the automatic doors.

"I'll have our lab clean up the video and bring out the details," Presley said.

Thomas didn't think it would make a difference.

"I need the names of everyone working last night," Thomas told the manager.

"I can get those for you. Harry Sims is here now. He's my assistant manager. Harry closed the store at midnight."

Sims remembered Adkins after Thomas showed him a picture of her driver's license.

"There were only two or three shoppers in the store after ten," Sims said, creasing his forehead as he remembered.

"Anyone following her or acting strangely?"

"No, but a van almost ran me over when I went outside to corral the shopping carts."

"What time did this occur?"

"Sometime between ten-thirty and eleven. I figured it was a kid hot-rodding through the parking lot."

"Did you get a look at the driver or read the license plate?"

"It was too damn foggy."

"How about the make and model?"

"Couldn't tell you. It was a dark color, maybe blue or black. Sorry I can't help more."

17

Raven followed Darren to the state park and left her black Nissan Rogue beside his truck. They split off after Darren noticed his trail cameras had arrived. Raven knocked on the door to Paul Phipps's cabin and didn't get an answer. She peeked through the windows. They hadn't made the bed before they left, and a stack of dishes littered the sink.

She followed the trail into the forest, intent on catching up to Darren. Now that they were away from LeVar and Scout, she wanted to tell him about the lacerations on Chelsey's chest. An unthinkable idea passed through her head. Was Chelsey cutting herself?

Darren was probably halfway to Lucifer Falls. The woods seemed darker than when she'd hiked with Darren. Being alone lent an ominous overtone to the forest. Leaves crunched in the distance as someone cut between the trails, breaking park rules by taking a shortcut. It could have been Darren, or a hiker in a hurry. Or the Lucifer Falls killer.

She stopped beside a tree and listened as the footsteps moved away. Then she heard nothing except bird calls and animals rustling through the gloom. This was a bad idea. Darren was too far ahead, and her nerves were frayed. As she turned back to the cabins, she spotted footprints in the dirt circling cabin three. She wouldn't have given the prints a second thought except they congregated in two places—outside the door and beneath the dusty window. It appeared someone had searched for a way inside the cabin.

She followed the prints and knelt to examine a cluster beneath the window. The prints fit a male sneaker, size ten or eleven.

Raven circled cabin three and knocked. Again, nobody answered. Most campers were out on the lake or walking the trails at this time of day, though she suspected some would return soon for lunch.

A dirt and stone path fronted the cabins and merged with the ridge trail. She walked down the path, her focus on the space between the cabins. Between cabins seven and eight, she found another set of prints. Again they converged beneath the window and at the door.

She stopped beside the prints and snapped a photograph with her phone. Everything appeared identical—the tread pattern, shoe size, and print depth. Someone was testing the locks on the doors and windows. This had to be the same person who swiped two-hundred dollars from Paul Phipps's wife. She searched along the window. The pane was off its tracks, as if someone jostled it open recently.

"What are you doing there?"

Raven swung around to a lanky man with gray, wispy hair, a white mustache, and glasses.

"Sorry to bother you, sir. But did you notice anyone circling the cabins or trying to break inside the last few days?"

"Can't say that I did, and I would have called the cops, anyhow. Who are you?"

"Raven Hopkins. I'm a private investigator with Wolf Lake Consulting."

"A private eye, eh? You got identification?"

"I have my driver's license, if that helps."

Raven removed the license from her wallet and showed it to the man. He narrowed his eyes.

"Looks like you are who you say you are. But that doesn't mean you're a private investigator. What business do you have at the camp?"

"One of your neighbors hired me after his wife had money stolen from her wallet."

"You don't say."

Raven removed a pen and notepad.

"May I ask your name, sir?"

"Shillingford. Cole Shillingford."

"Mr. Shillingford, have you or your neighbors lost any items of value over the last week?"

He called over his shoulder without taking his eyes off Raven.

"Aileen, come out here."

A gray-haired woman in a flannel shirt and jeans emerged from the cabin. She glanced at Raven and widened her eyes.

"Should I call the police, Cole?"

"She says she's a private investigator. Claims a camper hired her to catch the thief running around these parts." The woman edged away from the door and stood beside her husband. "Tell her about the money you lost."

Raven's eyes lit up.

"Someone stole your money, Mrs. Shillingford?"

"It wasn't much. Twenty or thirty dollars. I don't recall how much I left on the table before we took a walk."

"When did this occur?"

She glanced at her husband.

"Monday afternoon, wasn't it, Cole?"

He nodded and puffed out his mustache.

"How do we know you didn't take it?"

Raven stared at the couple.

"What?"

"You appear out of nowhere, flash a driver's license, and claim you're a private investigator. That's a pretty good story if you want to fool people. In the meantime, someone's stealing money from campers. Where's your badge?"

"I don't have a badge."

"Then there's no way to verify you really are a private investigator."

Raven took a composing breath.

"Look, I'm just trying to help. If I catch the person who's stealing from you, maybe I'll get your money back. I'm friends with Ranger Holt. He'll vouch for me."

Cole glared at Raven. Aileen shrugged her shoulders and sauntered back to the cabin.

Opening her wallet, Raven handed Cole a business card.

"This is the firm I work for. Should you see anyone hanging around the cabins who doesn't belong, call me. And be sure to tell Ranger Holt."

Cole turned the card over in his hands as Raven walked away.

18

Deputy Aguilar arrived for the swing shift at the same time Thomas returned from interviewing Paige Sutton again. He kept thinking about what the assistant manager at the supermarket said—a dark blue or black van raced through the parking lot around the time Justine Adkins went missing. Unlike larger villages, Wolf Lake didn't have traffic cameras scattered around town. He hoped someone would come forward and remember seeing the van.

Inside the kitchen, he stirred sugar into his coffee. Aguilar shook her head.

"You don't approve of coffee. I remember."

"It's not that I disapprove of coffee or caffeine. But you're loading it with sugar. You might as well chug a Coke or one of those heart-disease-causing energy drinks."

Thomas scowled down at the mug. He figured it was a good idea not to tell her he'd dumped two packets of cream into the coffee.

"What would you suggest? Diet soda?"

Aguilar palmed her face.

"Those are even worse. Artificial sweeteners are linked to brain tumors and bladder cancer."

"So the weight loss isn't worth the risk."

She propped herself up on the counter, not an ounce of fat on her chiseled arms.

"Believe it or not, those zero calorie sweeteners you're addicted to cause weight gain."

"Really?"

"Yes, really. Check out the science. You'll never put that garbage in your body again."

Thomas poured the coffee down the drain and scrubbed the mug clean.

"You convinced me."

She lifted her chin at him.

"Try green tea or matcha, if you need an afternoon energy boost. I drink tea first thing in the morning, then space out cups throughout the day. That keeps my blood sugar steady and cuts down on cravings."

"I could do that. I like green tea."

"And instead of wasting your money on an oily sub from the deli, make a protein drink for lunch. You're welcome to use my blender."

"Thanks, Aguilar. I appreciate the tips."

All at-once, she seemed to realize she'd engaged in casual chitchat with her superior. She cleared her throat and hopped off the counter. Thomas smiled to himself. He'd tricked her into talking.

"So," she said, sliding her food into the refrigerator. "What's the latest on your missing person?"

"Nothing new since Kane Grove PD found her vehicle in the grocery store parking lot. I'm about to drive over to Kane Grove and check out the place she's staying at. Why don't you ride with me?"

Thomas took the lake road back to the highway. It took a few minutes longer than cutting through the village center. But the view was worth it. Aguilar sat ramrod straight in the passenger seat, her radio on her shoulder, the hat propped on her head as her hair blew around. Thomas preferred to drive with the windows down.

"You should get a place down here," he said, tilting his head toward the water. "I saw two places go up for sale last week."

"I like my ranch house. These properties are too labor intensive."

He fiddled with the radio while she stared straight ahead through the windshield. Sifting through a catalog of conversation starters in his head, he glanced across the cruiser.

"I'm thinking about weight lifting."

It wasn't a lie, though he had no reason to bring it up, except to strike up a conversation.

"Oh?"

"I've got a spare room I'm not using. Figured it would be the perfect spot for a bench and free weights."

She lifted an eyebrow at him.

"Do you even lift, bro?"

He burst out laughing, and Aguilar couldn't help but grin. Good. He'd found the magic elixir for making her lighten up.

"This may be hard to believe, but I had a gym membership when I lived in Los Angeles."

"Probably one of those pink and purple gyms with treadmills and exercise bikes," Aguilar said, making air quotes around *gyms*.

"You'd be surprised. It was a hole in the wall near Manhattan Beach. My partner's brother owned the place. The gym was nothing but squat racks, pull up bars, and benches.

"I'm impressed. How often did you workout?"

"Two or three times per week at first."

"And then?"

He watched the lake pass by the window.

"Two or three times per year."

"Could have guessed."

When they passed a sprawling mansion on the west side of the lake, he spotted a florist delivery van parked in the driveway. Thomas snickered.

"That was the place that sold me the bouquet."

"The bouquet?"

"You know, when we attended the Magnolia Dance together."

The week after Thomas started working for the Nightshade County Sheriff's Department, Lambert convinced Thomas to ask

Aguilar to the April dance, Wolf Lake's most popular festival. Aguilar feigned coughing to cover a laugh.

"That was quite the night," Thomas continued.

"You picked me up late, sweating like a schoolboy on his first date. Ten minutes after we sat down to eat, you started a fight, and we had to leave."

"The fight wasn't my fault."

"Sure, it wasn't. Everyone who attends the Magnolia Dance ends up punking his ex's new boyfriend."

Chelsey attended the dance with Ray Welch, a heavy drinker who'd bullied Thomas during high school.

"You're twisting the facts, Aguilar. Ray Welch attacked me. As I recall, he said unkind words about you."

"So you defended my honor?"

Thomas laughed.

"More like I subdued him before you kicked his teeth in."

"That's more like it."

Thomas turned the cruiser onto the highway. The sign read four miles to Kane Grove.

"I miss this."

"I'm not sure what you're talking about."

"The two of us being friends, not just coworkers." When she didn't reply, he looked at her. "Just because I'm sheriff doesn't mean things need to change between us. Lambert doesn't treat me differently."

"You trust Lambert's judgment? He's the one who convinced us to attend the dance."

"Good point."

Thomas pulled the cruiser into the bed-and-breakfast's parking lot. The Orange Tulip was a sprawling three-story Colonial Revival home, painted in powder blue. The Nightshade River weaved through the countryside a hundred yards beyond the property, and a railed deck along the back offered a water view. Vehicles with license plates from all over the northeast choked the parking lot.

The manager's office resided inside an addition on the east side of the property. Thomas held the door open for Aguilar, who appeared ready to punch him if he performed another act of chivalry. Gene Maldonado, the Orange Tulip's manager, was a portly man with a soft chin. He had a snobbish habit of looking down his nose.

"You must be the sheriff who keeps calling me," Maldonado said, typing at his computer terminal as he avoided eye contact.

"Good afternoon. I'm Sheriff Shepherd, and this is Deputy Aguilar. We'd like to see Justine Adkins's room."

He sniffed.

"Do you have a warrant?"

"I can get one. But that will take time, which I don't have."

"Is Ms. Adkins in peril, Sheriff?"

"She's missing, yes."

Maldonado printed a sheet of paper and slapped it on the table.

"This is the amount Ms. Adkins owes me," he said, tapping a fat finger on the sheet. The balance read three-hundred dollars. "She paid for the first night up front. We bill the balance to our guests' credit cards upon checkout."

"Are you suggesting she checked out without paying?"

"Her belongings are still in her room. If she wants them back, she must pay."

Aguilar set her arm on the counter and asked, "How do you know her belongings are still in her room?" Flustered, Maldonado returned to his keyboard. "Is it standard protocol to enter your guests' rooms while they are away?"

Maldonado cleared his throat.

"After her car vanished from the parking lot, I feared she'd run off without clearing her balance. I had no choice."

Thomas met Aguilar's eyes. How often did the manager slip into rooms?

"We'd like to see her room now," Thomas said.

The manager plucked a key out of his desk.

"You're persistent. I'll give you that. Follow me."

Maldonado locked the office behind him and led them up a wooden staircase with a polished banister. Four doors stood on the second floor. He knocked on the third door, a courtesy Thomas doubted Maldonado afforded Justine Adkins before he sneaked into her room.

The quaint room was an odd mix of old world charm and modern conveniences, the antique dresser clashing with the flat screen television mounted on the wall. Glass double doors opened to a balcony overlooking the grounds and the Nightshade River.

"I'll leave you alone," Maldonado said, edging out of the room.

Aguilar closed the door in his face without replying.

A leather travel bag lay open on a made bed. Thomas and Aguilar donned gloves before touching anything. He aimed a flashlight inside. The bag held two changes of clothes, suggesting the woman intended to check out the following morning. There was a toothbrush, deodorant, and floss. As Thomas pawed through the bag, Aguilar opened the dresser drawers.

"I never want to visit a hotel again," Aguilar said.

"Why is that?"

"I wonder how often that happens. Hotel staff entering your room while you're out and looking through your belongings. Creepy."

"I doubt it happens often. What do you think of Maldonado?"

Aguilar closed the drawer.

"I wouldn't want him in my room. But he's too pretentious to abduct someone."

"Is that a rule? Kidnappers can't be snobs?"

She thought for a moment and shook her head.

"I can't picture Maldonado kidnapping Justine Adkins. What's his motivation?"

"What was Norman Bates's motivation?"

"Touché. Perhaps we should investigate Maldonado's mother."

Thomas spoke into the radio on his shoulder.

"Lambert, you there?"

"I'm right here, Sheriff," Lambert said over the radio.

"Find everything you can on Gene Maldonado, the manager of the Orange Tulip in Kane Grove."

"I'm on it."

"And after, cruise past Paige Sutton's residence in Wolf Lake before she vanishes too."

Aguilar and Thomas searched the room for any clue that would lead them to Justine Adkins. The path led to a dead end before Thomas felt something in the side compartment of Justine's travel bag. Unzipping the compartment, he fished two items out of hiding. The first was a folded receipt from a Wolf Lake florist. Who would Justine purchase flowers for?

The second hidden item made Thomas pause.

He picked up the beaded friendship bracelet.

19

T hunder groaned beyond the hills, as a black mass crossed the sky and blotted out the sunny afternoon. Scout gave a wary glance through the guest house window when the wind picked up, churning the lake.

She typed at the keyboard, ignoring the building storm. Thunder made her edgy. The deafening crescendos sounded too much like the crash that left her paralyzed from the waist down. Beside her, LeVar fiddled with his phone.

"I thought you wanted to help with this investigation."

He set the phone in his lap.

"I am helping."

"Ever since Anthony called, your head hasn't been in the game."

"Easy now, Ma." He turned the phone off and set it on the card table. "There. Happy now?"

"Don't call me Ma. If I want to *son you*, you'll know."

He leaned his head back and laughed.

"*Aight*, Scout. You don't gotta do me like that." He nodded at the screen. "This that alumni forum you were jawing about earlier?"

"The unofficial Wolf Lake alumni forum, yes."

He scooted his chair forward and scanned the thread topics.

"Ten bucks says this is more Tinder than Facebook."

"Couples looking to hook up and live out their high school days?"

"Bet."

She entered Skye Feron's name into the search bar and pressed the return key. LeVar squinted at the screen.

"Only four results," he said, tapping his fingers on the desk.

"Ah. I see the problem. The default settings only go back three months. We'll change that."

Scout clicked on the advanced search settings and changed the duration to six years. After she clicked the mouse, the results filled seven pages.

"That's more like it. What do the messages say?"

Scout clicked a message, in which a woman named Jessica prayed for Skye's safe return. Other messages offered theories about the girl's disappearance.

"These posters watch *Murder, She Wrote* too often."

"What the hell is *Murder, She Wrote*? That on HBO?"

"Never mind." Scout brushed the hair off her forehead and changed tactics. Typing Paige Sutton's name into the search bar, she scrutinized the results. "Lots of topics. Tell me if you notice her screen name."

"I don't see her. It's like she didn't create an account."

In a second browser window, Scout typed the web address for the Wolf Lake Library. She chewed a nail as she worked. Her eyes stopped on her quarry—a digital version of the Wolf Lake High School yearbook from Skye's senior year. Paige Sutton's face showed up everywhere. Candid photographs, the football and basketball cheer teams, the prom committee, student government. It didn't take a private detective to deduce Paige was incredibly popular.

And yet she wasn't active on the alumni forum.

Scout returned to the forum and located the screen name directory. She searched under P and S.

"That's weird. Why wouldn't the most popular girl at Wolf Lake High sign up for the alumni forum?"

LeVar rested his chin on his fist.

"Probably she's too good for them. Feels the forum is beneath her."

Scout issued a noncommittal groan.

"Or Sheriff Gray was right, and Paige Sutton has something to hide."

"Click on that yearbook again. I wanna check something out."

Scout brought up the yearbook window and slid the mouse to LeVar. After he located the cheerleader team pictures, he ran his finger over the names.

"Staring at the pretty girls, LeVar? Bet you're into pom-poms."

"Anyone ever tell you you're a sicko?"

"I've been called worse. What are you looking for?"

"Her," LeVar said, tapping his finger on the monitor. "That's Justine Adkins. She was on the cheerleader team with Paige Sutton. I bet if you examine the pages, you'll find Justine in as many pictures as Paige. Pretty and popular. Does she have an alumni account?"

Scout checked the forum.

"No."

"Damn. What are they hiding?"

"Let's try something else." Scout's fingers flew across the keyboard. "I'm querying the website for posts mentioning Paige and Justine together."

Their names appeared in posts dating back six years.

"Click on that one," LeVar said, gesturing at a thread titled, *Whatever Happened to Skye*?"

Scout sat forward. A poster named Webb-WLHS referred to Paige as a bitch and claimed Justine slept with half the school.

"Interesting."

"Some gals never get over the catty stuff."

"Hey."

"No offense. Whoever this Webb-WLHS is, she hates Paige and Justine."

"Or is Webb-WLHS a *he*?"

"Check the yearbook."

Scout couldn't locate anyone named Webb in the senior class. A check of the sophomore and junior classes came up empty too.

"Maybe Webb-WLHS missed picture day," said LeVar, studying the photographs.

"Or Webb-WLHS is a sock puppet account."

"A what?"

"You really need to learn about tracking people online, if you intend to go into law enforcement. A sock puppet account is a fake user name. They're usually generic sounding and help the user blend in."

"So is this person a former student disguising her name—"

"Or his."

"Or his," he said, rolling his eyes. "But is Skye's killer stalking the forum?"

"I'll check the person's profile." She clicked the user name. Whoever Webb-WLHS was, the person neglected to include a name, photograph, or class, as the other members had. "Nothing. This person is a fraud."

"The name could mean the user graduated in 2014. Now what?"

"We check what our stranger posted over the last several years."

LeVar shifted his chair and read the messages as Scout opened them.

"In every message, this person has something nasty to say about Paige and Justine. Check this out. *Those whores ruined Dawn's life.*"

Scout tapped her hand on the mouse.

"Who is Dawn?"

"She must be a classmate."

After a thorough check of the senior class, Scout and LeVar couldn't find anyone named Dawn. Nor did the girl exist in the underclassmen photographs.

"I don't know," Scout said, sitting back in her wheelchair. "It's conceivable this Dawn girl attended another school."

"Kane Grove or Harmon?"

"Those would be my guesses."

LeVar turned his phone on. As soon as it rebooted, the phone buzzed with new messages.

"Anthony again?" she asked.

LeVar chewed his lip.

"Yeah."

"What do you intend to do?"

"I gotta help him. Darren and Raven don't understand. He was like a little brother to me."

Scout turned the wheelchair to face him and set her hands on the chair arms.

"LeVar, promise me you won't go back to Harmon without talking to Thomas first."

"Bet."

"I mean it."

"Chill, Scout. You ain't gettin' rid of me that easy."

But as LeVar walked outside to return Anthony's call, Scout knew her friend was lying. She had to stop him. The Harmon Kings would kill LeVar on sight.

20

FRIDAY, AUGUST 13TH 4:10 P.M.

Maggie, the station's administrative assistant since Thomas was a high school intern under Sheriff Gray, was packing her bag when Thomas returned to work. She swiped her orange-brown hair off her shoulder and examined her face in a handheld mirror. Then she noticed him and stuffed the mirror inside her bag.

"Oh, Sheriff. There's a woman waiting to see you. Deputy Lambert showed her to the interview room."

"Any idea who it is?"

"Someone worried about Justine Adkins."

It had to be Paige Sutton. Thomas thanked Maggie and wished her a pleasant weekend. In the kitchen, he grabbed two bottled waters and carried them to the conference room, hoping the woman would open up to him this time.

Paige Sutton sat with her back to Thomas inside the interview room. He caught the woman chewing her nails as she peered through the window toward the village center. Afternoon sunlight poured into the room and painted yellow triangles against the carpet. The palm in the corner wilted from neglect.

Thomas rapped his knuckles against the door and pulled it open. Paige stood and straightened her skirt.

"Please, sit."

Paige gave him an uncertain nod and lowered herself into the chair.

"Water?" he asked, offering her a bottle.

"Thank you."

Thomas took the seat across the table from hers. The woman's eyes were drawn and girded by dark circles. She kept glancing at the window, as if she expected something to burst inside and drag her into the unknown. He'd run a background check on Paige Sutton and found a DUI from four years ago. Otherwise, her record was clean. She held a steady job with the Paris fashion company, and none of her neighbors complained about her.

"What can I do for you, Ms. Sutton?"

"Call me Paige."

"All right."

She stared at the table and composed her words. When she lifted her head, Thomas saw tears glazing the woman's eyes.

"You found Justine's body, didn't you?"

Thomas studied her from across the table.

"Why would you say that?"

"Because it's happening again. Just like six years ago when Skye went missing."

"What's happening again?"

"The kidnappings and murders."

Thomas set his hands on the table.

"We don't know where Justine Adkins is, and we haven't identified the body from the state park. Had you spoken to Justine since she returned to Wolf Lake?"

"Just once. Wednesday morning, we met for coffee in the village."

"I thought the two of you were friends."

Paige's hand moved to her wrist. She touched the friendship bracelet.

"We are."

"Before Justine returned, how often did you speak?"

Paige ran a hand through her blonde hair as her lower lip trembled.

"Not often."

"By not often, do you mean once a month, once a year?"

The woman looked away. She unscrewed the cap on her water bottle and drank, the bottle quivering in her hand.

"Not since high school graduation."

"Did something happen between the two of you?" She didn't answer. "Paige? If there's something important you're holding back that will help me find Justine, tell me now."

Paige's eyes wouldn't sit still. She kept glancing everywhere, except at Thomas.

"We drifted apart after we lost Skye. It was too difficult for us to bear." She pawed through her bag and dabbed a tissue beneath her eyes. "When I saw Justine at the cafe, it was like the old days. She's stubborn and keeps to herself. But she opened up to me. After I didn't hear from Justine, I sensed something was wrong. So I called her last evening and got her voice-mail. That's when I contacted your department."

Thomas wasn't sure how much he wanted to share with the woman. If someone kidnapped Justine, Thomas needed to find her quick. The first forty-eight hours were crucial, not only because murder rates increased beyond that time window, but also witness accounts grew foggy after two or three days.

"We found Justine's Acura at the KG Shopping Market in Kane Grove." He paused and studied Paige, waiting for a reaction. "According to her credit card company, she purchased groceries at ten-twenty-three, and the assistant manager remembers her."

"What happened to her?"

"That's what we're trying to determine. The assistant manager claims a dark colored van almost ran him down around the time Justine left the store. Do you know anyone who drives a black or dark blue van?"

Paige swallowed.

"Should I?"

"Paige, tell me who wanted to hurt Skye during high school. Because if the same person broke into your house and kidnapped Justine, you might be next. I can't help you unless you're straight with me." The woman didn't reply. Her haunted expression peered through the walls, as though viewing a reality only she could see. Thomas sighed. "When I sat down, you were certain we'd found Justine's body. Why?"

Paige shook her head. She fiddled with the bracelet, spinning it around her wrist.

"I'm just scared. That's all."

Thomas sat back.

"Three girls form a bond that lasts through high school. One goes missing, and the other two refuse to speak to each other again."

"But I—"

Thomas held up a hand.

"Yet you both hold on to your friendship bracelets, as if they're lifelines. Something happened during school that drove you and Justine apart, and I sense it got Skye killed. What aren't you telling me, Paige?"

She stood and swung her purse over her shoulder.

"Why am I on trial? I have nothing to hide. My friend is missing. Search for her instead of interrogating me."

"Sit down."

"I came here on my volition. You can't force me to stay."

"Paige, I'm trying to help you. Please." She tossed her purse on the neighboring chair and sat. "Now, let's go back to high school. I remember what it was like to be a teenager. Insecurities, peer pressure. We all made decisions we regret. Was there a boy you competed over with Skye and Justine?"

"I wouldn't steal a boy from my friends."

"Okay. How about a classmate the three of you had a run in with?"

"I told you. Everyone loved Skye."

"But did everyone love you?"

She examined her hands.

"You make me sound conceited."

"I'm simply asking who your enemies are. Someone bullied me during school. It's not unusual."

"There was no bullying at Wolf Lake High. We were a better school than that."

Thomas shrugged his shoulders.

"Then I'm uncertain what you want from me. You claim you have no enemies, and nobody would want to hurt you or your friends. Yet you believe someone murdered Skye, and that person took Justine."

Paige clasped her hands together.

"It's possible the intruder who broke into my house is the same person who kidnapped Justine and murdered Skye. I want protection. Can't you place a deputy in front of my house until you apprehend this psychopath?"

"We don't have enough deputies. I can't watch your home twenty-four hours per day."

"You can't, or you won't?"

"Tell you what. I'll call the state police barracks. They might have enough officers to stake out your neighborhood. But I can't make any promises."

The woman collected her belongings and strode to the door where she glared at Thomas before leaving.

"If you can't protect us, Sheriff, our blood will be on your hands."

21

FRIDAY, AUGUST 13TH 5:25 P.M.

"Yes, Mr. Middleton. I'm happy we resolved your dispute."

Chelsey held the phone away from her ear as Carl Middleton barked through the speaker. The man should have been satisfied she'd proved fraud in the Herb Reid case. But a jerk like Carl Middleton was never content. Now he wanted to sue Herb Reid.

"I'm sorry, but that's a legal matter. You have the video footage. I can't tell you how to proceed, but I feel you should take the win and call it a day."

The curse words flying out of the phone made Chelsey wince.

After Middleton finished screaming and hung up, she lowered her head and rubbed her aching neck. Bending her neck made the cuts on her chest flare with red agony. She unclasped her necklace and pushed it into her desk drawer.

Two missed calls awaited Chelsey on her phone. The first had come from a nurse at the incompetent doctor's office, the idiot who diagnosed her heart condition as anxiety. The nurse wanted Chelsey to schedule a followup appointment. Like hell she would waste another dollar on that doctor. The second call was Raven's. Chelsey set the phone on her desk and tapped the voice-mail icon, playing the message through her speaker.

"Hey, Chelsey. Just checking in on you."

I don't need you to check on me, Chelsey thought with a scowl.

"I need to run an errand in Syracuse this afternoon, then I'll drop by the office." Raven paused and composed her words. "There's something we need to discuss. Don't worry. I'm not lecturing you. I'm your friend, and all I want is to help." Raven's footsteps scuffed the sidewalk as she walked through the city. "I love you, Chelsey. Never forget it. If you're in trouble, you can talk to me."

Chelsey hit the delete icon. The last thing she needed was Raven mothering her. Raven had enough skeletons in her own closet—her drug-addicted mother, her gangster brother. Who was Raven to judge Chelsey?

She shoved her rolling chair back as she stood. The chair collided with Raven's desk and jiggled the mouse, activating the computer screen. Chelsey walked away and stopped. A digital map of the state park filled the screen, a green dot pulling her attention. She examined the satellite image of the terrain surrounding Lucifer Falls.

Chelsey moved the mouse before the screen saver reactivated. Studying the image, she let her arms fall to her sides. The green locater on the map marked where the sheriff's department unearthed bones beside the creek.

Why was Raven investigating the Jane Doe murder behind Chelsey's back?

CHARCOAL GRILLS SENT mouthwatering scents through the state park as Darren cut down the ridge trail. It was dinner time, and everyone at the camp had sat down to enjoy a meal except him. After placing the trail cameras earlier, he'd obsessed over them. Were they working? Three times he tested the cameras and walked through their fields of vision, then checked the footage on the computer in his office. There had to be a way to send the pictures to his phone. But he hadn't figured out the app. Raven would know what to do.

He checked his reception and dialed her number, pleased when she answered. A motor growled in the background. Raven was driving with the windows down.

"Hey, babe. Where are you?"

"I'm coming out of Syracuse now," she said. She raised the window and squelched the noise, making it easier for Darren to hear her. "I picked up two security cameras in the city. They're top of the line models. Scout should be excited. Once we set them up, we can monitor the guest house on our phones."

"Good work. I'm starting to dig this Nancy Drew, Scooby Doo mystery busting team. Speaking of cameras, I haven't figured out the app for my trail cameras."

She snickered.

"And you need my help."

"Yep."

"Ranger Holt, are you concocting reasons for me to visit you on a Friday night?"

"I'm rather helpless with technology. I need a strong, smart woman to set me straight. And do other things."

"Meow. Give me an hour. I haven't checked on Mom since breakfast, and I want to drop the cameras off with LeVar."

"All right, I appreciate the help. How's Chelsey today?"

Raven cussed.

"I completely forgot to stop by the office. Add that to my to-do list."

"Is everything okay?"

"Something is up with Chelsey, but I can't talk. I'm behind a dump truck, so this isn't the best time to discuss what's going on. We'll talk later."

"I'll be here."

He ended the call and stared at the phone. Something was going on. He'd heard the worry in Raven's voice when he mentioned Chelsey.

Waving away a curious bumblebee, Darren cut through the trees. Birdsong played through the forest, and the late afternoon light created a picket fence pattern through the trees. He was half a mile from camp when movement in the forest caught his eye. Darren pulled up and stood behind a thick maple tree. A hundred feet away, a shadow shifted in the woods. Hikers weren't allowed off trail. The forest held hidden dangers—dead falls, bramble, even the occasional bear. But he wasn't a stickler for the rules, provided the hiker complied after he asked the person to return to the trail.

What bothered Darren most was this person didn't seem like a hiker. Instead, the stranger moved from tree to tree, concealing himself. Darren checked the GPS on his phone. As he suspected, the unknown figure hid near a drop off that plummeted fifty feet into Wolf Lake. One wrong move, and the soft forest ground might give way.

Darren slipped out from behind the maple tree and jogged toward an oak, staying light on his feet to avoid spooking the stranger. He was close enough to see a man peering through binoculars toward the lake. What was he looking at? Darren waited until he was certain the man hadn't spotted him before he crept closer. It was eighty degrees in the shade, and the man wore a hooded sweatshirt with the string drawn tight to conceal his face.

As Darren climbed over a log, his foot came down on a fallen branch and snapped it in half. The man's head shot up. Before Darren cursed his carelessness, the man took off running up the hill. Darren cut across the forest, tree limbs whipping his face as he fought to keep up. He was in good shape, fitter than he'd been as a Syracuse police officer. But his quarry seemed to take two steps for every one Darren took, the stranger pulling away.

"Hey! Come back here!"

Darren leaped through bramble, the thorns tearing red streaks into his flesh. He knew shortcuts that would take him to any of the park's trails. But the man was too agile and fast. Near the campgrounds, Darren leaned against a tree and caught his breath. He'd lost sight of the stranger.

Wiping the sweat off his brow, he batted away a swarm of gnats and backtracked to where he'd first seen the unknown man. Maybe he'd dropped an item that would help Darren identify him. Darren's gut told him this was the state park thief. But a chill rolled down his back when he considered an alternative—he'd chased the killer who murdered the young woman beside the creek. Darn his incompetence with technology. Had he properly set up the trail camera application, he could have checked his phone. It was possible the man appeared on multiple cameras in the woods. If the stranger visited the grave site below Lucifer Falls, he'd have evidence this was the killer.

Darren edged down the ridge, walking sideways so his shoes didn't slip on the loose soil. Blues from the lake siphoned through the woods, as though an endless sky lay beyond the forest. He spotted the group of trees where he'd first seen the man. Darren knelt down and squinted at the footprints. This was where the man stared through his binoculars. Darren snapped a photograph with his phone. Then he stood in the man's tracks and parted the saplings. Darren flinched when he followed the man's sight line.

The stranger had been staring across the water at Thomas's house.

22

Water dripped, the darkness bleeding.

Justine jolted awake. The manacles snared her wrists and dragged her back to the wall. Stretched to the point of popping out of joint, her shoulders screamed. She'd hung forward, unconscious, with the chains yanking her arms back while she dozed. She didn't know her location or the day. But the fading light creeping around the window told her it was almost sunset. Soundproofing foam covered the rest of the window, and a reinforced door at the top of the basement staircase locked her in this black hell.

A tray of food lay at her feet. She'd refused the man's food since he abducted her from the parking lot and tossed her in the cellar. Now her stomach ached with acidic hunger, and she wished for anything to quell the stomach pangs. Her eyes dropped to the tray—a baked potato and a chicken thigh that smelled of vinegar and pepper. Reaching out with her foot, she dragged the tray closer, unsure how she'd retrieve the meal with her arms chained. Something scurried through her food. She pulled her feet back and retched when a cock-roach the size of her thumb skittered across the chicken and beneath the washing machine.

A shiver rolled through her body. The basement gloom would only thicken after sunset. Soon the basement would become a black abyss, and she wouldn't see the roaches and spiders coming for her.

Justine wondered about her abductor. He'd hung within the shadows so she didn't recognize him. Why take her? Was she just a random victim in the wrong place at the wrong time, or had he followed her through the store, patiently waiting until she ventured into the fog? This was fate's way of torturing her for her wrongdoings. Karma coming around to snatch her in its needle-fang jaws.

She'd asked for this. Not by returning to Wolf Lake, but by her inaction when Paige bullied Dawn and drove the poor girl to commit suicide. Justine could have stopped the madness. At the very least, she should have turned her back on Paige, as Skye had done months before. How ironic that Skye paid the price for their sins, when she was the only one brave enough to tell Paige she was out of control. Even then, it was already too late. Dawn hung herself in her bedroom, while her classmates looked forward to their final school-days and applied to universities. It should have been the happiest times of their lives.

Exhaustion and a malnourished body dragged her toward an unconscious state. It was silent above the ceiling. No footfalls scuffling across the floor. Perhaps her kidnapper had abandoned her to starve and die in this nowhere world. A *whoosh* drew her eyes to the far wall as the water heater turned on. A moment later, water poured through the pipes as the shower ran somewhere in the house. She wasn't alone, after all.

Be strong, Justine.

The words floated inside her head as she hallucinated Skye speaking to her. It wasn't the first time she'd imagined her friend in the same room. Since the weekend Skye disappeared, Justine heard the girl talking from the shadows when Justine teetered on the edge of sleep. Skye came to her in dreams and told her she was alive, that someday they'd be together again. Justine could show her faith and keep Skye's memory alive by wearing the friendship bracelet.

Donning the bracelet brought Justine closer to her lost friend. It wasn't a tribute to Paige.

Her head bobbed and dropped to her chest. The manacles stretched her arms taut as she pitched forward. Numb, she no longer experienced pain.

As her eyelids fluttered, a shadow disturbed the darkness. She blinked, suddenly awake and aware of her surroundings. Beyond the water heater, a foot scraped against the concrete floor.

Then she saw the eyes staring at her from the darkness. Twin moons of psychosis, leering at Justine.

She screamed. And no one heard.

THE SUN SET over Wolf Lake State Park and stole the security of daylight. Raven's nerves frayed with trepidation as she parked her Nissan Rogue at the visitor's center and crossed the campground toward Darren's cabin. Campers roasted marshmallows on sticks and made S'Mores. Somewhere, soft music filtered out of a radio.

Her eyes darted from one shadow to the next as she hustled toward the safety of the light. Darren opened the door before she knocked. He'd seen her coming.

"Sorry I took so long," she said, falling into his embrace.

He rubbed her back.

"You're like a powder keg ready to blow. What's going on?"

"It's more of the same. Anytime I'm alone, especially after dark, I freak out."

"Well, you're safe now."

He bolted the door and drew the curtain over the window. The homey cabin was Raven's sanctuary, and her heart stopped thrumming when the light caressed her skin and washed away the coming darkness. Darren led her to the couch. A small television sat atop his dresser, perfect for when he streamed movies. He didn't have cable or satellite. That was fine by Raven. Nothing but bad news played on those channels.

"I have leftover pizza in the fridge. By the time I tested the trail cameras, I was too tired to cook. So I stopped at Donatello's and grabbed a sheet."

"Maybe later," she said, leaning her head back. "How do the cameras work?"

"Great, but I still haven't caught our thief."

Raven, who'd drifted into a relaxed semiconscious state, snapped her eyes open.

"The thief came back?"

"Possibly," Darren said as he opened the refrigerator. He tossed her an iced tea and popped the top on a soda can. "While I was checking the cameras, I caught someone sneaking around the woods."

"It wasn't a hiker?"

"I don't think so. The guy took off running when he spotted me."

"Any idea who it was?"

"No. He wore a hooded sweatshirt, so I couldn't see his face. Whoever he is, he's as fast as the wind. Even taking all my secret shortcuts, I couldn't keep up with him."

"Damn. Then again, you're slow. I'd beat your cute butt in a race any day."

Darren slid beside her and set his soda on the floor.

"I don't doubt it. But I feel you're just fixated on my cute butt."

She slugged his shoulder.

"So the cameras didn't catch the thief?"

Darren sighed.

"I'm afraid not. The guy avoided the cameras, almost like he knew where they were." His forehead creased. "I wonder if he watched me setting them."

"Which means he followed you through the forest. That's unsettling."

"Just a tad. Now I regret not buying more cameras. I should record the cabins and catch him in the act."

"I'll grab another set in Syracuse tomorrow."

"I can go. You don't have to drive all the way to the city on my account."

"It's no problem. Besides, this is my case. The offer stands, if you're interested."

His eyes lit.

"Oh, I forgot. The guy left footprints all over the forest, so I snapped a photograph." Darren swiped through his phone and found the shoe print. "I took these near the drop off into the lake. The creep had binoculars."

"What was he looking at?"

"If I wasn't crazy, I'd say he was spying on Thomas's house."

Raven touched her forehead.

"What would a campground thief want with the county sheriff?"

"I might be wrong. He could have been looking at someone on the water."

Raven grunted. Examining Darren's photo, she recognized the tread pattern.

"I'll be darned."

"What's that?"

Raven removed her phone and called up the photographs she took around the cabins.

"It's the same guy," she said, placing her phone beside his. She zoomed in on the two pictures as Darren leaned forward. "I shot these while working the Paul Phipps investigation."

"So this guy robs cabins and hides out in the woods, watching houses across the lake. What's his motivation?"

Raven slapped her thigh.

"That settles it. We'll cover the cabins with cameras and catch our thief before he strikes again."

She set her phone aside, and he turned to her.

"Earlier, I asked you about Chelsey. You weren't ready to talk."

Raven wrung her hands. How much should she tell Darren? She suspected her friend was cutting herself. But there might have been a logical explanation for the lacerations on Chelsey's chest. Raven swallowed.

"My brother brought Scout by the office Wednesday morning. Chelsey was her usual self…well, the way she's acted lately. She hid in the kitchen and wouldn't say hello. Then she dropped her coffee mug and made a mess. After LeVar left with Scout, I helped Chelsey pick up. That's when I noticed her chest."

"What was wrong with her chest?"

Raven felt a sob coming on and placed a fist against her lips.

"It was covered with cuts. Like someone went at her with a razor."

Darren fell back.

"You think she's cutting herself?"

"I don't know. I mean, that was my first guess."

"She's acted strangely over the last month."

"I'm worried about her, Darren. What if her depression comes back?"

He rested his elbow on the couch and set his chin on his palm.

"What if her depression is already back?"

"Don't say it."

"It's common for people with histories of depression to relapse. Is she seeing a doctor?"

"If she was, she wouldn't tell me."

"Hmm."

Raven pushed her hair off her shoulder.

"Darren, did Thomas mention anything about getting back together with Chelsey?"

He dropped his brow.

"No. I would have remembered, given their history."

"Something happened between the two of them. Please keep this to yourself, but after I spoke with Chelsey last month, she decided she'd try again with Thomas."

"That guy is still in love with her. He'd never admit it, but you can see it in his eyes whenever she walks into the room."

"Exactly. So why would he drive her away?"

"He wouldn't. Something else must have happened."

Raven scrubbed her hand down her face.

"I might be way off base with this. Either way, we need to watch Chelsey and make sure she's okay."

"Raven, if Chelsey isn't in her right mind, we need to tell someone."

"Oh, God. What if I'm wrong and making mountains out of molehills?"

He touched her shoulder.

"What if you're right, and we don't step in before something terrible happens?"

23

LeVar patted Jack on the head as the big dog watched him fish two glazed donuts out of the box.

"Sorry, these aren't for you."

The dog cocked his head, tongue hanging out and beading with saliva.

As LeVar plated the donuts, Thomas shuffled into the kitchen and yawned. The sheriff wore baggy shorts, a T-shirt, and flip-flops, his disheveled hair messier than normal. He'd worked late poring over his notes on the Skye Feron and Justine Adkins cases. LeVar had glimpsed him through the window last night, guilty that he'd hidden their investigation from the sheriff. Until LeVar found concrete evidence, he needed to keep the investigation secret. Thomas wouldn't approve of their group, especially with Scout involved.

"I picked up a dozen donuts from the Broken Yolk this morning. Hope you don't mind me snatching a couple."

Thomas pawed through the box and grabbed a donut.

"Why would I mind? You paid. Take ten bucks out of my wallet."

"My treat, Shep Dawg."

Thomas smirked.

"Shep Dawg. I kinda like that. But I still want to pay."

"I don't pay full price. Ruth gives me a discount. You know how that goes."

He turned to leave before the sheriff asked any more questions.

"You want to grill later?"

"Say the word, *bruh*."

"All right." Thomas narrowed his eyes as LeVar slid the deck door open. "I'll check in with you after four."

LeVar winced as he closed the door behind him. Was Thomas on to their investigation club? He stopped himself from running and did his best to appear casual while he crossed the yard. Inside the guest house, he pulled the curtain on the front door and exhaled.

Scout was already scouring the security camera footage from last night.

"Find my prowler yet?" he asked.

She glanced over her wheelchair and shook her head.

"But I caught three raccoons scrambling between our yards. Oh, and a dozen deer."

Scout was all smiles as she ran through the footage on high speed.

"That's lit," he said, pointing at the screen with his half-eaten donut. "You can see the sun rising. See what I did there? Lit, sunrise?"

"Yeah, you're a real Chris Rock, LeVar."

He slid the plate in front of her.

"What's first on the agenda?"

"We should pick up where we left off yesterday."

"The girl Paige and Justine tormented. Dawn."

Scout called up two browser windows. One held a digital yearbook from Harmon High School from the year Skye Feron vanished. The second contained Kane Grove High's yearbook.

"I get the impression Paige wasn't as liked as she was popular," said Scout. "Dawn might have been a rival."

"We don't know her last name."

"It sucks, but we'll go through both yearbooks, name by name. If she's in there, we need to find her."

Outside the window, a family floated on the lake in kayaks. Scout returned to work, examining the two senior classes and running her finger along the names.

"I don't get it," said Scout, shaking her head. "There's nobody named Dawn in either yearbook."

"Weird. It's a common name."

"Not common enough. I'm unsure where to go from here."

The guest house turned quiet as they mulled over their decisions.

"Let's go back to Webb-WLHS and find everything we can on her."

"We scoured the unofficial forum." Scout slapped her forehead. "Why didn't I think of it?"

"What?"

Scout typed in a blur as she opened a new search window.

"People who hide behind sock puppet accounts often use the same name elsewhere."

"So we search the internet for Webb-WLHS."

"And we figure out who he or she is by following the breadcrumbs."

Scout scanned the results and stopped on a classified advertisement. LeVar pointed at the first link.

"Is that an advertisement from Wolf Lake?"

"It might be." Scout opened the link. "Someone sold a snowblower under that user name. But I don't see an address." Her eyes hovered over the contact information. "Bingo. There's a phone number."

"Scout, it's a 607 area code. That's our region."

As they considered their next move, LeVar tapped his foot impatiently.

"We should call this person."

"And say what?"

"Duh. That we want to buy the snowblower." He punched the number into his phone. "I'll call. I sound more like an adult than you. No offense."

"None taken, old man."

He grinned. In his ear, the phone rang. Switching the call to speaker, he set down the phone and waited.

"Hello?"

Scout mouthed, "Is that a woman?"

LeVar shrugged. The pitch was too neutral to determine gender.

"Is this the person selling the snowblower?"

A long pause followed.

"That's right. Who's calling?"

"Uh..." Scout slapped his arm to get him talking. "Benton Brickfield."

Scout dropped her head to her chest.

"What can I do for you, Mr. Brickfield?"

"My snowblower died last winter, and I need something new this year. What's the horsepower?"

The unknown person read the details over the phone.

"I didn't notice an address in your listing. I live in Harmon. You close by?"

"The address is 4890 County Line Road."

LeVar snapped his fingers and gave Scout a thumbs up. This person lived just outside Wolf Lake.

"The snowblower is one-hundred-fifty. Cash only. No checks."

"That's fair. When is a good time to pick it up? I can borrow my buddy's truck next week."

"How about Monday or Tuesday afternoon?"

"I can make that work, Mrs...."

LeVar drew the word out, prompting the person to give a name.

"Remember. Cash only. If you bring a check or credit card, no sale. See you then, Mr. Brickfield."

The caller hung up.

A grin formed on Scout's lips.

"I can't believe you used the name Benton Brickfield."

"Shut up. It was the best I could come up with on the spot."

"And you want to be a private investigator." She tutted. "You need to think fast under pressure. Are you really gonna drive to County Line Road?"

LeVar leaned back and closed his eyes.

"Naw. We gotta bring the sheriff in on this."

"Already?"

"We found someone on the forum harassing Paige Sutton and Justine Adkins, and this person lives outside Wolf Lake."

"That doesn't mean Webb-WLHS murdered Skye and kidnapped Justine."

"It's a solid lead." LeVar glanced over his shoulder at the A-Frame and groaned. Thomas wouldn't be happy LeVar had investigated the state park case with Scout. "I have to tell him."

Scout chewed her lip.

"If you say so. Do what you have to do."

24

Thomas opened his contact list. His finger hovered over Chelsey's name. She'd fallen off the face of the earth over the last month, and Raven always became quiet when Thomas brought Chelsey's name into the conversation. Something was happening to Chelsey. Thomas feared the depression was back, that he'd lose her forever if the sickness dug its claws into Chelsey and refused to let go.

He couldn't decide. Calling her uninvited seemed like a violation. She didn't want his company and made it clear. Even if he mustered the courage to click the send icon, she'd recognize his number. No chance she'd answer.

Thomas placed the call and reached Chelsey's voice-mail after several rings. He waited for her playfully sarcastic message to finish. When the tone rang in his ear, he swallowed.

"Chelsey, it's Sheriff...Thomas. Haven't spoken to you in a long time and wondered if everything was okay. Call me or stop by the office. Would love to get your thoughts on the skeleton we found below the falls." He didn't know what else to say. "Anyhow, if we put our heads together—"

His time expired. Thomas pushed the phone across the table,

feeling like an idiot. Jack lay at his feet with his snout resting on his paws, the dog sensing Thomas's discomfort. He leaned down and stroked the dog's fur, cursing his inability to find the right words whenever he spoke to Chelsey.

A knock pulled his eyes to the deck door. LeVar waited outside with the plate he'd borrowed. Thomas waved him in.

"Wolfed down those donuts pretty fast, I see."

LeVar's gaze flew to Jack at the mention of wolfing. The teenager set the plate on the counter and took a composing breath.

"I gotta be straight with you about something."

Thomas stood from his chair and circled the dining room table.

"What's going on?"

"I didn't eat both donuts. One was for Scout."

Thomas snorted, expecting a punchline. LeVar just stood there, examining his shoelaces.

"I don't get it."

"Thomas, we're investigating the Skye Feron disappearance."

Resting his back against the wall, Thomas opened his mouth and stopped. LeVar's admission caught him off guard.

"That's potentially a murder investigation, LeVar. I support Scout's interests as much as anyone. But her mother won't approve of Scout researching a homicide. Not after what happened in the Jeremy Hyde case. How long has this been going on?"

"Since yesterday morning."

LeVar glanced out the window.

"Something else you want to tell me?"

"Raven and Darren are involved too."

Thomas jiggled his head in surprise.

"The four of you are investigating the Skye Feron disappearance?"

"For real, for real. And the Justine Adkins case. We believe they're related."

Thomas wandered back to the table and fell into a chair.

"This isn't a game, LeVar. We might be dealing with two murders."

"We understand. That's why I'm coming to you now. Scout and I found something you need to see."

~

"TELL ME ABOUT THIS PERSON AGAIN," Thomas said, leaning over Scout's shoulder as she typed at the keyboard.

"We haven't determined the person's identity. He, or she, hides behind a fake user name and keeps attacking Paige Sutton and Justine Adkins on the Wolf Lake High alumni forum."

"I can't speak to Justine Adkins's personality. But I've met Paige Sutton, and I'm sure she ruffled a few feathers during her high school days. That doesn't make this poster a kidnapper or murderer."

"No," LeVar said, seated at the card table. "But trolling a forum under a fake name is sketchy."

"You're positive the name is fake?"

"We went through the high school yearbook, and there isn't anyone named Webb."

Thomas squinted his eyes at the screen.

"It's worth looking into. We don't have any leads yet. This Dawn the poster refers to...Dawn...why does that name ring a bell?"

"That's another mystery we haven't solved," said Scout, turning her chair to face Thomas. "We can't find anybody named Dawn in the yearbooks."

"Heck, I can't believe there's a secret Wolf Lake High alumni forum. I hadn't heard about this."

"That's why it's called a secret forum," LeVar grinned.

"But I attended that school."

"You became a cop. Maybe your old buddies don't want law enforcement snooping around, checking up on people."

Thomas waved the idea away and stared over the water. Dawn. Where had he encountered that name before?

"You copied the address?"

LeVar ripped the note off the memo pad and handed it to Thomas.

"County Line Road is right outside Wolf Lake."

"I'm familiar with the location." Thomas folded the note and slid it inside his pocket. "I'll swing past the house and tell you what I find."

Scout and LeVar shared a glance.

"Does that mean you're not angry with us?" Scout asked.

"I'm not angry. But I have to speak with your mother about this." Scout lowered her eyes. "As far as I can tell, all you did was sift through forum messages and fool someone into believing you want to buy a snowblower." Thomas smiled at LeVar. "By the way, if you ever use an undercover name like Benton Brickfield again, I'll purge you from the law enforcement database. You sound like a country club flunky."

"Told you it was weak," Scout said.

Thomas leaned toward Scout.

"Your mother still hasn't forgiven me for the Jeremy Hyde fiasco. Let me smooth things over. As long as you aren't investigating alone, and you have LeVar, Raven, and Darren monitoring your activity, it should be all right."

"Thank you for understanding."

Thomas patted his pocket.

"Thank you for the lead. Something tells me the two of you have long careers in law enforcement ahead of you. Just keep me in the loop from now on. Okay?"

25

Raven twisted the key in the lock. The converted house seemed to inhale as she stepped into the entryway and hung her sweatshirt on the coat rack. The afternoons remained warm in Wolf Lake, but the morning chill took longer to burn off, a sign autumn colors would return before long.

Hoping to catch up on her caseload, she strode down the halls of Wolf Lake Consulting. After turning the corner, she pulled up and touched her heart. Chelsey was already here, on a weekend no less. Her boss leaned back in a rolling chair with her feet propped on the desk.

"Chelsey, I didn't think you'd be here on a Saturday."

"When were you planning to tell me about the state park research?"

Raven swallowed and sat at her desk, Chelsey's stare shooting daggers across the room.

"That's off the books. I'm just—"

"Playing amateur detective with your friends." Chelsey swept her hair off her forehead. Her eyes sank into her skull, her face pallid and drawn. Was she eating? "We're swamped with cases, and you're adding to the workload."

"I can research the case on my own time. It's not an issue. Besides, it's not my fault we're so far behind."

"So it's my fault? I'm here on my day off."

Raven took a calming breath.

"Chelsey, you call in sick two, three times a week, and you never say no to a prospective client."

"We need to keep the momentum going. If we fall off, we'll lose business."

"Then hire a third investigator. I've told you this for months. Bring another investigator on board, or cut down on the caseload."

Chelsey tapped a pen against her palm and tossed it across the desk.

"It's difficult finding qualified applicants in a sleepy resort village. And either way, if you stopped playing around with your friends and focused on your work once in a while, we wouldn't be in this position."

Raven's fingers clawed at the chair. Incensed, she wanted to tear the upholstery. It took her several breaths before she readied herself to reply.

"I'm here a lot more than you, Chelsey. If anyone isn't pulling her weight, it's the sick chick who never sleeps."

Chelsey tugged at her necklace. Raven searched for the lacerations, but Chelsey's T-shirt concealed the cuts.

"I haven't felt well lately."

"Lately is going on a month. Are you okay? I mean, *really* okay? If you want to talk, I'm here for you."

"There's nothing to talk about. I'll be fine once the hot days end. I'm sure it's one of those summer flus."

Raven rubbed her eyes. Holding a logical conversation with Chelsey was impossible.

"Fine. No sense in me being here and catching your cold. I'll grab my case files and work from home."

Chelsey held up a hand when Raven stood.

"I'm trying to find another investigator."

"So why haven't you?"

"No luck yet."

Raven sat down and rolled her chair to Chelsey's.

"Hire LeVar."

Chelsey stared at Raven as if she'd grown a second head.

"Your brother?"

"Why not? He's majoring in criminal justice and taking classes."

"He's enrolled. Classes don't begin until the end of the month. We're talking about the enforcer for the Harmon Kings, right? The teenager I chased into an abandoned warehouse?"

"Give him a chance. If you'd seen him working with Darren and Scout—"

"How many people did you rope into your investigative team?"

"Just the four of us."

Chelsey dropped her head back and blinked at the ceiling.

"All right, go on."

"LeVar has a knack for investigative work. And you know he's fast enough to run anyone down. Who would mess with him? Just give him a chance." When Chelsey didn't reply, Raven touched her arm. Chelsey flinched as though shocked. "Come on, one interview. Do it for me."

Chelsey removed her feet from the desk and exhaled through her hands.

"One interview. That's all he gets." Raven reached out to hug her friend. Chelsey backed away. "But it has to be this afternoon. My schedule is booked solid next week."

"I'll tell him. How does two o'clock sound?"

"Deal. Raven, if he isn't here by two, I'm leaving. No second chances."

THOMAS WATCHED the guest house through the bedroom window, worried he'd made the wrong choice. Naomi was unhappy with her daughter. But she allowed Scout to work on the investigation, provided Darren, Raven, and LeVar monitored her activities.

LeVar's shadow passed over the window. Scout was in the guest house, no doubt working on the case and drawing one step closer to an unknown murderer. Which made Thomas's spine stiffen.

And that name. Dawn. It lay inside a forgotten memory.

Picking up his phone, he dialed Gray and nestled into his chair, letting the idyllic lake view relax his nerves.

"Pretty soon, I'll have to take my old job back," Gray laughed. "What is it this time?"

"You probably heard Justine Adkins is missing."

"I have. Nasty business, Thomas. Those girls held a secret, and it's coming back on them."

"I have a lead. It's a weak one, but it's all I have. Are you aware there's an unofficial forum for Wolf Lake High alumni?"

"Sure, everyone knows about it."

Not everyone, Thomas thought. He told Gray about Webb-WLHS.

"I'm not surprised someone had it in for Paige and Justine. Those girls are trouble. Well, Paige Sutton is. I got the impression Justine was along for the ride, a bystander. But neither girl told me anything that would have helped us locate Skye Feron, so they're both guilty, as far as I'm concerned."

"There wasn't anyone with the last name Webb in their graduating class."

"Hmm." Thomas pictured Gray tugging his mustache in thought. "Did you check the sophomore and junior classes? Maybe this person was younger."

"No one named Webb in those classes, either. The poster kept bringing up someone named Dawn. That name seemed familiar, but I couldn't place it."

Gray sucked in a breath.

"Dawn Samson."

"You remember her?"

"That was a terrible summer, Thomas. Dawn Samson hung herself. The suicide destroyed the community. Before we came to grips with the loss, Skye Feron disappeared a few weeks later."

Thomas remembered now. He read about the suicide while working in Los Angeles, shocked a Wolf Lake student took her life.

"And nobody connected the cases?"

"There wasn't a connection. Dawn had a rough home life. Both parents were alcoholics, and child services kept showing up after the neighbors complained the Samsons were beating their children."

Thomas sat forward.

"So Dawn had a sibling."

"A brother, yes. Alec Samson. He was a year younger than Dawn."

"Did the kid have a record?"

"Nope. You'd figure a kid who suffered through that much torment would get into trouble—fights, drugs, something. But he was clean as a whistle. Anyhow, we tried to link the Dawn Samson and Skye Feron cases. It was a dead end road."

"You're certain Dawn's suicide wasn't foul play."

"I trust Virgil's opinion. As I recall, the ligature marks on her neck indicated suicide. A chaotic pattern would have suggested someone tied the rope around Dawn's neck and fought her. That wasn't the case."

"And with Skye..."

"She just vanished. There was no evidence to tie her to Dawn Samson, though I always worried we'd missed something important."

A black crow flew past the window and set down atop the guest house, its head swiveling as the sun dissolved into the bird's black eyes.

"Sheriff, this Webb-WLHS person claims Paige and Justine tortured Dawn." Gray went silent. "Did you hear what I said?"

"My God, Thomas. That's the missing link. Did those girls drive Dawn to suicide?"

26

L eVar stood before the mirror and scowled. He looked like a penguin.

"You're very handsome," Naomi said from behind, straightening his jacket. "I'd hire you in an instant."

"I don't know." LeVar pushed his hair back. "Should I hide the dreads inside the jacket?"

The horrified look Naomi gave him in the mirror answered his question. Watching from the front room of the guest house, Scout snorted. Naomi shot her daughter a warning glare not to upset LeVar.

Not that it mattered. His heart pounded, and he couldn't breathe with the tie cinched up to his Adam's apple. Even when Ruth Sims interviewed him for the Broken Yolk job, he'd been a hot mess. But this was the real deal. The big leagues. Three months ago, he was a street kid living on borrowed time. After today, he might have a full-time job in his dream profession.

If he didn't blow the interview.

After Raven called with the good news, he'd borrowed a navy blue jacket, matching slacks, a white dress shirt, and a tie from Thomas. Fortunately, LeVar still had his dress shoes from two years ago when Trey died. LeVar almost quit the Kings after someone gunned down his friend in Harmon. The police never found the shooter, though LeVar suspected the rival Royals gang murdered Trey.

Staring into the mirror, he wiped his clammy hands on his jacket and forced his best smile.

"Just relax and be yourself," Naomi said, picking lint off his shoulder. "You know Chelsey."

"Yeah, and she hates me."

"She hates everyone," said Scout, wheeling herself down the hallway. "Don't take it personally."

"Thanks a ton."

"She doesn't hate you," Naomi said, tugging on the jacket sleeves. No matter how hard she worked, she couldn't alter physics. LeVar was two sizes larger than Thomas. This was the best they could do on short notice. "Thomas says Chelsey is going through a tough time. All the more reason she needs someone reliable to help her at the office. I'm sure Raven put in a kind word for you."

LeVar's mouth was too dry to swallow. As if she sensed his discomfort, Scout tossed him his iced tea.

"Thanks." He took a swig. "I owe you one. Both of you."

"You buy the pizza after your first paycheck," Scout said.

"I low-key can't wait until I get this interview done with. At least I still have the Broken Yolk if today goes south."

"Positive thoughts," Scout said, drawing a nod from Naomi.

He gave the mirror one last glance.

"Okay. I can do this."

As he fidgeted with the cuffs, Naomi rounded Scout's wheelchair.

"Let's give LeVar space so he can get ready."

His hands refused to sit still. He straightened the tie for the hundredth time, tucking the end into his jacket. The tie was like an ill-mannered snake that refused to stay in its cage.

"Call us when it's over," Naomi said, patting his shoulder as they headed out the door. "You'll knock her socks off."

The door closed, locking him inside the silent house. Alone with his thoughts.

Was this actually happening? If Chelsey hired LeVar, he wouldn't need a college loan. He pictured his mother's face if he won the job. Despite Serena's differences with Raven, she always expected her daughter to achieve success. But not LeVar.

Until now.

He peeked out the window. Naomi pushed Scout up the walkway Thomas carved last spring. His heart warmed. For the first time in his life, he had dependable friends and an extended family to pick him up when he was down. People believed in him, and he wouldn't disappoint them. His car, a black Chrysler Limited that had once been the most feared vehicle in Nightshade County, waited in Thomas's driveway. He calculated the drive to Wolf Lake Consulting in his head, intent on arriving five minutes early, even if he encountered traffic. Which meant he needed to unlock his frozen knees and get moving.

He inhaled deeply and let the breath out.

Grabbing his keys off the counter, he pocketed his wallet. Then the phone rang.

LeVar considered letting the call go to voice-mail. What if it was Chelsey changing the appointment time?

He answered without glancing at the screen.

"LeVar, I'm in trouble."

Anthony.

LeVar set his hand on the jamb. He'd been seconds from walking out the door.

"Now is not a good time, bro. I got things to do."

"It's Rev. Somehow, he found out. He's gonna kill me and my mom."

LeVar closed his eyes. Not now.

"Are you sure about this?"

"Kilo pulled me aside, man." Kilo was the new enforcer for the Harmon Kings, the thug who took LeVar's spot. He'd earned his moniker by pushing drugs in Harmon, another reason LeVar left the Kings. "Says Rev heard I was tryin' to get out. He ain't playin', LeVar. This time it's for real."

"Where are you?"

"In my apartment. They're outside. The Kings. At least seven of them surrounding the place. I can't find my mom. She won't answer her phone, and I don't know what to do."

"Call the police, Anthony."

"What? Hell, no."

"You have to."

"What happened to you, LeVar? Four months ago, you wouldn't trust a cop if he was your great uncle. Now you livin' in luxury, and suddenly, you think the police are our friends. No cop gonna help me or my mom."

"I told you, Anthony. I can't get you out of this one. Just make the call. Don't tell the police who you are. Give them the address and say the Harmon Kings surrounded the apartment with guns. They'll—"

"Oh, shit. They're coming, LeVar. Rev, Kilo, all of them. I think Kilo set me up."

LeVar pushed through the door and ran toward the car.

"Stay away from the windows and lock the doors. I'm on my way, little bro."

Anthony yelled a second before a window shattered. The line died.

27

SATURDAY, AUGUST 14TH 1:30 P.M.

A guilar set a berry smoothie in front of Thomas. He sat at the small table inside the kitchen at the Nightshade County Sheriff's Department, the blender blades whirling behind them as Aguilar waited for her afternoon snack. He took a sip and grimaced.

"Too sweet?" she asked.

"No. It's cold. How many ice cubes did you put in this smoothie?"

"Suck it up, Sally. I'm sure you can tough it out. There are thirty-five grams of protein in that drink. You want to support your workouts, right?"

"Well, yeah."

"Then you need protein. Drink up."

He took another sip and swallowed. Not bad, except the drink numbed his throat. Spreading his notes on the table, Thomas jabbed his finger at the address Scout and LeVar gave him.

"The house belongs to Cathy Webb. Age twenty-nine, born and raised in Syracuse. She moved to County Line Road six years ago."

Aguilar poured her smoothie into a mason jar and joined Thomas at the table. She frowned.

"That's around the same time Skye Feron vanished. Might be a coincidence."

"I don't think so." Thomas removed a photocopied yearbook picture of Dawn Samson's brother, Alec. The boy looked like every teenager—acne dotting his forehead, an uncomfortable smile, dark hair styled into a mid fade with the sides buzzed and the top combed back. But there was something wrong with the boy's eyes. A hidden devilry Thomas couldn't define. "Cathy Webb's place is also the last known address for Alec Samson. According to my records, Webb is Alec's cousin."

"The brother of the girl who committed suicide. Does he still live with his cousin?"

"That's the strange part. He closed his account at the First National Bank of Harmon four years ago. Since then, no tax returns, no employment, and his driver's license expired. It's like the boy fell off the edge of the earth."

"Like Skye Feron. Maybe someone killed him too."

"Don't say it."

Aguilar drank her smoothie and wiped her lips on a napkin.

"Cathy Webb must be the Webb-WLHS writing all those nasty things about Paige Sutton and Justine Adkins. Can't say I blame her, if those women drove her cousin to commit suicide. What's wrong with teenagers?"

Thomas thought back to Ray Welch. Ray bullied Thomas for years, and nobody stopped it.

"Right now, she's our number one suspect."

"What about Gene Maldonado?"

"The manager at the Orange Tulip?"

"Lambert looked into Maldonado's background and found something interesting."

Aguilar passed a case folder to Thomas. He scanned the documents and arched his brow.

"Shoplifting at seventeen."

"Check out what he stole."

Thomas ran his finger down the document and paused.

"A girlie magazine. So he was a teenage boy with raging hormones. That doesn't make him a predator."

Aguilar crossed her legs.

"What do we know about serial rapists? Lying and stealing are common traits for future rapists. Many are loners who engage in impulsive activities."

"Maldonado's job allows him to avoid people for most of the day. He handles a few people checking in. Otherwise he's always alone."

"And he admits he sneaked into Justine Adkins's room. That's damn impulsive and creepy. By the way, Maldonado drives a blue Honda Odyssey."

Thomas set his drink aside.

"That might be the vehicle that sped through the parking lot outside the supermarket. Why do you believe Maldonado attacked Justine Adkins?"

"It's just a theory. But if he raped Justine, he had good reason to get rid of her. Lock her away or kill her so she couldn't go to the police."

"This feels like a stretch."

"Imagine the situation from Maldonado's perspective. How many single women get rooms at the bed-and-breakfast? And of the few that do, do any of them have Justine's looks? He must have drooled on the floor the second she stepped foot in his office."

"So we add Maldonado to our suspect list."

"That's my suggestion. What now?"

Thomas grabbed Alec Samson's photo and studied the boy's dead eyes.

"Let's visit Cathy Webb and find out what happened to Alec Samson."

28

L eVar punched the steering wheel when Chelsey didn't answer her phone. He'd called her five times in the last half-hour to explain what was happening. No chance she'd reschedule the interview. He'd been right about Chelsey—the woman hated him and would never trust the former enforcer for the Harmon Kings.

He climbed out of the Chrysler and stepped into the McDonald's parking lot. The busy fast-food restaurant sat two blocks from Anthony's apartment. The Kings would recognize his vehicle if he parked too close to his quarry, but he blended into the crowd here. Sweet scents of baked apple pies mingled with greasy fries and burgers as LeVar glanced around the lot. Nobody paid him attention, despite the dress clothes, expensive shoes, and look of wary apprehension. His paranoia heightened as he studied the hidden shadows between the vehicles.

Someone squealed. LeVar dropped below the hood and wiped the sweat off his forehead. It was just a girl skipping across the blacktop and holding her father's hand, a boxed happy meal swinging from her arm. The father eyed LeVar as he rose out of his crouch. LeVar feigned retrieving a dropped coin and walked toward the restaurant.

When the father looked away, LeVar swerved in the opposite direction and cut down a side street lined with bars, dingy-lit restaurants, and consignment shops. He hadn't set foot in Harmon since spring. The streets he ran in April seemed foreign to him, as if entire generations had passed while he was away. He kept his pace to a brisk walk, not wanting to draw attention. He might not recognize the faces on the street. But he bet they recognized his.

He dialed Anthony's number again and pressed the phone to his ear as he jogged through an alley. A block ahead, the boy's brownstone apartment grew out of the pavement like a post-apocalyptic fortress. The call went to Anthony's message. LeVar cursed and shoved the phone into his pocket.

He needed to be careful now. The Kings had to be close.

Stopping beside a family run grocery market, he cocked his head around the corner and pulled back. Kilo and Lawson milled outside Anthony's apartment building. LeVar had considered Lawson a friend while he ran with the Kings. But the muscular boy with the shaved head would put a bullet in LeVar's skull without blinking, if they caught him in Kings territory.

LeVar glanced up and down the street. There had to be more gang members around, but he only saw Kilo and Lawson. Something wasn't right. Why would the two boys hang out in front of the apartment if they'd already killed Anthony?

He ran to a parked car and knelt beside the bumper. Traffic buzzed past, the wind from passing vehicles whipping his dreadlocks. He'd forgotten Harmon's smells—fuel, garbage, concrete, and fetid hopelessness. Maybe he'd never noticed it before. Four months of living beside a lake changed his perception of normal.

LeVar wished he'd brought a gun. Conceding to Thomas's wishes, LeVar got rid of his weapons before he moved into the guest house. He still owned a hunting knife, which he concealed beneath his mattress. Four months of luxury hadn't stopped LeVar from sleeping with his eyes open, a survival tactic for anyone who'd lived inside Harmon's ganglands.

Where were the other members? Rev should be here. Not that LeVar was sorry not to see the leader of the Harmon Kings. Rev was volatile, prone to crazy decisions. LeVar recalled the time Rev's psychotic delusions got the best of him. The Kings recruited a former college football linebacker named Derek. Rev got the crazy idea Derek was an undercover cop and pummeled the recruit behind the strip club on Fifth. Derek was a big guy. But nobody was tougher than Rev. By the time Rev finished with Derek—the other members were too scared to stop Rev—the guy's face looked like raw meat. LeVar always wondered what became of Derek. Rev's enemies had a funny way of disappearing.

A police officer walking his beat moved down the sidewalk, drawing Kilo's attention. Kilo swatted Lawson's arm and lifted his chin at the cop. Then the boys meandered down the sidewalk with their hands in their pockets until the officer passed. LeVar took advantage of the opportunity. With Kilo's back turned, LeVar hurried around the brownstone apartment. He didn't trust the front doors. The Kings would post someone inside. But a shattered window behind the complex allowed access to the basement.

He swung his head left and right. When he didn't see anyone, he kicked a shard off the pane and slipped through the window, dropping hard to the concrete floor. The dress shoes did little to comfort his fall, the impact reverberating through his knees. Thick chemical cleaner scents filled the basement. A laundry room stood at the end of the hall, a dryer grinding away. He ran in the opposite direction and scrambled up the stairs, his breath held every time he moved past a blind corner. A heavy steel door opened below. Footsteps. Someone coming.

LeVar found Anthony's floor and edged the door open. Peeked down the dimly lit corridor. Music thumped from behind a closed door, loud enough to cover his steps. His heart pounded as he approached Anthony's apartment. He tried again to call the boy. This time Anthony picked up.

"Why the hell don't you answer?"

"I had to hide," Anthony said, his voice trembling. "They came through the window, so I hid in the crawlspace."

"Who was it?"

"Dunno. Kilo and Lawson, I think."

"They're outside. You're cool now. I'm coming in, *aight*?"

LeVar turned the knob. The idiot kid had left the door unlocked. That thought played through his head as the apartment revealed itself. Was this a setup?

Not taking any chances, he locked the door behind him and bolted it. A cluttered living room with a chipped, wooden coffee table dominated the room's center. A green upholstered couch with tears in the fabric stood on the far side of the coffee table, large enough to hide someone with a gun.

"Anthony?"

No answer.

He crept through the living room and swiveled his gaze toward the kitchen. Saw the shadow on the wall a second before the gun barrel pressed against his temple. Anthony grinned.

"Hands in the air. Don't make me pull the trigger, LeVar."

LeVar complied.

29

County Line Road might have lurked a million miles from Wolf Lake. Nothing but an expanse of wilderness, interrupted by the occasional farmhouse. Thomas peered at Aguilar over the cruiser, feeling the same dread his partner did.

Cathy Webb owned a sagging, gray two-story home with a broken step leading up to the porch. An ancient swing sat in the corner, swaying ghostly when the wind blew. The grass grew past their shins, and the shrubberies circling the yard threw gangling branches toward the sky, as though praying to a malevolent god.

"Are you sure someone lives here?" Aguilar asked, angling toward the stairs.

Thomas glanced at the empty driveway. The stone path led to a tilted garage behind the house. No way to determine if the closed door hid a vehicle. Stuffed with catalogs and coupons, the mailbox hung askew beside the door. Scattered pieces of mail fluttered through the overgrown grass.

The hair stood on the back of his neck when Thomas ascended the steps, careful not to crash through the broken plank. He checked the curtained windows, certain someone watched from inside. Aguilar's hand hovered over her gun as Thomas knocked on the door.

After thirty seconds passed, he knocked again, straining his ears when a thump came from deep inside the house.

"I don't like this," Aguilar said.

Thomas nodded.

"Nightshade County Sheriff's Department," he called before banging his knuckles on the door for a third time. "Anybody home?"

The wind whistled around the eaves, a mournful sound.

"What should we do?"

"Maybe she's out back," Thomas said, though he doubted it. He wanted an excuse to search the backyard and peek inside the garage. "Keep your eyes open."

Thomas and Aguilar circled the house. He used blackout curtains in his bedroom so the sun didn't wake him after he worked overnight shifts, and the same style of curtain concealed every window on Cathy Webb's house. There was something blocking the cellar windows.

"See that?" Aguilar pointed at the basement window.

"Looks like foam insulation. Ms. Webb is pretty secretive for a single woman living in the boonies."

A warped picnic table stood behind the residence. Sitting on its benches would leave the unsuspecting victim with dozens of splinters piercing his backside. No garden, no shed. It was the garage that commanded Thomas's attention.

"Watch my back," he said. "I'm checking for a van."

Aguilar eyed the windows as Thomas moved toward the garage. The garage door didn't have windows. He tugged the handle but found it locked. Next, he searched for a murder weapon. Dr. Stone had been convinced the killer murdered their Jane Doe with a pick ax. As he rounded the building, the back door opened on the decrepit two-story.

"What are you doing back there?"

Thomas and Aguilar raised their eyes. A large shouldered woman filled the doorway. Thomas couldn't see her hands or determine if she held a gun. She stood in the shadows, beady eyes burning holes through Thomas. His heart pounded as he remembered the gangland shooting in Los Angeles, the attack that nearly killed him. The bullet had missed his spine by a hair.

"You Cathy Webb?"

"I'm Webb. Why are you on my property?"

"Sheriff Shepherd, Nightshade County Sheriff's Department. This is my partner, Deputy Aguilar. We knocked first."

"Get away from my garage. There's nothing back there for you."

"We'd like to ask you a few questions."

"What about?"

"Your cousin, Alec Samson."

The woman's eyes narrowed. There was something wrong with her blocky, angular face. Despite the afternoon heat, she wore a bulky sweatshirt, rugged blue jeans, work boots, and a knit cap over her head. He swore he'd met her before, though he couldn't imagine when.

"Alec doesn't live here anymore."

Thomas shared a glance with Aguilar as they approached the back stoop. The woman edged deeper into the shadow, ready to slam the door in their faces.

"I'd like to speak with you about Alec, all the same."

Webb moved her eyes from Thomas to Aguilar. He still couldn't see her hands. The air grew tense, the sensation one experienced before lightning struck. Thomas breathed again when Webb strode out of the house. Her callused hands weren't strangers to yard work. She didn't hold a gun.

"What's Alec gone and done now? Is he in some kind of trouble?"

Thomas and Aguilar approached the woman. Her eyes darted to the garage, a giveaway there was something she didn't want them to see.

"We want to speak with Alec."

She scoffed.

"Good luck with that. I haven't seen my cousin in years."

"Our records state this is Alec Samson's last known address," Aguilar said.

"That's right. Alec moved in with me after high school. Had to get away from his parents. The living situation wasn't good for him. His family packed up and left last year. Moved to Michigan, I believe."

"How long did Alec live with you?"

She furrowed her brow.

"A few years. Alec left three or four years ago."

"Where is he now?" asked Thomas, peering over the woman's shoulder at the curtained windows.

"Last I heard, he was working on one of those oil rigs off the Alaskan coast. Doubt he kept that job for long. Alec never could keep a job."

"You haven't spoken to him since?"

"Not a peep. But if you find my deadbeat cousin, tell him he owes me four-hundred dollars. Alec has a way of disappearing whenever he owes someone money. Knew I shouldn't have trusted him."

The woman scratched her scalp, wisps of short, black hair spilling from beneath the cap.

"When did you move into your house?" asked Aguilar.

"Six years ago. A year after Dawn died. I grew up in Syracuse."

"What made you choose this area?"

Cathy Webb scowled.

"With all that was happening, I was the only family Alec had." Her eyes glistened. "After Dawn committed suicide...the poor girl... Alec was lost. Someone needed to care for the boy."

"Dawn's suicide must have come as a tremendous shock to everyone," said Thomas, softening his eyes. "Did Dawn leave a suicide note?"

"Didn't need to. Those girls at Wolf Lake High drove her to it. Vultures, both of them."

"Which girls, Ms. Webb?"

"Paige Sutton and Justine Adkins. They terrorized our Dawn for years, and the school did nothing to stop it. They murdered Dawn and should pay for their crimes."

"Are you familiar with the Wolf Lake High alumni forum?"

A vein pulsed inside Webb's neck.

"Why do you ask?"

"Ms. Webb, we saw your messages on the forum." Webb shuffled her feet. "You're quite upset with Paige and Justine."

"So? Wouldn't you be, if Paige and Justine drove your cousin to suicide?"

"But you grew up in Syracuse," Aguilar said, setting a hand on her hip. "Your profile name is Webb-WLHS, as in Wolf Lake High School."

Webb shrugged.

"Nothing illegal about snooping around a forum. Those girls never show their faces on the forum, anyhow. They're guilty."

"What can you tell us about Skye Feron, Ms. Webb?" asked Thomas. "She disappeared six years ago, around the same time you moved in."

"If you're implying I had anything to do with Skye's disappearance, you're wrong."

"I noticed you didn't include Skye's name when you implicated Paige and Justine."

The woman's eyes bounced between the house and the garage.

"Alec didn't mention Skye, only Paige and Justine. So I assumed they were the girls torturing our Dawn."

"And yet Skye vanished. How would you describe your cousin? Was he ever violent while he lived with you?"

"Never. Alec wouldn't hurt Skye."

"Why do you say that?"

"Because my cousin isn't a killer. He had a tough upbringing, and the boy went through hell with his parents and sister. But he's not crazy."

"How did Alec feel about Paige and Justine? He ever talk about revenge for what the girls did to Dawn?"

Webb puffed out her chest and lifted her chin.

"Alec didn't hurt anyone, Sheriff. But I wouldn't blame him for hating those girls. I have no regrets for calling them out on a public forum. Everyone needs to hear what they did to Dawn. Now, if you don't mind, I have work to do. The next time you set foot on my property, bring a warrant."

Before Thomas or Aguilar replied, the woman turned and stomped inside the house, slamming the door in their faces.

Aguilar glanced at Thomas.

"She's hiding something. What do you make of her story about Alec moving to Alaska and working offshore on an oil rig."

"It makes sense. Alaska is a great place to hide, if you're on the run. The questions I have are, what did Alec do that made him run, and did he return to Wolf Lake?"

"As much as I detest the woman, I admit I'm worried about Paige Sutton."

"She'll have State Trooper surveillance until we find enough bodies to monitor her house. But I agree. Paige Sutton is the only friend who hasn't disappeared yet."

The curtain swung shut when Thomas glanced over his shoulder. Someone was watching them from the window.

30

"I got the fool. Get up here."

Anthony ended the call and pushed the gun barrel against the back of LeVar's head.

"Have a seat," Anthony said, gesturing at the chair beside the kitchen table. "And keep your hands where I can see them."

LeVar glared over his shoulder at Anthony.

"You sound like a cop. Why are you doing this?"

"It's like Rev says. Nobody leaves the Kings."

"I helped you, Anthony. I saved your ass from Rev after you mailed that package to the press."

During April's murders, serial killer Jeremy Hyde approached Anthony and paid him to mail a cardboard box to the newspaper. The box contained the severed head of Hyde's victim.

"Things changed after you abandoned us to live beside the lake. I moved up the ladder." Anthony chuckled. "Who knows? I might have your old position before long."

Right. Soaking wet, Anthony was half LeVar's weight. And by the way he handled the weapon, he wasn't good with guns. No way Rev would promote an idiot like Anthony to be his enforcer. But Anthony held all the cards now. One wrong move by LeVar, and Anthony would end his life.

Or would he?

Gunfire attracted attention in a crowded apartment building. Even if Anthony escaped unseen, he'd forever be on the run after the police investigated the murder scene. He'd never see his mother again. Despite the kid's brash demeanor, he loved his mother and wouldn't put her at risk by murdering a former gang member inside her kitchen.

He had to think fast. Kilo and Lawson were on the way, and Rev was probably with them. They'd lead LeVar down the stairs and take him out through the basement to avoid attention. Then they'd drive him to a remote location outside Harmon and put a bullet in his head.

LeVar stared at Anthony, focusing on the kid's trembling hand.

"Rev won't promote you, fool. Don't you get it? He's using you to get to me. As soon as this is over, he'll get rid of you. You seen too much."

"Shut up."

"I ain't bullshitting you. You know how crazy Rev is. He's taken out smaller threats than you over the years."

"Rev wouldn't do me like that. After we put you down, we might take a ride over to that pretty lake house of yours. Blow holes through that pig sheriff and the pathetic crippled girl next door."

LeVar's muscles twitched. How dare the Kings threaten his friends? He wanted to punch the smile off Anthony's face.

"Rev would've buried you four months ago over the Jeremy Hyde nonsense, if I hadn't talked him out of it."

"Don't try to change my mind, LeVar. No more talking."

Anthony pushed LeVar's head forward with the gun. The kid's arm trembled as if the floor shook beneath him. LeVar worried Anthony might fire the gun by accident and spray his brain all over the kitchen. A steel door squealed open and closed down the hallway. They were coming.

As the kid held him at gunpoint, LeVar glanced at the window. If he cocked his head, he could look into the parking lot behind the complex.

"What the hell? Why would Rev bring a Royals member with him?"

The moment Anthony took the bait and looked out the window, LeVar wheeled around and slammed his palm against the kid's wrist. He deflected the barrel a second before the gun fired. The bullet blew a hole through the window and shattered the glass. As the shards rained onto the kitchen floor, LeVar rammed his forehead against Anthony's nose. A sound like eggshells cracking. Blood streamed from Anthony's nose as his eyes rolled back in his head.

LeVar caught the boy before he smashed headfirst against the linoleum. He eased Anthony to the floor. Someone pounded on the door as LeVar swung his head around. Kilo and Lawson must have heard the shot.

As the gang members yelled from the hallway, LeVar climbed out the window. Not good. Too far to jump unless he wanted two broken legs. The door burst open inside the apartment. A second window stood five yards away. The neighbor's apartment. Muttering a prayer, LeVar leaped for the ledge and grabbed hold of the bricks before he lost footing. He wobbled backward, one arm pinwheeling as the other hung on for dear life. When he got his balance, he placed his foot against the pane, prepared to kick through the glass. That's when he noticed the window was open a crack, the summer breeze swaying the curtains.

He yanked the screen off and tossed it into the parking lot. Angry voices shouted from inside Anthony's kitchen. If Kilo stuck his head out the window, he'd spot LeVar. With the screen removed, LeVar crouched upon the ledge and yanked the window open. He crawled inside the apartment before the gang members spotted him.

LeVar glanced around the apartment. He stood inside a kitchen, a mirror image of Anthony's, though the neighbor kept this kitchen tidy. A vase on the table held roses, and a fan over the stove buzzed. LeVar peeked his head into the living room. Didn't see the neighbor. The bedroom door stood closed.

He crept across the floor and edged the front door open. A woman in the corridor shouted for someone to call the police. When she turned her back, LeVar spun into the hallway and sprinted for the stairwell.

"Stop that kid!"

A man's voice. Gruff and irate.

LeVar bounded down the stairs, the dress shoes slowing him down until he kicked them off.

He escaped through the cellar as the first police siren wailed through the city.

31

SATURDAY, AUGUST 14TH 3:10 P.M.

Raven lifted her chin and strode into Wolf Lake Consulting, prepared for an argument. She couldn't fathom why LeVar had blown off the appointment. Now she needed to defend her brother to Chelsey, and her boss had sounded like a time bomb ticking down to zero on the phone.

Chelsey was at her desk when Raven entered the room.

"That was his only chance, Raven. I need dependable workers, not people like your brother."

"That's not like LeVar. There has to be a reason he didn't show."

"Whatever the reason, he lost his opportunity. And that's the last time I take advice from you on who I should hire."

Rage, emotional fatigue, and a month's worth of frustration boiled to the surface inside Raven.

"You know something, Chelsey? You've turned into a real b—"

She cut the insult short when the door opened. Saturday visitors were unusual. It had to be LeVar. Chelsey glared at Raven, as if daring her to complete the curse. Raven held her hands up in exasperated surrender.

Paul Phipps, the camper who'd hired Raven, rounded the corner.

"Mr. Phipps, you should have called instead of driving into the village."

Phipps glanced between the two women. Chelsey rocked in her chair, watching Raven, no doubt hoping she'd make a mistake with Phipps. Then Chelsey would have an excuse to fire Raven. Maybe that was for the best. A few weeks ago, Raven had considered Chelsey her best friend. But she wouldn't work another day beside this version of Chelsey.

"What's the latest on my case? Have you caught the thief?"

"Please sit," Raven said, gesturing at an open chair.

"I prefer to stand."

Raven brushed the hair off her forehead as Chelsey's glare cut into her back.

"We have a lead, Mr. Phipps. I'm working with the park ranger, and we've covered the campgrounds with surveillance cameras. If the thief returns, we'll catch him."

Phipps sniffed.

"Sounds to me like you're nowhere near finding the brigand. What sort of operation do you run here?"

Raven turned her head to Chelsey, who lifted her brow and raised her palms, as if echoing Phipps's question.

"I assure you, we're close to catching him. We discovered shoe prints, and the ranger spotted him in the forest. But I must ask, Mr. Phipps. Is this case worth your money? You've already paid twice what the thief stole from your wife's wallet. Even if we find your money—"

"It's not about breaking even. This is a matter of principle. I want the outlaw brought to justice."

Raven sighed.

"As you wish, Mr. Phipps. I promise I'll give you an update by Monday."

"I'll expect progress."

Phipps gave Chelsey a curious look before turning away. The door closed, and an awkward silence settled over the room.

"Well handled, Raven," Chelsey said, her expression blank as she clapped. "Bravo. Perhaps you should enlist your mystery-solving team to catch the campgrounds outlaw and save the day."

"I'm doing my best. Lay off. Instead of criticizing me, why don't you help? We could use an extra set of eyes on the camp."

Chelsey shook her head and slung her bag over her shoulder.

"I don't have the time or patience."

"Where are you going now?"

"Home. I don't feel well and shouldn't have come in today."

Raven couldn't take it anymore. She rounded on Chelsey and blocked her from exiting the room.

"You're not going anywhere until we discuss what's happening with you."

Chelsey threw up her hands.

"Nothing is happening. I caught the flu. You should back away before you catch it too."

"Don't lie to me. I know you better than anyone. You aren't sleeping, you refuse to leave the house, and you're falling behind at work. These are classic signs of—"

"Don't say it."

"Why? You need help. Hiding from the truth won't make you better."

"I'm not listening to this." Chelsey moved past Raven. Raven shifted her body and placed a hand on Chelsey's shoulder. "Move."

"No. You can't push me away this time." As Raven held her friend in place, the neckline of Chelsey's T-shirt dipped and revealed the inflamed lacerations. Raven flinched. "Tell me about your chest."

Chelsey's face twisted.

"My chest? What the hell are you talking about?"

"You're covered with cuts from your neckline to your chest." Raven took a breath. "If you're hurting yourself..."

Her friend's eyes narrowed before widening with understanding.

"Oh, my God. You think I'm cutting."

"That's what it looks like."

"You're...I can't believe...Oh, this is priceless." Chelsey wrestled with the clasp on her necklace. When the hooks refused to unfasten, she grabbed the necklace and yanked it off, snapping the clasp in half. A piece clinked off the floor and skittered under the desk. "The cuts are from the necklace, for God's sake." When Raven glanced at Chelsey in question, Chelsey rolled her eyes and slapped the necklace on the desk. "It's a family heirloom. My great aunt passed it down to my aunt, and now I own the damn thing. I was stupid and wore it to sleep. The pendant slices into my chest whenever I roll onto my stomach. Jesus, Raven. I'm not cutting myself."

Raven bit her lip. Was Chelsey lying, or had she been wrong about the cuts? Guilt slumped Raven's shoulders.

"Stay and talk. I'm so sorry for jumping to conclusions."

"I'm leaving. The next time you accuse someone of cutting, do five seconds of due diligence before you make a fool of yourself."

32

A noise upstairs jerked Justine out of a nightmare. In her dream, spiders and cockroaches covered her body as she curled on the dark floor of the basement, bugs skittering in and out of her ears, crawling into her nose. She jolted and tried to swipe the imaginary spiders off her body. Justine found her wrists chained as before, her body pitched forward with her shoulders bearing the weight. With a moan, she adjusted her feet and leaned back, careful not to scrape against the wall. She'd learned the hard way that cobwebs and dust covered the concrete, draping off the ceiling. They took up residence in her hair, her nose, her clothes. The filth was a part of Justine now, as much as she was one with the dark.

She squinted at the thin line of light burning around the sound barrier over the window. Judging by the strength of the light, it had to be afternoon. As she tested the manacles and searched for a weak spot, footsteps descended the staircase above her head. She'd heard her abductor moving through the house since he locked her in the basement. But he hadn't visited since morning, again standing in the shadow so she couldn't recognize his face. Was this man someone from her past?

She recalled the kidnapping through a malnourished haze.

Justine had walked out of the supermarket and into the fog. As she pushed the shopping cart to her car, she'd noticed the man in the wheelchair struggling to load his groceries into the van. A cast covered his leg. All a ruse. He'd fooled her, taken advantage of her soft spot for the disabled. All she'd wanted to do was help, and look where it got her. She'd made it easy for him, falling for his trick when he asked her to fish the crutch out of the van. Then he struck her head. Who was the man? He wasn't injured or disabled. Even the cast had been a fake. Was she a random victim, or had he targeted her?

The days and nights blended together. Justine had no idea how long he'd locked her in the basement. Days, weeks. Her gaze searched the rear of the basement where the water heater stood. The heater had become her silent partner, the only thing in the darkness that kept her company besides her delusions. She shivered when she remembered the crazed eyes staring at her from behind the water heater. She assumed it was her kidnapper. Yet she swore he'd been somewhere in the house moments before. Whoever the person was, real or imagined, the stranger wasn't here anymore.

Her eyes fell to the floor. Despite the gloom, her vision adjusted. She discerned shapes and shadows. While she'd slept, he'd removed the tray and taken it upstairs. Except for nibbling on a crusty piece of bread, she hadn't eaten since he locked her in this inhospitable dungeon. Her stomach lurched with hunger as she swallowed the sickness crawling into her throat.

A cupboard opened and closed. She imagined him fixing a sandwich, cutting through the bread with a sharp knife. Little droplets of mustard spilling off the bread as he lifted the sandwich toward his mouth. It seemed impossible the man could eat a meal or sleep through the night with a prisoner locked in his basement. Carrying on with his life without a care. If she died, he'd find someone to replace her. A new pet.

Defeat slumped her body forward, and the chains snapped her arms behind her again. She cried out. Stars filled her vision.

As she pulled herself erect, he spoke. The ceiling muffled his voice, made it impossible to make out words. Perhaps he was on the phone.

Then a second voice responded. A woman's voice.

Justine straightened and concentrated on the two voices. Had someone knocked on the door? No, she would have heard. The woman was inside the house. Adrenaline surged through Justine's body. She wanted to believe...no, *needed* to believe the woman wasn't working with the man to keep her trapped. It was possible the woman didn't know Justine was locked in the basement. Justine opened her mouth to scream, and a raspy groan emanated from her chest. Her parched throat refused to respond.

Tugging on the chains, Justine shuffled forward until the manacles stopped her. She stood directly beneath them. Closing her eyes, she listened. His raised voice silenced the woman, forced her to comply. A whimper followed. He'd upset the woman. Was she another kidnapping victim? Or was this his wife or sister, living in submission, too petrified to question why he locked unsuspecting women in the basement?

Footsteps, lighter than his, trailed up the staircase to the second floor of the house. A door closed. Silence pervaded.

Justine waited for the man to move again. A minute later, footsteps crossed overhead, and the sink ran. Water trickled through the basement pipes.

Then a key twisted in the basement door. Until now, she hadn't realized the reinforced door opened with a lock and key. Any hope she held for escaping her prison faded away.

The door opened. A rectangle of light pierced the darkness and forced Justine to avert her eyes. The brightness seared her vision as his shoes thumped against the stairs. He was coming for her.

Justine dropped her head to her chest and pitched forward. She bit her tongue when her shoulder joints threatened to tear. Closing her eyes, she pretended to be asleep as he shuffled through the gloom. She could smell him now. The musky scent of his cologne, tinged with a sharp aftershave. Squinting one eye open, she spied his silhouette amid the black, swaying as though blown by an unseen wind.

"You're awake. You don't need to pretend."

He stepped closer and held out his hand. She'd correctly pictured the man making a sandwich. It rested on a plate.

"Eat. If you don't eat something, you'll die."

Justine's eyelids fluttered. She locked her gaze on the plate, didn't want to look into his face and spy the monster who'd captured her in the fog. Still, the voice tickled her memory. He'd sounded familiar in the parking lot too, though she had no friends or family in Kane Grove.

He picked the sandwich off the plate and pushed it toward her lips. She turned away, though her mouth watered. Seasoned roast beef, lettuce, a sweet pickle. It amazed her how much her nose discerned from one whiff.

"You must pay for what you did. Even inaction is a crime. But I won't harm you, if you cooperate and make amends."

Justine's eyes shot to his silhouette. He'd echoed the guilt she'd felt since high school.

"I'm sorry," she sobbed.

"I know you are, and that's why you're still alive. But you need food and water, if you're to survive another day."

He pressed the bread against her lips. She opened her mouth and bit down on the sandwich, chewing as the flavors hit her tongue. He might have poisoned her. One last trick. But she didn't think so. For whatever reason, he wanted her alive. She needed to escape and warn Paige. If the man was avenging Dawn's suicide, Paige would be next on his list.

She swallowed and coughed after eating too fast. The food struck her hollow stomach and sizzled, threatening to make her nauseous. As she steadied herself, he placed a glass against her dry, caked lips. The water hit the back of her throat. She gulped hungrily as he tipped the glass, his arm extended, face always hidden behind a veil of darkness.

Justine choked and spewed water. Her lungs spasmed as she

sucked air, chest wracked by another coughing fit. He waited until she finished. Then he offered her the glass again. She blinked the tears out of her eyes and cleared her throat, accepting the water.

The stranger fed her until only the corner of the sandwich remained on the plate. She'd consumed all the water in the tall glass. Her chest heaved as though she'd climbed a mountain.

"Who are you?"

He stepped back, as though afraid she'd recognized him.

"Someone who will help you atone for your sins."

Justine cried out.

"Please don't hurt me. I should have helped her."

"Yes, you should have. But here we are, all these years later, and you still need to pay for what you did."

He turned before she could reply and spoke over his shoulder.

"I will bring you another meal this evening. You did well, Justine. But death is forever. You're never leaving."

The door closed, and the key twisted in the lock.

33

The escalator carried Chelsey to the second floor of the mall. Two college age females approached with shopping bags, the girls laughing about something that happened at last night's party. Chelsey moved aside and let them pass. They were too consumed by conversation to pay attention to people around them.

Finding a bench in front of a store selling classic board games, Chelsey slumped onto the seat and sipped her soda, people watching as soft music played through the speakers. Two rails divided the corridor. She glanced over the closest rail, giving her a birdseye view of shoppers hustling down the lower corridor. It was good to relax. After lying to Raven about going home, she'd driven to the mall outside Harmon, craving retail therapy.

Her phone buzzed in her pocket. She eyed the screen and glimpsed Raven's message. Chelsey flicked the phone into silent mode and ignored the text, still fuming over the ridiculous accusation. Cutting herself? Even at Chelsey's darkest moment, when her friends had abandoned Wolf Lake for college and her parents didn't know how to reach her, she hadn't disfigured her body. She'd only wanted the nightmare to end, to find a way out of the dark tunnel she'd fallen into. There were nights when she closed her eyes and didn't care if she never awoke. Yet she'd never considered suicide. Not seriously. Nor had she sliced her body with little razors and hid the lacerations like secret friends.

Who was Raven to accuse Chelsey of self-harm? Her mother jammed needles into her arm for a decade, and LeVar ran the Harmon streets with his thug friends. Raven was the last person who should lecture someone about her demons. Chelsey had even given LeVar a chance, and the teenager blew off the interview. She'd predicted he'd call moments before the appointment with some excuse, some lame reason for postponing the interview. So, when his name had appeared on her phone, she'd ignored his calls. No second chances. She climbed out on a limb for Raven's brother, and he made a fool of her.

Chelsey tossed the soda in the trash and wandered up the corridor, hugging close to the rail to avoid the throng of weekend shoppers. Cold sweat trickled down her forehead after a burly man in a hurry almost trampled her. He looked too much like Herb Reid, the construction worker she'd investigated. Memories of the attack came unbidden to her. Head swimming, she leaned against the rail and caught her breath as shoppers passed, a few eyeing her warily.

You're okay, she told herself. It took a while before the floor stopped undulating. After she steadied herself, she continued on. Her growling stomach reminded her she hadn't eaten since breakfast. Sweet and savory scents wafted out of the food court.

Outside the Disney Store, a man and woman embraced. She swore it was Thomas and Naomi until the man turned his face toward Chelsey, sensing her glare. Chelsey lowered her head and hurried away, feeling stupid. And jealous. Against her will, she pictured Thomas and Naomi beside the lake, her arms wrapped around his shoulders, both of them smiling into each other's eyes. They'd celebrated a joyous occasion—Thomas professing his love to Naomi, no doubt.

Let them be together. Despite her jealousy, despite the hurt burning through her heart, she wanted Thomas to be happy. Naomi seemed like a good person. Chelsey admired the woman for caring for a wheelchair-bound teenager by herself. If anyone deserved Thomas, it was Naomi.

A tear crept out of her eye. She flicked it away in anger. Why was this upsetting her?

As she weaved between teenagers, a memory flashed of the night she met Thomas at the high school football game. He'd offered her his sweatshirt to keep her warm. Long after the game ended and the bleachers cleared, they sat and laughed, oblivious to the chilling autumn wind. She'd loved the boy from the moment she set eyes on him, adoring his quirky mannerisms, never once considering he had Asperger's, and not loving him less when she learned the truth.

Throwing her friends and family out of her life had been a huge mistake. But breaking up with Thomas had crippled her. He was her rock, her steadying force. With Thomas by her side, she would have broken out of her depression sooner. She wouldn't have wasted a decade of her life, wandering the country, searching for a love she'd tossed away. She'd convinced herself she didn't need friends to lean on, and all those lies drowned beneath a battering wave of truth.

A teenage boy and girl held hands on a bench. The girl giggled and kissed the boy on his cheek. Another tear forced its way past Chelsey's defenses. Every store she passed reminded Chelsey of her ruin. The jewelry store, selling love on credit. The greeting card store. A shop that emblazoned the names of loved ones on stuffed animals. At that moment, she might have been the only person alone in the world.

She lowered her head and picked up her pace, not noticing how hard her heart was slamming against her chest until her vision blurred and her legs buckled.

The next thing Chelsey remembered was lying on her back, the cold rail brushing her cheek, her hair splayed out like spilling blood. A woman leaned over her.

"Miss, can you hear me?"

Chelsey couldn't reply. The mall somersaulted as her breath came in quick gasps.

"Someone call 9-1-1! I think she's having a heart attack!"

Concerned shouts. People circling, staring down at her like she was some strange piece of art they couldn't grasp. Chelsey's heart screamed in warning. It thrummed at hyper-speed, jack-hammering into her throat as her vision moved in and out of focus. Unlike her attack during the Herb Reid investigation, pain seared through her body this time. A vise clutched her heart and squeezed, shooting pain down her limbs. Her left arm fell numb as a stabbing sensation trailed from her neck to her shoulder. As her life flashed before her eyes, she understood the implications.

"Does anyone know CPR? Get security!"

This was it. She was dying.

The physician hadn't listened to her. She should have called a cardiologist. Like everything in her life, she'd waited too long to act.

A woman in a white and black security uniform knelt beside her and spoke words Chelsey couldn't understand.

She blacked out.

34

When someone turned the knob on the guest house door, LeVar snatched the knife from beneath the mattress and slipped it into his back pocket.

The lake mirrored the blue sky, making it seem impossible that danger could reach him here. But someone had broken inside the guest house already. He couldn't think straight. Too many worries crawling through his head. What if the Kings attacked Scout and Naomi, or shot Thomas when he intervened? LeVar had invited danger into paradise. The blood of his family and friends would be on his hands if something unthinkable happened.

He waited behind the wall. The lock jiggled.

LeVar slipped the knife out of his pocket, fingers wrapping around the hilt. A knife was a poor choice in a gunfight. But it was the only weapon he possessed.

He let out a breath when someone knocked. Rev or Kilo wouldn't rap their knuckles on his door. They'd kick the door down and shoot the first person they encountered.

LeVar leaned his head around the wall. Raven peered between the curtains with worry and irritation on her face. As he approached, her eyes fell to the knife and widened.

"What's with the knife?" she asked when he opened the door.

"Just being careful."

He led her inside and gestured at the chair beside the window. She set her hands on her hips.

"I'm not here for a social call, LeVar. You aren't answering your phone, and you never showed for the interview."

LeVar fell into the chair and lowered his head, elbows on his knees, dreadlocks concealing his face.

"Something came up."

"I went out on a limb for you. Chelsey's angry as hell, and she blames me for wasting her time. I don't get it. You wanted that job."

He slung his hair back and rubbed his temples.

"Anthony Fisher called just as I left."

"I told you to let Thomas deal with Anthony. You didn't go to Harmon, did you?" He glanced out the window. His silence answered her question. Raven fell into the chair beside him when he scooted over to make room. "Talk to me."

"I'm an idiot, okay?" He clenched his hands. "Anthony set me up. Half the crew was waiting for me."

She opened her mouth to reply. Her haunted eyes fell to the floor.

"How did you get away?"

"Still got a few tricks up my sleeve, Sis. They shoulda known better than to mess with their muscle."

"Please tell me you didn't..."

"Naw. I didn't kill no one. Busted up Anthony's nose and broke into some lady's apartment. But that's all."

"So just a few minor infractions. Great. We should call the police."

"And say what? That the former enforcer for the Kings beat the snot out of some kid for pulling a gun on him? That'll go well for me."

Raven cast a worried glance at the door.

"What if they come here?"

LeVar leaned over and touched the mouse on Scout's computer. The views from the security cameras appeared on the screen. He tapped his finger against the monitor.

"I'll see them. But my guess is they already have."

"The break-in."

"Right. Now that I have eyes on the guest house, ain't nobody sneaking up on me again."

Raven eyed the knife.

"I don't want you fighting. If you kill somebody, even in self-defense, you'll go to prison. And if they kill you...I can't live without my brother."

She rested her head on his broad shoulder. He stroked her hair.

"Nothing gonna happen to me. I'll take care of it. Like I always have."

"That's what I'm afraid of. At least tell Thomas. This is his property. He deserves to know what's going on."

LeVar enlarged the security camera views, zooming around the yard.

"I'll tell Thomas." LeVar raised his eyes to Raven's. "But if Rev shows his face, it won't end well for him."

SHARP PAIN SPREAD down Chelsey's arms and legs. Her body tingled.

A nurse wearing too much aftershave removed the oxygen mask from her mouth. She grabbed his hand, her lungs struggling for air.

"I...can't...breathe."

The golden-haired doctor glared down her nose at Chelsey.

"Yes, you can, Ms. Byrd. You're hyperventilating. The more you depend on the mask, the longer it will take for the gases in your blood to return to normal."

The nurse wheeled a machine forward as Chelsey sat on an uncomfortable cot in the emergency room.

"What's that for?"

"We'll run an echocardiogram and check your heart," the doctor said, motioning for the nurse to prepare for the examination.

"Don't you give people shots or something when they're having a heart attack or stroke?"

It felt as if a million tiny hands squeezed Chelsey from the inside. Cutting off the blood flow in her veins. Clutching her heart.

"You're not having a stroke."

"But my left side. It's numb."

"Give me your leg," the doctor said, tapping her left knee. Chelsey raised her leg as the doctor held her foot. "Push against me. Good. Now your arm."

Chelsey bent her arm at the elbow and resisted as the woman pulled.

"Good thing for me we aren't arm wrestling," the doctor said. "Because you would have already won. You're not having a stroke. I can run a CT and an MRI. But the signs of a stroke or heart attack aren't there." The doctor held Chelsey's eyes. "You're already relaxing, Ms. Byrd. All you needed was to hear you aren't dying, and the blood returned to your face. How's your heartbeat?"

"It's still really fast."

The doctor took Chelsey's wrist and checked her pulse.

"About a hundred beats per minute. Elevated, but not dangerous. You hit a hundred beats per minute every time you walk uphill. Even someone in good physical condition will push one-hundred-twenty or higher climbing stairs. But you think nothing of it because you expect your heart rate to rise."

"I'm sitting down. My heart rate shouldn't be a hundred."

"Stress will make your heart beat faster. When I was in medical school, we studied people watching tense scenes in action and horror movies. We measured heart rates of ninety to one-hundred, even though they were seated."

Chelsey lowered her eyes. Had she done this to herself?

"We'll give you an echocardiogram and run a few more tests, just to be sure. But I'm ninety-nine percent certain you aren't having a heart attack or stroke."

"Ninety-nine isn't one-hundred."

The doctor patted Chelsey's arm as if she were an inconsolable child. She had Chelsey remove her shirt while the nurse turned his back. Then Chelsey held out her arms so the doctor could slip a pale blue hospital gown over her.

"All right, Ms. Byrd. I'll have you lie on your back to start."

With a pillow beneath her head, Chelsey stared at the ceiling as the doctor pushed the cold transducer probe around her chest. Then she lay on her side, facing away from the monitor while the doctor repeated the procedure. Her lips quivered from cold and sadness. What had become of her life?

After the doctor finished, she told Chelsey to sit up.

"You're not having a stroke, and your heart is healthy."

"So what's happening to me?"

"Have you experienced a lot of stress lately, Ms. Byrd?"

Chelsey glanced away.

"There are things going on in my life."

"My guess is stress caused your attack. We'll keep you a while longer and monitor your condition. But you need to relax. You aren't dying."

35

Scout felt summer slipping away. The sun set a few minutes earlier every night, and the darkness was complete by the time she set her phone on the nightstand and pulled herself from the wheelchair to the bed. Crickets sang through the cracked open window. Usually, she stayed awake until midnight during the summer. After spending the day scouring forums, tracking Webb-WLHS, Paige Sutton, and Justine Adkins, she couldn't force her eyes to stay open. She'd outlasted her mother, who turned in a half-hour ago, complaining of a headache. Now Scout dragged her atrophied legs across the bedsheets, hauled the covers to her chest, and lay back with her arms propped behind her head.

To her side, the phone hummed with an Instagram notification. She ignored it. Yesterday, she'd overheard her mother on the phone with her father. Her chest tightened. It had been months since she last saw her father. Scout had almost forgotten what he looked like. She twiddled her thumbs over her stomach as she considered calling him. How would he react? Enraged that she interrupted his sleep, or thrilled to hear her voice? What sort of father abandoned his daughter after a crippling automobile accident?

She picked up the phone and scrolled to his number. He woke up early, even on Sundays. During the week, he began work at six in the morning, and he maintained an early schedule through the weekend. The green call icon beckoned. She set the phone down, undecided, then picked it up again. Calling Glen entailed risks. If he spurned her, it would be forever, and she couldn't bear losing hope.

Scout was about to give up when a red alarm icon appeared on the screen. The security camera outside her window detected movement. Propping herself up with her elbows, she opened the app and stared at the screen. The yard leading to LeVar's house appeared empty. But she didn't trust the shadows spilling across the grass. It was probably nothing. The alarm triggered whenever a deer ran through the picture, or a raccoon scurried past. She zoomed in and studied the pools of darkness cast by the trees, the sharp moonlight reflecting off LeVar's windows.

For five minutes she studied the screen. Had Raven and Darren received the same alert? The lights were off inside the guest house. Scout hadn't seen LeVar since the interview, so he must have received bad news. Scout didn't understand Chelsey. LeVar was the obvious choice to fill the vacant investigator position, and Wolf Lake Consulting had fallen behind on their cases.

A silhouette darted out of the trees. Scout swallowed and moved the phone closer to her face. Someone approached LeVar's door, staying close to the wall. She urged LeVar to wake up. Watching the real-life horror movie play out on the screen froze her with indecision.

Minimizing the app, she called LeVar's phone and got his voicemail. Dammit. She fired him a text.

Someone is outside the guest house. Stay away from the windows.

LeVar didn't respond.

Scout dragged herself off the bed, cursing her useless legs. It took too long to struggle into the chair. Even if she reached LeVar in time, she was no match for the prowler. Pulling open the bedroom door, she pushed the wheelchair through the kitchen to the deck door. She spied the stranger in the night, testing the windows as he moved around the guest house.

Scout jolted when the phone rang, dropping it into her lap as the shadow crossed behind the house, searching for a way inside. Raising the phone to her ear, she answered.

"I see him," LeVar said.

"Why didn't you answer?"

"'Cause I didn't want him to know I was awake. Don't come out here, Scout." She imagined LeVar peeking through the window, spying her beyond the glass deck door. "Get away from the glass and call Thomas."

"What will you do?"

He answered Scout by ending the call.

"LeVar?"

Her mouth went dry. The prowler moved to the door again, crouching below the window as he tested the knob. The pane exploded as LeVar punched through the glass with a T-shirt wrapped around his fist. Stunned, the stranger fell back on his palms and crab-walked backward. The door flew open as the unknown man fished a gun from his pocket.

"No!" Scout screamed.

The gunshot split the night.

LeVar ducked and dove for the ground, anticipating the shot. The bullet whistled past his ear and tore into the black sky as his assailant scrambled away. LeVar leaped to his feet and threw a punch, striking the hooded figure's face. Blood spurted from the man's nose, the stranger pinwheeling his arms as he stumbled backward with the gun still in his hand.

"That you, Anthony? Come back to finish the job?"

Floodlights flicked on behind the A-Frame. The hooded man took off running as LeVar tumbled to the ground. Whoever it was, the man was fast. Kilo or Lawson? Rev or Anthony?

LeVar righted himself and sprinted after the figure, the night swallowing his assailant. The man's sneakers pounded the trail as he fled toward the state park. LeVar hoped Darren had seen the security camera alert. If the park ranger cut the stranger off, he'd have no escape.

Barely breaking a sweat in the warm and humid night, LeVar kicked into another gear, pumping his arms and legs, gaining ground on the fleeing suspect. Fear whispered in his ear. If the man turned back with the gun, he'd have a free shot at LeVar. But if he missed his shot, he'd never escape LeVar's wrath.

The fleeing man vanished when he ran beneath a tree grove. LeVar searched the night, blinded by darkness. Footsteps squished over soggy terrain, telling LeVar his intruder had cut toward the lake shore. LeVar burst through a tangle of branches and leaped debris, pulling up amid the trees when he couldn't find the man. As fast as he was, the man in the hooded sweatshirt ran like the wind.

LeVar spun in a circle. Darkness converged from all sides.

He'd lost the suspect.

The snap of a branch gave LeVar no warning before the next gunshot exploded.

36

SATURDAY, AUGUST 14TH 10:05 P.M.

cross the lake, Raven heard the gunfire. After pleading with her mother to stay calm, promising nothing bad had happened to LeVar, Raven jumped into her SUV and raced toward the gunshots, sickness eating away at her stomach. The Kings had come to settle the score.

In the deep gloom behind the sheriff's property, she placed a hand to her forehead and prayed her brother was all right, that he wasn't shot and dying in the forest.

"Don't worry," Naomi said. "I'm sure LeVar is fine."

"He just ran into the night?"

Raven paced a groove into the lawn. She peered toward the lake, the trail, the cloaking forest leading to the state park. Naomi stood beside Scout and Thomas in the backyard as the sheriff spoke into his radio. The flashing lights of the cruiser whirled across the grass as Deputy Lambert arrived.

Raven dialed LeVar's phone, and it rang inside the guest house. He'd left it behind. Now she had no way to track her brother.

The words rang hollow. How ironic it would be, if LeVar became a victim of gang violence after leaving the Harmon Kings and moving to Wolf Lake. Safety was an illusion. Raven turned to Scout.

"Did you see who broke into the house?"

The girl shook her head.

"It was too dark. LeVar kept the lights in the house off because he'd received the security alert too."

Raven kicked herself. If she'd noticed the alert...

Then what? She couldn't have reached LeVar in time. The attack happened too fast.

Deputy Lambert hurried to Thomas. The two officers shared a brief conversation. The grim look on Lambert's face told Raven the deputy had bad news. She braced herself, understanding nothing would save her sanity if LeVar was already dead.

"I spoke to Deputy Aguilar," Lambert said. "Aguilar and the ranger are searching the state park grounds. The campgrounds are on lock down. So far, we've found no one. No sign of LeVar."

"Find him," said Raven. "He might be injured."

Thomas flicked on his flashlight.

"We'll take the trail along the lake and meet up with Darren and Aguilar. With any luck, we'll trap the suspect between us." And find LeVar alive, Raven prayed. "Do you have your gun on you?"

Raven nodded and patted her holster. Thomas handed her a radio.

"Keep it on at all times, and don't let Naomi and Scout out of your sight."

"Gotcha."

Thomas took a deep breath and touched Raven's shoulder.

"We'll find LeVar. I promise."

Raven steeled herself.

"Bring him home, Thomas."

Thomas and Lambert took off for the trail. Raven's body thrummed with tension as she cupped her elbows with her hands. She wanted to be in the park with the search team. Raven held the flawed belief that she could alter fate by joining the hunt. As she struggled to remain calm, she spied the terror on Scout's face. She needed to be strong for the girl. Kneeling before the wheelchair, Raven took Scout's hand in hers.

"You did great, Scout."

"No, I didn't help him."

"He's alive because of you. Darren and I missed the alert. If it wasn't for you, we wouldn't have known someone tried to break into the guest house."

Naomi rested a hand on Scout's shoulder. The girl sniffled and swiped her hand beneath her nose.

"I just want him to be okay. He's my friend."

A part of Raven broke inside. Since he'd left the Harmon Kings, her brother had touched so many lives. Not just his family's. That he'd befriended a paralyzed fourteen-year-old made her even more proud of what he'd become.

"He loves you, Scout. LeVar has a funny way of showing affection sometimes. But he's a teddy bear at heart. I see how he looks at you."

Raven turned away when Scout broke down. As much as she wanted to comfort the girl, Raven couldn't watch Scout sob without falling apart. She faded into the shadows where the others wouldn't see her cry.

A shout pulled Raven around. She shared a glance with Naomi, then she ran toward the lake trail, stopping when LeVar walked out of the darkness.

"LeVar!" Scout cried out.

Raven breathed again. She wrapped her arms around her brother and hugged him close, never wanting to let him out of her sight. The honeymoon didn't last long. Remembering he'd run after his assailant like a reckless fool, she shoved his shoulder.

"Don't do that again. You risked your life for nothing."

"I had it handled."

"Oh, really? He shot at you."

LeVar glanced over his shoulder.

"Well, he's not a good shot, 'cause he missed."

Raven shook her head.

"Think with your head, not your fists. Did you see who it was?"

"Nah, I didn't get a good look at him. It must have been one of the Kings. My guess is Rev or Kilo."

Scout called to LeVar. He met the girl's eyes and hugged her tightly, planting a kiss on her head.

"We thought we'd lost you," Scout said, on the edge of tears again.

"Takes more than a prowler to put me down." LeVar brushed the hair off her forehead. "If he's stupid enough to return, we'll catch him."

"No, you won't. Leave it to Thomas," said Naomi. Raven nodded in agreement. "This is a police matter. Thomas and the deputies are in the state park with Ranger Holt now."

"Yeah, I passed them on the way back. They won't catch the guy, though. He's too fast."

"Promise me you won't do anything stupid like that again," said Raven. "You're not expendable, LeVar. Everyone cares about you."

"Don't worry, Sis. Like I said, I got it handled."

Sure you do, Raven thought. Fire burned in her brother's eyes. If the Kings returned, he'd be prepared. What if LeVar found a gun and shot somebody? Worries fluttered through Raven's head as LeVar spoke with Naomi and Scout. How would Raven explain tonight's events to Serena without worrying her sick?

Before Raven called her mother to break the news, her phone buzzed with an incoming text. She stared at the screen. When it rained, it poured.

"What's wrong?" asked Naomi, coming to Raven's side.

She put the phone away and exhaled.

"That was Chelsey. She's in the emergency room."

37

R aven ignored the speed limit on her way to the hospital. She'd worried something like this would happen. Chelsey had grown sicker by the day, and Raven fretted over the myriad of possibilities. Was her friend stricken with a disease, or had the crippling depression returned?

She sprinted into the emergency room, but the receptionist wouldn't allow Raven inside because she wasn't family. After a lot of persuasion and arguing, Raven stood aside until a family gathered at the receptionist's desk. Then she slipped through the emergency room doors before anyone noticed. She hurried to room four, the room Chelsey claimed she occupied in her text. A doctor with a gray mustache turned when Raven entered. There was nobody else in the room.

"Who are you looking for?"

"Chelsey Byrd. She messaged me and told me she was in this room."

The doctor scrunched his brow.

"The woman who occupied this room is in surgery."

Raven's stomach dropped. No, this wasn't happening.

"Are you certain?"

"Well, yes. They rushed her into surgery five minutes ago." He narrowed his eyes. "Are you immediate family? You shouldn't be here."

"I'm her coworker...I mean her best friend."

A confused expression fell across the doctor's face.

"Coworker? I would have expected she retired years ago."

"Wait, are we talking about the same person? My friend is thirty-two. Dark hair down to about here." Raven touched her shoulder.

"Oh, my. You have the wrong room. The woman I examined was much older than your friend."

It took several minutes to sort out Chelsey's location. She'd given Raven the wrong room number. Figures, Raven grumbled to herself as a nurse found Chelsey in her database. The hospital had moved Chelsey out of the emergency ward and into her own room.

Raven finally located Chelsey on the fourth floor. Cleaning solutions tickled her nose as she knocked before entering. Chelsey's head was turned away as Raven walked inside. She spotted the black circles around her friend's eyes, the sickly pallor of her drawn face.

"Chelsey. Are you okay?"

Raven set a hand on Chelsey's arm. Her friend turned her head toward her.

"It's back. My depression." She sniffled and stared at the ceiling. "I'm such a basket case, Raven."

"Slow down and tell me what happened."

Chelsey lifted a shoulder and lowered her eyes.

"The doctor said I had an anxiety attack. I was at the mall, trying to relax and get away from work for a while, and it hit me all at-once."

Raven brushed Chelsey's hair off her face.

"What hit you?"

"It was terrible. My heart started racing out of control, I couldn't breathe, and I was too dizzy to keep my balance. Next thing I remember, I was on my back with some mall cop leaning over me and radioing for an ambulance."

"That sounds terrifying. The doctor checked your heart, I assume."

"Yeah," Chelsey said, choking on the word. "They ran all sorts of tests. My heart is fine, and I'm fit enough to run a marathon." She wrung her hands. "This is just like when I was eighteen. Suddenly, my mind refuses to sit still. I did this to myself, Raven. All of it."

"This isn't your fault."

"Yes, it is. It's always my fault. Everything I touch goes to hell. And now I'm right back where I was fourteen years ago. I can't go through that again."

"You won't, if I can help it." Raven turned Chelsey's head to face hers. "You're my best friend, Chelsey. I won't let anything happen to you."

"It's out of our control. Depression isn't a switch I can turn on or off."

"Has anything like this happened before?" Chelsey chewed her lip. "Chelsey?"

"Once. During the Herb Reid investigation. He grabbed for my camera, and my heart kinda went nuts."

"Why didn't you tell me? This isn't a game. You need to take care of yourself."

"Like I said, I'm a mess."

Raven rubbed her eyes.

"What did the doctors say? Are they treating your anxiety attacks so it doesn't happen again?"

"He wants me on an antidepressant." She sighed. "I thought I was done with these medications."

Raven held Chelsey's eyes.

"It's not forever. They're preventing a repeat of what happened to you as a teenager. Listen to your doctors, take your medication. And most of all, stop pushing your friends away. We're trying to help."

Chelsey's eyes narrowed.

"Don't you realize you can't help? I lost out on everything. College, family, friends. You have no idea what it's like. You weren't there."

"No, I wasn't. But I care for my mother every day and make sure she's stays on the straight and narrow. She'll always be an addict, and each day is a new test. If she can conquer heroin, I'm certain you'll get through this."

Chelsey snatched a tissue from the table and wiped her eyes.

"Yeah, on my own. They're kicking me out of the hospital in an hour. I lobbied to stay this long."

"Why would you want to stay? Wouldn't you be more comfortable in your own house?" Chelsey wouldn't admit it, but she didn't want to be alone. "Why don't you stay with us tonight?"

"You don't have the room."

"Then I'll call my brother and have him watch Mom. I can stay at your place."

"It's no use. Go home, Raven. I shouldn't have called you here. I'll handle this on my own."

"You don't mean that."

"Why? I've always looked out for myself."

"Right, you've always shouldered everyone's problems, including your own. And this is where it got you. It doesn't have to be this way. You're overworked and wound tighter than a cheap watch. Take time for yourself and hire a third investigator."

"If I ever find dependable help, I will."

Raven groaned and leaned back. Chelsey was impossibly stubborn, forever concocting excuses to refuse help.

"I didn't want to say anything. But my brother almost died today. That's why he missed the appointment."

Chelsey's face twisted.

"He almost died?"

"The Harmon Kings don't let their members walk away. Seems they've targeted LeVar."

Chelsey stared at her hands.

"I didn't know. Now I feel bad. Still, he should have called."

"He called. You refused to answer. Give him another chance, Chelsey. I'm vouching for my brother, and despite everything you've said about me over the last month, you know I've never steered you wrong. LeVar will work harder than anyone else. And we need a male presence at the firm, a tough guy capable of banging heads together when things get rough."

"Isn't that what I hired you for?" Chelsey cracked a grin. Finally, a sign that Raven's best friend was hiding beneath her shell. "Tell your brother I'll interview him soon. Not this coming week. I've got too much on my plate. But I'll give him a fair shot."

Raven smiled.

"You won't regret it. LeVar is exactly the person we need to fill the open investigator's position." A nurse wheeled a patient down the hallway. "Hey, why don't I stay until they release you? I'll follow you home. Maybe you'll reconsider and let me spend the night."

The sullen Chelsey returned. Kneading the blanket covering her legs, she turned away.

"I don't need you watching me. Go home, get some sleep. I'm not a suicide risk. We'll get back to work Monday morning."

"Are you sure?"

"I am."

"So, are we cool now?"

"We're friends, Raven. But this isn't something you can fix."

38

T he tree outside the window drew misshapen shadows across the ceiling. Sleep welcomed him with inviting hands, but he couldn't follow.

Thomas Shepherd's A-Frame was three-quarters glass. Experience warned him Uncle Truman's house would get cold come winter. Year round, it invited the light inside, whether it was sun or moon. Tonight, it left him exposed.

He interlaced his fingers behind his head. His mind raced and wouldn't allow him to fall asleep. Through the window, he could see the guest house with one light shining inside the bedroom. LeVar was still awake. The teenager almost died today when LeVar's past came back to haunt him. Though Thomas fretted over the boy, he also needed to consider Naomi and Scout. As long as the Harmon Kings sought revenge on LeVar, Naomi and Scout would be in the line of fire.

He kept his Glock on the bed stand tonight. Loaded and ready.

After speaking with Darren, he'd copied the web address for the security camera footage. Now he flicked his phone out of hibernation and checked the cameras. He had to hand it to Scout. Blanketing the backyard with cameras was a smart idea. The high-definition camera yielded a crystal clear view of the guest house.

If only he'd caught the person breaking into LeVar's house. The man had been too fast, outrunning LeVar and escaping through the park before Thomas hemmed him in.

Satisfied the criminal wasn't coming back tonight, Thomas set the phone aside and closed his eyes. Twenty minutes after he drifted asleep, the shrill ring of the phone jolted him upright. Confused, he stared at the clock before answering.

"Shepherd," he said, reaching for the water glass beside the bed.

"Sheriff Shepherd, I'm sorry to bother you at this ungodly hour. But my team had a breakthrough with your Jane Doe."

It took a moment for Thomas to recognize Dr. Astrid Stone. He hadn't spoken with the forensic anthropologist since Tuesday. He swung his legs off the bed and set his bare feet on the floorboards, squinting after he switched the bedside lamp on.

"I'm listening."

"Now that we've reconstructed the skull, we compared Skye Feron's dental records with our Jane Doe."

"Go on."

"Teeth, Sheriff, are among the body's hardest structures. They preserve well and provide us with vital clues about a person's identity. Your Jane Doe has what we call a class 2 malocclusion."

"An overbite."

"Very impressive, Sheriff."

"What does that tell us?"

"Jane Doe is not Skye Feron. Feron's dental records show she wore braces in elementary school to correct a crowding issue. But the braces came off in ninth grade. The girl never had an overbite."

Thomas ran a hand through his hair.

"So who did we dig up below Lucifer Falls?"

"That remains a mystery. But it isn't Skye Feron."

The damn cop hadn't budged in over an hour.

Paige Sutton peeked between the living room curtains. The night held too many secrets, too many places to hide. After the county sheriff informed her a state trooper vehicle would park outside her house, she'd felt some measure of relief. Finally, the police were taking the matter seriously. Now, they just needed to find her friend. Forty-eight hours had passed since anyone heard from Justine. A pall blanketed Paige. Something terrible had happened. It was all spinning out of control again, just like six years ago, when Skye vanished on a night eerily similar to this one.

The cruiser slumbered beneath an oak tree with long branches that brushed the curb like the claws of some ancient devil. She made out the officer's silhouette and little else. He was probably asleep. She waved to the man and whipped the curtains shut after he didn't respond. To hell with him. She'd considered bringing him coffee or something to eat.

Sitting on the couch, Paige couldn't relax. Not with the window behind her. She swiped through her phone, hoping against hope that Justine would message Paige and let her know she was safe. Then she gave up and moved to the recliner, wanting an unrestricted view of the door.

Something brushed against the house. A scraping sound like claws dragging across a tombstone. She sat up and moved her eyes from one window to the next, then to the stairs. The memory of the break-in clung to Paige, made her jump at every sound, every shadow. One more glance out the window. No movement inside the cruiser. If the trooper had seen someone, he'd already be in pursuit of the suspect.

She chided herself. If she lost her mind over every noise, she'd never sleep tonight. Returning to the chair, she pulled a blanket over her bare legs and curled up with her feet tucked beneath her, the notebook computer in her lap and pumping warmth through her shivering body. She opened the Wolf Lake High School alumni website and snooped around in incognito mode, as she always did.

Nobody needed to know she was here, reading the comments, searching for messages targeted at Paige and Justine.

It didn't take long before Paige found another angry post from Webb-WLHS. Who did this woman think she was? Nobody named Webb had graduated with Paige's class. The woman was an impostor, a troll looking to stir up trouble. Paige had done some digging after contacting a friend who worked for the county. Dawn Samson had a cousin named Cathy Webb. The woman moved outside Wolf Lake the summer someone took Skye. Was Cathy Webb the person who broke inside Paige's house and left the friendship bracelet? How did she come upon the bracelet, if she wasn't responsible for Skye's disappearance? It didn't add up. If anyone wanted to avenge Dawn, it was Alec Samson, the bitch's brother. But he'd vanished too.

Now someone wanted to terrorize Paige and make her pay for her rivalry with Dawn. The same person had taken Justine. And Skye? Maybe it was time Paige paid Cathy Webb a visit and showed the woman she wouldn't be intimidated.

Paige scrolled through the woman's posts. The heat leapt off the screen. Cathy Webb blamed Paige and Skye for Dawn's suicide, as if a little harmless ribbing could push a girl to kill herself. Post after post of unsubstantiated rumor and hearsay. Yes, Paige would pay Cathy Webb back for her personal attacks. The woman couldn't hide behind a fake screen name forever.

Frustrated, Paige slammed the laptop shut. The hedges rattled outside her house. Her spine stiffened as she crept to the window. The yard drowned in deep shadow, as if a black tide rolled through the neighborhood. Overhead, a street lamp flickered and died. Perfect. Just what she needed. Whatever had crawled through her yard, it wasn't there now.

Accepting sleep wouldn't come to her, even with the trooper stationed outside, Paige padded barefoot to the kitchen and searched the refrigerator for a snack. She settled on a Greek yogurt and set it on the island. The deck door rattled. Her eyes flew to the glass as a shadow vanished from view.

Paige's heart was a jackrabbit. All speed and terror as she edged away from the glass. A tree cast a grotesque shadow against the deck door, amplified by the moonlight.

Grabbing her phone, she dialed the state trooper's barracks. The dispatcher sounded half-asleep and irritated she'd called. He assured her she was safe as long as the trooper remained outside.

"But there's someone behind the house. The officer can't see my backyard from the street."

Footsteps crunched through the grass below the kitchen window. She yelled out and backed into the living room.

"He's circling the house. Tell the officer the intruder is here, the psycho who broke into my home."

"Remain calm, ma'am. I'm sure it's just an animal pawing around the yard. I'll radio the officer and have him take a look."

Incompetent fool. Paige ended the call and swung her gaze from the door to the upper landing. Instinct told her to flee while she had the chance. Fear kept her rooted in place, her legs blocks of ice that refused to respond.

A knock on the door snapped her head up. It must be the officer checking on her.

She unfroze her body and hurried to the door. Peered through the peephole. Saw nobody on her stoop.

Was this some kind of trick?

She craned her head toward the cruiser and spied the officer in the front seat, his face bathed in darkness, the moonlight glimmering off the hood. The lazy ingrate hadn't bothered to check her property.

Paige huffed and marched to the kitchen, intent on calling the dispatcher again to give him a piece of her mind. Instead, she snatched her sweatshirt off the table and pulled it over her head. She donned sandals and exited the house, her glare arrowing at the officer. Paige threw up her hands as if to say, "Well, are you going to do anything about the prowler?"

Hands stuffed in her pockets, she crossed the lawn and bee-lined toward the cruiser. Her scowl should have warned him he was about to get an ear full. Yet the window didn't descend, and the officer stayed put in his seat, ignoring her.

"Hello? Did you not see the person knocking on my door? What the hell is wrong with you people?"

Oh, heads would roll tomorrow. She'd call the officer's supervisor, the idiot sheriff, the mayor. A dog barked from a few houses away as she rounded the vehicle. The officer leaned against the headrest. Paige issued a mirthless laugh. The son-of-a-bitch was asleep on the job. No wonder he hadn't responded to dispatch. She bet the jerk had turned his radio off so he could snooze. Meanwhile, the prowler might be inside her house.

Paige pounded her fist against the hood. A blast like a kettle drum. Hoping to jostle the trooper out of his dream, she paused when he didn't stir. Strange.

She moved to the window and tapped her fingernails against the glass. The driver's side window was halfway down to let in the summer air. As she tried to get the officer's attention, his head lolled over and struck the glass. Blood, as black as midnight, curled down from his neck and soaked his uniform. Paige opened her mouth to scream when footfalls thundered behind her.

She whirled and raised her arms as the pick ax arced through the night. The pointed end buried into her skull, splashing fresh blood against the macadam. Paige's hands grasped the air as though a ladder to heaven descended from the sky. Her knees buckled. Eyes rolled back in her head.

Paige Sutton crumpled against the blacktop as the shadowed killer vanished into the night.

39

SUNDAY, AUGUST 15TH 12:25 A.M.

Aguilar was already on the scene when Thomas drove into Paige Sutton's neighborhood. A throng of state troopers and Harmon police officers canvassed the block, shining their flashlights at every shadow and into every hidden corner. The police presence always grew with a killer at large. But when an officer died, the magnitude of the search increased tenfold. An air of hostility hung over the officers. They wanted to tear the neighborhood apart, piece by piece, and hand out frontier justice. Payback for taking one of their own.

Thomas hopped down from his truck and met Aguilar on the curb.

"What have you got?"

"A neighbor discovered Trooper Jamie McBride dead in his vehicle with his throat slashed outside Paige Sutton's house."

"Anybody see anything?"

"The woman across the street claims she heard a scream a little after eleven. She peeked out the window, expecting kids were screwing around, and noticed the state trooper cruiser. Assuming the situation was under control, she closed the curtains and went back to her television show. Rocky Cooper, who lives three doors down from

Paige Sutton, got home from the late shift at eleven-thirty. Says he thought Trooper McBride had fallen asleep. Cooper stopped his car and spotted the blood. A cruiser was already on the way, because McBride hadn't responded to calls from dispatch."

Thomas glanced at Paige Sutton's house. The door stood open, the house lit like a landing strip while officers searched the residence. The investigation team hadn't moved McBride's body. He sprawled in the driver's seat while the crime scene techs worked. A crowd gathered along the curb and gawked. A pair of officers held them behind the barricade.

"Take pictures of everyone in the crowd," Thomas said to Aguilar. "Be discreet. Don't let them know you're shooting photographs."

Sometimes killers returned to the scene. A few offered help and interjected themselves into the investigation. If their killer was in the crowd, Thomas wanted the maniac on camera. Aguilar weaved between the massing officers and lifted her camera.

Thomas turned his attention to Trooper McBride. No officer adjusted to the initial shock of seeing a dead person. Especially someone who fell victim to a violent murder. That McBride was a fellow officer wrenched Thomas's insides. Frailty. Every officer was one gunshot, one stab wound away from a funeral.

"Sheriff Shepherd?" Thomas turned and faced a mahogany-skinned trooper with specks of gray in his mustache. He towered six inches over Thomas, his body wiry, eyes hard. "Jordan Baker, New York State Police, Troop E. I knew your predecessor, Sheriff Gray." Baker's gaze traveled to the cruiser where the techs worked. He shifted his jaw. "Whoever did this is a monster. McBride had a wife and an eight-year-old daughter. Who's gonna explain to her that her daddy is never coming home."

"I'm sorry for your loss, Trooper Baker. Did you know the officer well?"

"For over ten years. Our families got together last winter for a ski trip. Always talked about hanging out more. Thought we had all the time in the world."

Thomas nodded.

"Any idea what happened here?"

"As far as we can tell, the killer sneaked up on McBride and slashed his throat while he was inside the cruiser. The window was open. He probably wanted fresh air to keep him alert."

Thomas eyed the blood splashed across the blacktop.

"That can't be McBride's."

"The blood appears to belong to another victim. Could be the killer's. But given that the home owner is missing..."

Baker cast a wary glance at Paige Sutton's house.

Had Paige witnessed the attack, run outside to aid the officer, and fallen victim to the killer? Or had she ventured outside to check on the officer, only to find his throat sliced while the killer watched her from the darkness?

The radio on Trooper Baker's shoulder crackled. He turned to Thomas.

"I'll be back in a second, Sheriff. Then we'll catch this scumbag. We can't let him escape our net."

The street was a mass of flashing emergency lights. Two ambulances parked along the curb amid the army of law enforcement vehicles. Camera in hand, Thomas angled his lens between two technicians and snapped a photograph. McBride's eyes were open, mouth agape. His hands had fallen to his lap. But blood covered one hand, coagulating between his fingers, suggesting he'd clutched at the gaping wound and attempted to stem the tide streaming out of his neck. Thomas couldn't help but wonder if Trooper McBride had been thinking about his wife and daughter, planning a late-summer trip, before his killer approached from behind. The psychopath must have taken McBride by surprise, as Thomas didn't see signs of a struggle. The kill was quick and efficient.

A female trooper with ebony eyes tipped her cap at Thomas from the curb. He nodded back at her, recognizing the woman from the Jeremy Hyde investigation. The state police had collaborated with the sheriff's department and Harmon PD during a citywide search for the murderer. So much loss had befallen Wolf Lake since spring.

His head swam. Thomas fought to keep his footing as the Los

Angeles shooting flashed before his eyes. He recalled the swirling emergency lights, the paramedic leaning over his twitching body as flies buzzed around his head, the winged parasites waiting for his heart to stop. But that wasn't the source of his panic. The screams around him drove him toward the edge of insanity. Unable to move, he didn't see who was injured and dying, could only fear the worst. How many officers had the bullets struck?

Without realizing what he was doing, Thomas placed a hand against the small of his back and winced, eyes squeezed shut. He drew stares from the other officers.

"You all right, Sheriff?" Aguilar's voice brought him back to the present. "Did you hurt yourself?"

"It's nothing." She raised a skeptical eyebrow. "Did you get pictures of the crowd?"

"Everybody."

"We'll comb the neighborhood. Someone must have seen a stranger hanging around Paige Sutton's house. In the meantime, find out where Cathy Webb was tonight."

40

The antique grandfather clock clicked from the hall. Inside the study, the counting seconds were the only sounds. Try as he might to ignore the clock, Thomas found his heartbeat following the swinging pendulum, regulating itself to his surroundings.

Heat poured through the vents despite the summer temperatures. His father, Mason Shepherd, slouched in his chair across from Thomas with a blanket over his legs, limbs quivering. The man's face had turned a sickly gray over the last month. Thomas didn't need a doctor's opinion to know time was short.

"How is the woman working out?" Mason asked.

He followed his question with a phlegm-choked cough into a handkerchief. Mason grimaced, folded the cloth, and stuffed it into his pocket.

"Naomi is doing well. She'll lead Shepherd Systems to its best quarter in company history."

Mason issued an uncommitted groan. He'd been against the hire, wanting Thomas to lead the company.

A glass clinked from the kitchen. Thomas wished his mother would join them and provide a buffer. He'd already asked his father the standard questions—how do you feel? Is there anything I can do to help?—but understood Mason Shepherd preferred not to discuss the progressing cancer, the black hand sealing his fate. Yet the lung cancer was the elephant in the room. The topic seemed unavoidable.

"I want you to know Shepherd Systems will always be in good hands," Thomas said, straightening his pants.

"It's a shame I won't be around to see it." Mason's eyes traveled around the room, taking in all he'd created via his wealth and power. He reached for his tea. The cup jiggled in his hand, liquid spilling down his lips as he sipped the hot drink. "I didn't do right by you, son."

Thomas lifted his head.

"Father?"

"I should have allowed you to follow your own path. Instead, I wasted years directing you." He set the tea aside and placed his gnarled hands over his knees. "Don't hate me for how I treated you."

"I could never hate you. I love you."

Mason pressed his lips together. His eyes glistened, and for a second, the natural color returned to his cheeks.

"Your mother and I wanted to protect you. It was a tactical mistake, one I should have recognized from the start. A parent's job is to keep his child safe. But it's also his job to step aside and let that child fly when he's ready. You've been ready for years. I was too stubborn to admit the truth."

Thomas slid his chair toward his father's and touched the man's hand. Mason, who'd turned sixty last month, appeared in his nineties. The disease had robbed the once powerful man of his vitality.

"You don't have to be scared for me."

"Don't I? You've already been shot, Thomas. And a murderer broke into your house and nearly took your life. Death follows you, and it scares the hell out of me."

Thomas glanced down. Liver spots covered his father's hand. The man withered away with each swing of the clock's pendulum.

"I've made it this far."

"Because you're a Shepherd." Meeting Thomas's eyes, Mason firmed his chin. "Long after I'm gone, the people will recognize you as the greatest sheriff this county has ever seen."

Thomas's throat constricted. Over the thirty-two years of his life, his father had been loath to compliment him.

"I'll make you proud, Father."

Mason Shepherd smiled.

"You already have."

RAVEN SET her keys on the desk and slid into a chair inside Wolf Lake Consulting. She was the only person inside the building, and her senses were on high alert as she perceived danger around every corner. Would she ever adjust to being alone?

She couldn't predict if her plan would work. A half-hour ago, after she'd talked with Thomas and confirmed he wasn't dating Naomi Mourning, she phoned Darren with her plan. Realizing Chelsey would ignore her calls, she had Darren call instead. Darren told Chelsey that Raven was alone at work and knee deep in cases. Raven hoped Chelsey had taken the bait. She hated lying to her friend. But this was the only way to get Chelsey alone.

The clock ticked past ten with no sign of Chelsey, as Raven fiddled with the computer and studied the topographic map of Wolf Lake State Park. The interconnecting trails convinced her the camp-ground thief and LeVar's intruder were one and the same. If fortune smiled upon Raven, she'd solve the Paul Phipps case and catch her brother's attacker. Sipping her coffee, she jumped in her seat when the front door opened and closed. Keys jingled, followed by footsteps.

She rose out of her chair as Chelsey turned the corner.

"Thanks for coming in," Raven said, extending her arm at the open chair.

Chelsey glanced suspiciously around the office.

"Darren said you couldn't keep up with today's cases. What's going on here?"

"Have a seat."

Chelsey opened her mouth to argue and bit her tongue before lowering herself into the chair. She folded her arms over her chest and glared.

"So you had Darren lie for you. Why? Last night wasn't enough? You need to watch me spiral out of control again?"

"You're not spiraling out of control. I understand what you're going through."

Chelsey scoffed.

"Nothing ever bothers you."

Raven crossed her legs at the ankles.

"What if I told you coming here alone terrified me?" Chelsey, who'd lowered her eyes, looked up. "I should have told you from the beginning. After Damian Ramos and Mark Benson kidnapped me, I started having panic attacks every time I was alone."

"I didn't know."

"Because I hid it from you. I confided in Darren. No one else knows."

"What is it you're afraid of?"

"I worry Ramos and Benson are following me, that they'll grab me the second I'm alone."

"But you have nothing to worry about. If the court gives them an early release, or they escape, we'll hear about it."

"The logical side of my brain realizes that. But the other side has a powerful voice." Raven leaned in and touched Chelsey's arm. "I didn't live through major depression. But I know a little about how our minds turn on us. You're not falling apart, anymore than I am. Now, let me help."

Chelsey's legs bounced with nervous energy.

"Raven, I don't think I can do this alone."

"You won't have to. We're in this together. But you need to be honest with me. What precipitated your anxiety attacks?"

Glancing away, Chelsey shrugged.

"My life has been one disappointment after another this last year."

"You've built a successful business, and you made a friend." Chelsey smiled back at Raven. "Life is never as bad as we fear. But we all need help from time to time. You're taking your medication?"

"Yes."

"I won't allow a repeat of what happened to you at eighteen. It's different this time, Chelsey. Doctors have better treatments for depression. You won't go into battle alone."

Instead of replying, Chelsey chewed her nails.

"Last month, you decided to try again with Thomas. We talked for over an hour about your decision. Then you went cold and refused to speak to me. What happened?"

"I was a fool for believing we could be together again. A guy like Thomas...he has his life under control. He's interim sheriff, he led two successful murder investigations, and now he owns Shepherd Systems. What would he want with a basket case?"

"Thomas has everything under control? His father has stage four lung cancer, and his parents almost died at the hands of a serial killer. And for the record, Thomas wants nothing to do with the family business. He signed the papers to save Shepherd Systems from falling apart."

"Either way, what we had ended fourteen years ago. We were foolish teenagers. Neither of us understood life."

"Yet you wanted to rekindle your relationship. I don't understand what changed."

Chelsey lowered her head and set her hands on her knees.

"Last month, after the Thea Barlow case, I drove to the lake. Believe me, I intended to make things right and finally tell Thomas how I feel."

"Why didn't you?"

"After I knocked, I searched for Thomas in the backyard and saw him beside the lake with Naomi and Scout. Thomas was embracing Naomi. They looked so happy together. I'd waited too long." Chelsey waved a hand through the air. "Not that it matters. Naomi is a kind woman, and Thomas deserves someone like her. I eliminated my friends from my life again."

The pieces fell into place in Raven's head. She slapped her forehead.

"I'm still here, and Thomas and Naomi aren't together."

"But I saw them on the shore."

"No, you saw Thomas offering Naomi a job. She's running operations at Shepherd Systems now."

Chelsey slung her hair off her face and creased her forehead.

"What?"

"Naomi fell into financial straits over Scout's medical bills. The poor woman lost her health insurance and accepted part-time jobs to put food on the table. Thomas recognized her value and brought her aboard. Chelsey, they were celebrating her job. They're not in a relationship."

For once, Chelsey was speechless.

41

L egs extended as he sat on the deck, a notebook computer balanced in his lap, Thomas scanned the digital case notes. There were no days off, no weekend breaks until he found Trooper McBride's killer and figured out who captured Justine Adkins and Paige Sutton. He wanted to believe the women were still alive. With so much blood spilled across the blacktop, he knew in his heart the attacker murdered Paige. But where was Justine?

He didn't trust Cathy Webb. But he also doubted her motivation to avenge Dawn Samson. Sure, she wanted justice for her cousin. But murder? If anyone wanted Dawn's tormentors killed, it was Alec Samson, the brother no one had heard from in years. Thomas needed a fresh perspective on Cathy Webb, a different opinion.

Dawn's junior year photograph filled his screen. Her kind, thoughtful eyes made Thomas wonder why anyone would hurt her.

Curtains fluttered inside LeVar's house as hip-hop thumped from the stereo. Which meant Scout was inside. The two shared recommendations on their favorite hip-hop artists, weighing the merits and weaknesses of each musician. The debates often turned into arguments, yet always ended with Scout and LeVar laughing.

Thomas carried his laptop to the guest house and knocked. The music stopped, and LeVar poked his head out of the door.

"Sorry, Chief. We too loud for y'all?"

"Not at all. I'd like your expert opinions on something."

"Well, then. Mi casa, su casa. Literally, since you own the place."

Thomas followed LeVar into the sitting room. Scout sat before the computer, the Wolf Lake High alumni website open in the browser.

"We're on the same wavelength this morning," Thomas said, gesturing at the monitor.

Scout shared a look with LeVar.

"We reached a dead end," she said. "I copied every message posted by Cathy Webb. Now I'm unsure where to go from here, or how to connect Webb to Skye Feron."

"What if I told you the skeleton in the park didn't belong to Skye Feron?"

They swung their heads to Thomas.

"For real?" LeVar asked.

"This stays between the three of us. We're not ready to release our findings to the press."

"We got you."

"I won't say anything," Scout said, nodding in agreement.

"So who's the girl in the state park?"

Thomas shifted his jaw and sat at the card table.

"I wish we knew. Something tells me Cathy Webb is involved. But we don't have evidence implicating her."

"Is she the person who killed that state trooper?"

"Possibly," Thomas said, though it didn't feel right. He opened his laptop and tapped the screen. "The issue is Cathy Webb's background. Her history is as much a black hole as Dawn Samson's brother's is."

LeVar took the chair across from Thomas and set his muscular forearms on the table.

"How so?"

"Webb grew up in Syracuse, graduated high school, then skipped college and moved outside Wolf Lake after Dawn's suicide."

"Okay."

"Thereafter, she moved Alec Samson into her house. A few years after that, Alec Samson's driver's license expired. No tax returns, no income. He disappeared."

"So how is his background similar to Cathy Webb's?" asked LeVar.

"Cathy Webb's license lapsed two years ago. She pays her taxes. Other than that, nobody knows her. She's just a hermit living outside the village."

"What happened to Dawn Samson's brother?"

"Webb claims Alec moved to Alaska."

"Sounds like dude is running from something."

Scout scrunched her face in thought.

"Is it possible someone murdered Alec Samson too? What if we're looking at this from the wrong angle, and the person who killed Skye also killed Alec?"

"What was the killer's motivation?"

LeVar snapped his fingers.

"There are two killers. Check this out. So Alec Samson goes crazy after his sister's suicide and gets revenge on her bullies by killing Skye. Then someone avenges Skye and murders Alec, hiding his body where nobody will find it."

"That makes for a good story," said Thomas, sitting back and clasping his hands over his belly. "But I'm not buying it. We can't even prove Skye Feron is dead. Why would Alec's killer target Paige and Justine next?"

The room turned quiet as LeVar and Scout considered the question. Outside the window, a motorboat raced across the lake and churned the water.

"Maybe we're asking the wrong question," said LeVar, sitting forward. "What made Cathy Webb turn into a recluse? Was she a loner in high school, or did something terrible happen to her? There must be some reason she became a hermit."

Thomas pushed a hand through his hair.

"Interesting idea. I checked Cathy Webb's yearbook. She doesn't have a class photo, so perhaps she really was a loner."

"Doesn't mean she's not in the yearbook," Scout said, wheeling around to the computer. "Kids miss their portraits all the time."

Scout typed at light speed and pulled up the digital yearbook from Webb's high school. As Thomas and LeVar watched, Scout scrolled past the portraits and skipped ahead to the athletic teams and clubs. Thomas scooted his chair forward as Scout paused over a student government picture. Five girls and three boys gathered around a table. The school banner draped over the edge. Scanning the names, Scout drew a breath.

"I found her. Cathy Webb was vice president of the senior class."

LeVar folded his arms.

"That doesn't sound like a loner to me. Cathy Webb was one of the popular girls."

Thomas slid his chair beside Scout and asked, "Can you zoom in on her face?"

"I'll try. But this is a low resolution photo. Don't expect wonders."

The blown-up version appeared blocky, too noisy to make out the girl's blurry face. Still, Thomas didn't recognize this girl as the woman he'd met outside Wolf Lake. People changed between their teens and twenties. But this girl didn't resemble the adult Cathy Webb at all.

"Find me another photograph."

Scout whipped through more pages, speed reading the names as her eyes processed the faces. Thomas was about to give up finding a different photograph of Cathy Webb when Scout stopped. Two dozen students in jogging shorts and leggings massed together in the woods, posing for the cross-country team photograph.

"There she is," Scout said, moving aside so Thomas had a better view.

"You're amazing, Scout."

This photograph appeared sharper than the student government picture. The lens zoomed in tight, yielding an unobstructed profile of Cathy Webb's face. The high cheekbones and bashful eyes were a perfect match for Dawn Samson. Even the hair was a similar length and style.

Except for one key difference.

Thomas's lips moved in silence as he stared at the girl's picture.

"You all right, Shep Dawg?"

He didn't register LeVar's question. The screen pulled him in, the puzzle slowly resolving itself in his mind as he recalled Dr. Stone's words.

"Your Jane Doe has what we call a class 2 malocclusion."

His mouth hung open as Thomas picked up the phone. Cathy Webb's prominent overbite commanded his attention. She was their Jane Doe, the murdered girl in the state park.

So who was the woman living in Cathy Webb's house? He recalled the unknown woman's sharp, black eyes and cropped dark hair, the sensation he'd seen her before. He had.

Alec Samson had never left Wolf Lake.

42

LeVar radioed Darren and Raven across the state park. Daylight made its last stand as trees encroached on the trail, boxing him in. Normally, he would have enjoyed the tranquility. But the fading light gave the forest a secretive, ominous quality that troubled him. Five minutes ago, the security cameras picked up a man in a hooded sweatshirt sneaking around the cabins. A screaming woman chased him off, and the prowler fled into the woods, a half-mile up the trail from LeVar's position.

He crouched between two hemlock trees and concealed himself within the spreading darkness, worried about Scout and Naomi. Chelsey Byrd had volunteered to stand guard over Naomi and her daughter, a sign the private investigator was coming out of her shell. But if a cold-blooded killer like Kilo threatened the family, would Chelsey pull the trigger and put the gangster down?

Thomas Shepherd's sudden departure an hour ago concerned LeVar. One moment, they'd studied Cathy Webb's picture. The next, Thomas grabbed his laptop and bolted for the door with a warning to stay together and keep the doors locked until he returned. That proclamation flew out the window when a hiker reported a suspicious figure watching the cabins from the forest. The sheriff had found his killer. It was plain on his face. What had Thomas learned from Cathy Webb's photo?

LeVar knew the Harmon Kings gang member who attacked him was the person stealing money from the cabins. It made sense. The state park provided cover and allowed the hood to watch the guest house from across the lake. While he was there, he pilfered money from unsecured cabins. Two birds, one stone. His radio squawked.

"Still there, LeVar?"

Darren's voice.

"Right here, bro. What you got?"

"Got a report of an unknown man hiding along the lake trail about a quarter-mile from your position."

"*Aight.* He's not getting past me."

"Don't engage him," Raven butted in. "He might be armed."

LeVar glanced at the hunting knife sheathed to his hip. He was armed too.

"Don't fret over me, Sis. I know everything about the Kings and how they roll. They won't surprise me."

Last week, while Raven purchased the security cameras in Syracuse, she also picked up three handheld radios. Perfect for communicating in areas of spotty cell coverage.

"We're moving in your direction," Darren said. "Flush him toward me and I'll take him down."

"Bet."

Except LeVar didn't intend to flush anyone out. The Kings set him up and tried to murder him in Harmon. They broke into his house, invaded his territory, and threatened his friends and family. The nightmare wouldn't end until he finished the fight. That meant cutting off the snake's head by taking out Rev.

An owl hooted from the hemlock. While he hid amid the foliage, the sun fell below the ridge line. Shadows thickened through the forest, obscuring his vision. LeVar blinked and rubbed his eyes, forcing his vision to adjust. He'd only get one shot at catching his attacker. Once the hood realized they were onto him, he'd stop using the state park and attack LeVar from a new angle.

He rose out of his crouch just as a branch rustled. Pulling back, he placed his body against the tree and peered around the side. The empty trail wound into the darkness. Blue dusk covered the sky.

"LeVar?"

He flinched at Raven's voice and flicked the radio off. It was just him and the gang member now. Two warriors who once fought together on the violent streets of Harmon. Only one of them would walk out of the forest tonight.

His eyes traveled to where he'd heard the noise. Saw only forest and thickening gloom. Something shifted at the edge of his vision. How had he not seen him before? The gangster hid behind the undergrowth a hundred feet from LeVar. He must have heard the radio, for the hood hunkered down, head swiveling as he took in the forest.

LeVar edged out from behind the hemlock and stepped toward a pine, his footsteps silent on a bed of fallen needles. The air was thick with humidity and evergreen scents. Animals scurried out of hiding and fled.

That's when he realized he didn't see the gangster anymore. He'd vanished from his position. Concerned his attacker was headed toward Raven and Darren, LeVar toyed with radioing them and breaking his silence. Too risky. This might be a trick. Staying in the woods, stepping across the soft forest bedding, LeVar was a silent predator. His skin prickled, body coursing with adrenaline. A few steps from the trail, he stopped and moved his gaze through the forest.

The fist exploded out of the dark and caught LeVar's chin, snapping his head back. Before he reacted, the shadowed figure leapt out of hiding and barreled his shoulder into LeVar's stomach, sending him backward. His spine collided with a fallen bough. The jagged end stabbed his flesh and drew blood as he scrambled away.

"Think you could walk away?" LeVar recognized the voice. The Kings hadn't sent Anthony, Lawson, or Kilo. Rev had come to finish the job. "I been watching you for weeks. Waited for this for too long."

The booted foot caught LeVar's head and whipped him sideways.

He sprawled in the dirt and leaves, fingers clawing at the soil as the forest spun around him. The next kick struck his ribs. Hot agony wrenched his body as he drew his knees to his chest and curled into a ball.

"You were my enforcer? What a joke. I could've bled you anytime I wanted, bitch."

As LeVar crawled to his knees, Rev pounded LeVar with a punch to the face. Blood spurted from his nose. He pushed himself to his feet before his knees buckled, the woods a confusing pattern of whirling motions. He swung blindly, intent on knocking Rev's head off his shoulders. The blow whipped harmlessly through the air. A low chuckle behind him revealed Rev's position. Too late for LeVar to react. Hauling LeVar up from behind, Rev snaked his powerful forearms around LeVar's neck. He squeezed, sapping LeVar's strength. Rev was going to kill him.

The arms around his throat constricted. LeVar gasped for air and reached out, desperate for a makeshift weapon or something to grab hold of. His hand fell to the sheathed knife. Rev hooked one arm around LeVar's elbow and pulled back, preventing LeVar from reaching his weapon. The other arm choked his life away as a cracking sound came from LeVar's neck.

"You're a nobody, LeVar. You never should have walked away from your real family. Shame. But when a dog goes bad, you gotta put her down."

LeVar whipped his head back and smashed it against Rev's face. Bones crunched in the gang leader's nose. Stunned, Rev's grip weakened. LeVar swung an elbow and caught Rev in the stomach, driving his attacker back. LeVar sucked air as Rev stumbled through the dark, fighting to regain his senses.

The forest turned red in LeVar's vision. As his strength returned, he zeroed in on the feared leader of the Harmon Kings. Rev doubled over, one arm wrapped around his stomach as he coughed blood. LeVar thought of the knife on his hip.

No. A quick kill would be too easy. He wanted the sociopath to suffer. Pay for the lives he stole while running Harmon's streets.

Rev recovered and raised his head a split-second before LeVar launched into him. His shoulder drove through Rev's midsection. The gangster's legs flew out from under him. He crashed back-first against the forest floor with LeVar atop him, fists raining down on his face. Rev raised his arms to cover up. But there was no stopping LeVar's fury.

"You shouldn't have threatened my friends." LeVar's punch snapped Rev's head backward. Blood flew from the man's mouth as LeVar smashed his fist against Rev's cheek. "I knew you were too stupid to leave me alone, Rev. You're a coward. You never would have survived Harmon without me watching your back."

Rev snatched the knife off LeVar's hip. The blade slashed at LeVar's arm and gashed his flesh. He cried out and fell as the gangster gasped for air and retched. LeVar covered his bleeding arm as Rev found his footing. The gangster stood hunched over, one hand on his knee, the other clutching the knife like a lifeline. A cruel smile twisted his lips. Instead of coming at LeVar with the knife, Rev tossed it aside. It landed somewhere between the trees. For a moment, LeVar thought Rev meant to settle the score with his fists. An unwise decision, even for a hardened criminal like Rev. Then Rev drew the revolver from his pocket.

"It's over, LeVar. First, I blow a hole in your head. Then I shoot that pig forest ranger you like so much and fuck your sister. I'll kill you slow, let you watch me rape the bitch."

A branch snapped on the trail. Rev swiveled his head toward the sound, giving LeVar the opening he needed. LeVar threw himself at Rev as the leader of the Harmon Kings raised the gun. The shot exploded and ripped past LeVar's skull. Taken by surprise, groggy from the battle, Rev lost hold of the gun. LeVar drove his fist against Rev's jaw. The gangster stumbled and propped himself against a tree as LeVar converged on him. Somewhere in the night, Raven shouted for LeVar to stop. He couldn't. Not until he finished Rev and ensured the psycho never threatened his family and friends again.

LeVar lifted Rev like the man was a rag doll. Hoisting the gang leader over his shoulder, LeVar spun and drove Rev against the ground. A gasp escaped Rev's chest. He lay wide-eyed and defense-less, the breath stolen from his body. He couldn't defend himself against the punches LeVar delivered. The gangster's eyes rolled back as LeVar pummeled the man's face. LeVar was a rabid dog, a force of nature Rev shouldn't have underestimated.

As LeVar raised his fist for the killing blow, someone dragged him off the unconscious gang leader.

"It's over, LeVar. Let him go."

Darren pulled LeVar to his feet, the former police officer unable to keep hold of LeVar. It wasn't until Raven rounded on her brother and pressed her hands against his cheeks that LeVar snapped out of his haze.

"Stop fighting. I won't lose my brother to prison over a stupid gang rivalry. Are you listening?"

LeVar blinked and glanced down at his bloodied hands, realizing he would have murdered Rev had Darren and Raven not stopped him. He thought of his new family—his mother, Scout, Naomi, Thomas. He couldn't let them down. This wasn't who LeVar was. Not anymore.

A choked sob came from his throat. He threw his arms around Raven's shoulders and cried for a long time.

43

Thomas checked his mirrors. Since he'd driven out of Wolf Lake into the depthless night, he'd sensed eyes on him. The road lay empty, the distant hills black monstrosities looming over the horizon. He had Aguilar on speaker phone as he rushed toward Cathy Webb's address on County Line Road.

"I'll arrive at the courthouse in fifteen minutes," said Aguilar. She would get the judge's signature at the courthouse to expedite the warrant. "Don't make a move until I join you." He didn't reply. "Thomas?"

"I heard you."

The centerline extended into the unknown, a line pulling him toward hell. For six years, a murderer had lived outside Wolf Lake with no one's knowledge. As he directed the cruiser around a curve, he remembered the real Cathy Webb's face. Except for the teenager's overbite, she looked exactly like her cousin, Dawn Samson. Dawn's suicide had driven Alec mad. The boy murdered his cousin, the kind woman who'd invited him into her house, because she was a carbon copy of his dead sister. A chill slid through Thomas.

Killing the headlights before he reached the decrepit home, he eased the cruiser onto the shoulder behind a stand of trees. He slipped into the night and watched the house through the branches. The screaming face of a full moon hung over the rooftop, the garage colored in deep azures. Silencing his phone and radio, he followed the tree line along the driveway. One light shone on the second floor. The silhouette of a woman brushing her hair played over a drawn shade. Thomas squinted at the figure. Inside, a speed metal rock song rattled the windows.

When the silhouette moved away from the window, Thomas crept down the driveway to the garage. Checked the door. Still locked. He rounded the garage and felt along the walls until he found what he sought. A crack in the wood, just large enough for his flashlight. He cast an eye at the house, worried he'd attracted Alec Samson's attention. Then he directed the light inside the garage. He stopped the beam on a dark blue Honda Odyssey. Flicked the light at the windshield and read the registration sticker —expired four years ago. No license plate. Just a paper copy mimicking the temporary license plates car dealerships placed on their vehicles.

Thomas doused the light and stepped away from the garage. He couldn't wait much longer for the warrant.

ALEC SAMSON APPLIED lipstick at the bedroom mirror. One leg crossed over the other with black fishnet stockings ending at mid-thigh, he puckered his lips and turned his face one way, then the other. He grinned at his profile.

The girl bleated from the neighboring bedroom. He turned the music louder to drown her out.

"You can't keep me locked in here!"

She pounded a fist against the bedroom door. Normally, he allowed his pet to wander the house as she wished. The doors locked from the inside and required keys. Concealed behind the blackout curtains, steel bars covered the first-story windows. Without a lower roof overhang, a leap from the second floor would guarantee shattered bones. It had been a few years since the girl last attempted escape.

But tonight was different. She raged against the bedroom door, screamed for release. He'd made a mistake last week, forgetting to lock the basement. She'd seen Justine. It snapped his pet out of her submissive state and reminded her of who she was, of what she once had. During her teenage years, she'd stood idly by and allowed Paige to torture his sister. He required repayment for her sins. A lifetime's worth.

Alec's hands curled into fists. His body trembled as he struggled to contain his fury. So many times he'd wanted to slam the girl against the wall and strangle the life out of her, glaring into her panicked eyes as he squeezed.

"You will be quiet now, or there will be punishment."

The pet turned silent for a moment. Then the pounding began again. This time with greater purpose, as if she meant to smash through the wood. The corner of his mouth twitched.

"Silence!"

His command had no effect. The walls shook as she threw her weight against the door. The sound like bombs exploding. Boom, boom, boom. His hands shook as he ran the brush through his gnarled hair. This is the way Cathy had responded after he locked her in the bedroom. She'd discovered his secret—the shack in the woods where he chained his pet and kept her hidden. Cathy finding out turned out to be a blessing in disguise. By eliminating his cousin, the girl who looked so much like Dawn, he had the house to himself. No more need for the shack. He moved his pet into the house, secured the doors and windows, and beat the girl into submission whenever she tried to flee.

But his world was falling apart tonight. It wasn't the infernal pounding that drove him mad. He sensed a change in the pattern. A drop in the pond, pushing concentric waves across the water, disturbing what lay hidden. His instinct told him to move away from the window.

Now he stood in the bedroom entryway as the girl hurled her

emaciated frame against the locked door across the hall. By now, she must have thrown her shoulder out of socket or cracked her collarbone. Yet her fervor intensified.

"Let me out!"

Heavy metal music blared through the hallway. Deafening. He clutched his ears, a breath away from ripping twin slices of flesh and cartilage off his head.

"Stop it." He screamed. "Stop it! Stop it!"

That's when the light flashed outside the bathroom window. A pinprick of illumination between the sill and the drawn shade. It was so subtle, it might have been a firefly.

Yet Alec Samson knew better. The break in the pattern. A fly caught in the spider's web.

He shuffled toward the window and stared out toward the garage.

"Here, piggy piggy."

44

Thomas grabbed his firearm when the screaming started. Though it was difficult to discern over the thundering music, there was no mistaking the woman's cries.

He checked his phone for Aguilar's message. She hadn't gotten the judge to sign the warrant yet. He radioed his position to dispatch and called for backup, knowing no one was coming. Aguilar was on the opposite side of Wolf Lake, and Lambert was home. It would take a half-hour for either of his deputies to reach County Line Road, and just as long before the state police arrived.

Then he was running at the leering fun house. The overgrown, dewy grass wicking his pant legs. Night hurtling past his face as deafening booms exploded upstairs, as if someone pounded holes in the walls.

He sensed, though he didn't see, the double bolted locks on the back door. He kicked the door open. It whipped into the kitchen and bashed the wall as he shone the flashlight over the dark interior.

"Nightshade County Sheriff's Department!"

The music mocked his pronouncement. Shook the walls and forced Thomas to place a hand over one ear. Loud noises had always disturbed him, a symptom of autism. The affect had worsened after the Los Angeles shooting.

Oblong light from upstairs fell over the lower landing. He aimed his gun up the staircase.

"Justine Adkins. Can you hear me?"

The hammering continued. Between the blasting music and the explosions reverberating through the walls, he couldn't tell where the sounds came from. Intent on climbing the stairs, he swung around when a woman cried out. From beneath his feet.

He peered down at the floorboards. The basement.

Gun raised with the barrel aimed up the staircase, he retreated from the speed metal and returned to the kitchen. Sweeping the flashlight across the kitchen, he spotted a door in the corner leading down to the basement. Two locks secured the door. They required keys.

"Justine Adkins, this is Sheriff Shepherd with the Nightshade County Sheriff's Department. You're safe."

"Get me out of here. He'll kill me!"

Thomas glanced around the room, hoping against hope the keys hung in the kitchen. No luck. He tugged the handle and found the reinforced door impossible to budge. Darkness crept inside the kitchen and slithered up to him, embracing his body with cold, dead hands. He swung his gaze over his shoulder. Knew Alec Samson was somewhere in the house and aware of Thomas's presence. Options flew through his head. He dare not shoot the locks without knowing the layout of the basement or where Alec Samson held Justine Adkins.

"Tell me where you are."

"I'm in the dark! He chained me to the wall. Open the door!"

"I need the keys, Justine. Stay calm. I'll be back for you as soon as I can unlock the door."

"Don't leave me down here. Please, please, please! Sheriff!"

Thomas hated to abandon her in that private hell a second longer. But he had no way to break into the basement, and a murderer was somewhere in the house.

The disorientating music and pounding pummeled his ears. Another scream. He thought it was Justine again. But this cry came from elsewhere. Another prisoner inside the house.

He hurried across the kitchen toward the threshold. Recognized the blind spot beyond the door. Always the most dangerous place. Breaths flew in and out of his chest as he pressed his back against the wall. Turned the corner and aimed the gun up the staircase. Then swung the weapon toward the darkened living room. The upstairs seemed too bright, almost as if the upper floor was ablaze.

As he stepped toward the stairs, the lights went out. Suffocating black. Interrupted only by the flash beam as he swept the light from the chipped plaster to the wobbling banister. Alec Samson had snuffed the power somehow, though the infernal music continued. Battery operated radio. Somehow, the music and explosions sounded louder in the dark.

He considered withdrawing to the kitchen. Shooting the locks out on the basement door, despite the risks. Then what? Shoot the chains off Justine's wrists and leave the second prisoner upstairs until help arrived?

A soiled shirt draped over the steps. He brushed it aside and waited for his eyes to adjust.

The cacophony masked his approach. A door stood open straight ahead. His brain resolved the familiar shapes—a sink and faucet with a toilet in the corner. Two closed doors to either side of the hallway. The one on his left buckled each time the prisoner threw her body against it.

"Who's out there?" The second prisoner's voice. "Please, I know someone is there. If you can hear me, my name is Skye Feron."

Thomas spun his head toward the door. Skye Feron. Impossible. Had Alec held the girl prisoner all these years?

He moved to the top of the staircase. One thin wall between him and whatever hid in the dark. The flashlight still shone. He considered turning it off so Samson wouldn't see his approach. But he couldn't bear that much black and place himself at the killer's mercy. Two danger areas. The bathroom and the open bedroom. If Samson wasn't inside either room, he'd fled to the attic crawlspace. Thomas's eyes widened until his head hurt.

He set his back against the wall. Reached out and tested the knob on the closed door. It wouldn't open. Like everything else in this murder house, it opened with a key. The jiggling handle got Skye screaming again. She knew he was on the other side of the door, that he represented freedom, escape, safe harbor. It killed him to leave her. He needed to eliminate the threat first. Then find the keys.

The plaster crumbled as he slid along the wall. He remained blind to the inside of the bathroom, except for the sink and toilet. The bedroom was a black abyss. And the noise. The slamming drums and screeching guitars.

Something reached out and touched his back. He spun with the gun aimed. It was just the jamb surrounding the bathroom entryway. Thomas swerved back and aimed at the bedroom. If he couldn't see Samson, the murderer couldn't see him. No movement. Not that it was possible to discern the killer shifting inside the bedroom, it was so dark.

His breaths came too fast and pushed him toward hyperventilation. First step. Clear the bathroom.

He swung into the room and swept the gun into the space. Moonlight bled around the drawn shade and pooled on the sill. Thomas rotated his body and directed the gun at the shower. Reached for the shower curtain a second before Alec Samson ripped the curtain aside and leapt at Thomas. In the split second it took him to react and squeeze the trigger, he spotted the pale white face, the wild eyes and mad leer, the knife.

Four blasts threw Samson backward and sprayed blood over the walls. He hung there for a moment, as if suspended by an invisible hand, then slumped into the tub, painting a long, red streak. Over the maddening music, he choked. "Kill them...both. For what they did. Kill them...pig."

Samson's eyes hung open long after the life fled his body. Thomas didn't want to turn his back on the murderer. He nudged Samson with his foot. The madman's neck lolled at an inhuman angle.

He swung the flashlight at the wall and flipped the switch, forgetting Samson had cut the power. Turned on the faucet and splashed water over his face. He stared at his silhouette in the mirror, wondering how different Alec Samson was from him. Tragedy pushed us over the edge. Did a monster lie dormant in each of us, hibernating until a crippling life event awakened the beast?

"Please! Open the door!"

Skye's voice snapped him out of his thoughts. He found the portable stereo in the bedroom and shut off the music. His ears rang. The girl beat her fists against the locked bedroom door with less fervor now.

"I need to find the key," he said from the other side.

"No, you can't leave me alone with him!"

"He's dead, Skye. I shot him."

A pause from the other side, the quiet suddenly loud.

"You can't kill death."

"He's just a man. He can't hurt you anymore."

45

Thomas never found the keys to unlock the doors. The state police broke the bedroom and basement doors down, and Deputy Aguilar led Skye Feron out of Alec Samson's house of horrors. Now in her mid-twenties, the emaciated, rail-thin girl hardly resembled her athletic former self. The haunted looks she shot Thomas, Lambert, and the male troopers at the scene spoke to the horrors she'd endured.

The media converged on Cathy Webb's house. How they found out so quickly, Thomas could only guess. They rushed the property with microphones and cameras and bright lights. Two vans with satellite dishes mounted on the roofs blocked traffic. Lambert forced the drivers to move the vans so the ambulance could reach the scene. It was a zoo. Worse than the scene outside the coroner's office after Dr. Stone excavated Cathy Webb's bones from the earth. That day, they'd all believed the skeleton belonged to Skye Feron. That she was alive stunned Thomas.

Bolt cutters broke the manacles securing Justine Adkins to the basement wall. The terrified woman stumbled through the front door with an army blanket draped over her shoulders. Three troopers drove the media back as flashbulbs lit the yard like lightning, and frantic voices begged for an interview, a sound bite, anything to boost ratings.

Neither Skye nor Justine lifted their eyes toward the law enforcement officers leading them to the ambulance. The women converged outside the emergency vehicle and stared at each other in stunned silence. Then Justine threw her arms around Skye as more cameras flashed. An overexuberant reporter with a razor-shaved face and perfect hair rushed the women. Aguilar forced him back with a warning.

A heavy hand clasped Thomas's shoulder. He turned around to Trooper Baker, the man he'd met outside Paige Sutton's house after Samson murdered Trooper McBride.

"Well done, Sheriff."

Thomas shook his head. He'd done nothing except pull the trigger. Were it not for the troopers, it would have taken hours to free the women.

"I don't understand. What drives a man to hold two women hostage and murder his own cousin?"

"You scored a touchdown for all of us. We want you to know we appreciate what you did here tonight. Can't have cop killers getting away with murder." After Thomas didn't respond, Baker cleared his throat. "We found a pickax in the garage with dried blood on the tip. Forensics took it away. You think that's what he used to kill Cathy Webb?" And Paige Sutton, Thomas thought. "Also a dark blue Honda Odyssey with an expired registration sticker. It matches the description the assistant manager at the supermarket saw the night Samson kidnapped Justine Adkins. All we lack is the murder weapon he used on Trooper McBride."

A shout from inside the house pulled their attention. Aguilar, Lambert, and two troopers were already sprinting toward the house. Lights shone from every window now that the power was on.

Thomas was the last to enter the home and climb the stairs, following the path he took before he shot Alec Samson. The crawlspace door hung open. A carrion stench rolled through the opening and overwhelmed the second floor. A mustached trooper turned and covered his mouth as the slender officer on the ladder motioned Thomas to climb up beside him. He followed the flashlight beam to Paige Sutton's body, stuffed in the crawlspace's corner and gathering flies. The woman's eyes stared at him, lifeless, frozen in perpetual horror.

"Tell Virgil he'll have a busy night," the trooper said.

Gallows humor, common among cops. Thomas heard too much of it from the homicide detectives in Los Angeles. He understood its purpose. You had to laugh at the dark and whistle while you passed the graveyard. Otherwise, the horrors would debilitate you.

"Virgil is on the way," Aguilar said behind him.

Thomas descended the ladder, the coppery scent of blood thick in the air. They'd found the last missing friend.

46

The news crews from the murder scene converged on the hospital as the clock passed the witching hour. Three officers stationed outside the emergency room doors prevented reporters from entering. Inside, a mix of friends and family members of the victims huddled together on uncomfortable vinyl couches, some in bathrobes, others with ruffled hair, shirts hanging out over their pants.

Spotting Aguilar near a door with DO NOT ENTER written across the front, Thomas veered around the throng. She tilted her head toward a blonde woman in a sweatshirt and pajama bottoms. A man in bifocals rubbed the woman's shoulder and whispered into her ear.

"That's Skye Feron's parents," said Aguilar.

"Have they seen their daughter?"

"Briefly. The mother refused to leave her daughter's side until the doctors forced her out. They're running tests, and a psychiatrist is coming in to evaluate Skye."

"So it doesn't appear she's going home soon."

"Afraid not." Aguilar held his eyes. "What about you? How are you holding up?"

He smirked.

"I'm sure Dr. Mandal will tell me. She always does."

"It's not a joke, Thomas. You've shot three murderers since April. One is enough to play with anyone's head. Are you sure you're okay?"

He released a breath. No, he wasn't sure. His thoughts meandered back to his father's words. Did his parents worry about Thomas falling victim to a stray bullet, or the daily stresses of the job catching up to him? Both paths led to destruction.

"I'll get through."

"Go home. Get some sleep. You look like death warmed over."

"I feel like it too." He brushed his hair back and studied Skye Feron's parents. Wondered what they must be thinking. They must be relieved Skye was back in their lives, yet terrified Alec Samson had stolen her sanity. "Not until I interview the women."

"They won't let you speak to Skye Feron. Not yet."

"Then I'll start with Justine and stay until the psychiatrist clears Skye."

"I can conduct the interviews, Thomas."

"Of course, you can. And when you decide you want to be sheriff, I'll hand the responsibility over to you."

"You're not thinking about quitting, are you?"

He touched her shoulder.

"Not yet."

Justine Adkins lifted her eyes when Thomas entered her room. The nurse outside the door gave him ten minutes to speak with Justine. Not a second longer. The woman's auburn hair appeared colorless beneath the florescent strip lighting. Almost black. Her curls matted against her face. A bandage wrapped around her head.

"Ms. Adkins, I'm Sheriff Thomas Shepherd."

She lowered her eyes and nodded.

"You're the one who shot Alec."

"Do you remember Dawn Samson's brother?"

She issued a choked sob and swiped a tissue under her nose.

"Vaguely. He said little during school. The kids used to claim his parents beat him."

Thomas gestured at the bandage.

"How's the head?"

"I'll be fine. I'm more worried about Skye. They won't let me see her."

"In time, you will. The doctors are checking her now. Be patient."

She fidgeted in the chair, favoring her shoulder.

"Is it true? Alec murdered Paige?"

Thomas shifted his jaw.

"I'm sorry."

Justine broke down and sobbed into her hands.

"We asked for this. All of us. But I never imagined it would end in murder."

Thomas pulled a chair beside Justine's and turned it around. He rested his elbows on the chair back.

"Can you tell me what happened?"

As Thomas took notes, Justine recounted the kidnapping in the supermarket parking lot and her imprisonment in Alec Samson's basement.

"I didn't recognize him from high school. We barely knew each other, and he'd changed a lot since graduation. Still, I realized it had to be Alec after he spoke about Dawn." Justine's eyes traveled to the wall and seemed to look toward a different time and place. "I didn't do enough to stop Paige. We'd been friends for so long—Skye, Paige, and me—and I didn't want to lose our friendship. But the bullying had gotten out of hand. Paige wouldn't listen, so I went to Dawn instead."

Thomas raised his eyes.

"Can you explain?"

"I wanted to be her friend. Dawn didn't trust me at first. Who could blame her? I ran with Paige, after all, and I'd stood by while Paige bullied Dawn at the tennis courts. We should have reported Paige, should have talked to her parents. I'll take the guilt to my grave. Dawn kept me at arm's length because of the trust issues. After several weeks, she realized I really was her friend. The problem was, I couldn't watch her twenty-four hours a day. It seemed Paige was always there to harass Dawn whenever I wasn't around to help."

"That must have upset Paige. You befriending her enemy."

Justine pushed her hair out of her eyes.

"She never found out. Dawn and I hid it well. I don't even think Alec knew."

"Did Skye?"

She shook her head.

"I'd meant to discuss it with Skye. She'd come to me many times, concerned over Paige's treatment of Dawn. Skye and Paige drifted apart. Skye always claimed she was too busy with sports to hang out. In the end, Alec blamed all of us for what happened. He was right to do so. But he realized Skye wanted to help back then, and I suspect that's why he kept her alive." A shiver rolled through her body. "He held Skye for six years and nobody found out."

Except Alec's cousin, Cathy Webb. And she paid the ultimate price.

47

L eVar peeked out of the alleyway as Anthony Fisher exited his apartment complex. The boy shot an anxious look across the street, as though he sensed eyes on him. After checking both ways, he jogged across the busy street, snatched a newspaper off a cafe table, and tucked the stolen item under his arm. His paranoia gone, the kid didn't appear to have a care in the world until he cut between the buildings and found LeVar waiting.

Anthony pulled up and reached behind him.

"I wouldn't do that if I were you," LeVar said, strolling up to the boy with an easy swagger. Anthony was more likely to shoot his own foot than put a bullet in LeVar. "It's time you and I talked."

Anthony took a step back and glanced around. There was nobody to help. A rancid smell rolled out of a rusty dumpster. Greasy scents blew through a restaurant fan.

"Don't want no trouble, LeVar. You know I was following orders."

LeVar backed Anthony against a brick wall and trapped the boy. Standing a head taller than Anthony, LeVar looked the gang member up and down.

"You set me up."

"I didn't have a choice."

"Did you threaten my friends on Rev's orders? Or was that the gangster wannabe in you talking?"

Anthony's eyes fell to his sneakers.

"I wouldn't have hurt nobody. Rev told me to put a scare into you."

"Rev told you," he scoffed. "Bad decisions will get your ass killed."

Anthony lifted his chin.

"Yeah? You gonna do it?"

LeVar grabbed Anthony by his shirt collar and shoved him against the bricks, one muscular arm pinning the flailing boy against the wall.

"If I bled you right here, nobody would care. You're just another gangster living on borrowed time. Shit, you didn't even pay for the damn newspaper." Anthony glanced at the paper tucked under his arm. LeVar tugged it away. "You don't know who I am, do you?"

"The enforcer for the Kings. We brothers."

"*Were* brothers. You and me stopped being blood when you talked shit about my own. And for the record, I was a lot more than the enforcer. Long before Rev came on the scene, I was the security that kept every Kings leader alive." LeVar swept an arm around the city. "None of this would be possible without me. Without LeVar keeping the wolves at bay, the Royals would've owned all this." LeVar's hand crept to Anthony's neck and gave a squeeze. Just enough pressure so the kid understood LeVar could snap his neck if he chose. "Hell, Rev would've carved you up and left you to the dogs had I not stepped in. I saved your ass, so that makes me your god, boy. We didn't have a sit down conversation about you. We had an understanding. Rev stayed in his lane, and he didn't get trucked by LeVar."

Anthony's knees buckled when LeVar released him. LeVar patted the boy's cheek.

"Ain't no Harmon Kings no more. Kilo and Lawson, they don't have stomachs for this. Now that Rev's gone, y'all gonna scatter like cockroaches when the Royals take over. This is your opportunity to change your ways. Take your Mom and get out of Harmon. Move up north with your family. Nothing here for you anymore."

LeVar held the boy's eyes for a second longer. Then he strode away with no fear Anthony would pull his gun now that LeVar had turned his back.

"You remember what I told you, lil bro," he said over his shoulder. "Don't make me come looking for you. Next time, you'll meet your maker."

48

FRIDAY, AUGUST 20TH 4:15 A.M.

Thomas jolted out of sleep. He sat up and caught his breath with Jack curled beside him. The big dog lifted his head and studied Thomas, who wiped his forehead on the bedsheet. A sliver of half-moon shone over the hills, starlight turning the lake silver.

In his dream, he'd been inside Alec Samson's house. While he directed the gun across the darkened upper landing, the doors shook with an inhuman fury. The pounding hurt his ears, forced him to cower. He feared what hid behind those doors. Somewhere, a woman screamed inside the house. And in the strange way of dreams, he'd known it was Chelsey. The fly caught in the spider's web.

He shook his head. Jack licked his hand and looked up at Thomas with his big doggy grin. Jack's smile had a way of disarming Thomas and setting him at ease. Sighing with the knowledge he'd never get back to sleep, Thomas rubbed Jack behind his ears.

"Wanna go outside, boy?" Jack apparently did, for he jumped off the bed and stood on his hind legs, pawing at the bedroom door. "All right. Let me get my shoes on first."

The morning was cool, dawn still two hours away. Fog curled off the lake and concealed the guest house. Jack did his business while

Thomas stood in the grass with his robe pulled tight, hands rubbing the chill off his arms. Summers had a way of slipping away in upstate New York. You needed to appreciate them while they were here, for tomorrow the leaves would fall, and the wind would bring snow and cold and a desolate landscape.

For a frozen moment, Jack stood still, tail erect, his eyes staring into the night. Thomas shuffled to the dog's side and followed his gaze. Something was in the fog.

"What is it, Jack?"

The dog didn't growl. Just glared into the mist, unmoving, ready to bound forward if a threat emerged. A splash followed as an unseen animal descended into the lake. Jack turned away and whined up at Thomas. He patted the dog's head.

His laptop sat open on the dining room table when Thomas returned inside. Locking the deck doors behind him, he filled the kettle with water and set it on the burner. From the cupboard, he removed a green tea packet and tore it open on the counter. While he waited for the water to heat, he jostled the computer out of sleep mode and called up the website for the *Bluewater Tribune*, Wolf Lake's newspaper. Scanning the headlines, he stopped on a story chronicling the Alec Samson case. The Psycho House. That's what the reporter called Samson's home.

Despite the sensational headline, the article focused on the Feron family's reunion with their daughter. Skye Feron would undergo years of therapy to come to grips with what happened. Thomas scratched his head and wondered how Skye's parents would bridge the chasm between them and their daughter.

The kettle whistled. Thomas poured the water into a travel mug and set the tea inside to steep. He'd attempted to interview Skye Feron at the hospital. By then, the woman had crept back into her shell and refused to speak with anyone. Except Justine. As Thomas understood it, the two women shared private conversations before the hospital released Skye.

The first hint of morning lay beyond the hills when his phone rang. He glanced down, saw the call was from his mother. A sick knowledge crawled into his belly. There was only one reason his mother would call this early.

"Mother, is everything all right?"

"He had a terrible night, Thomas. I'm talking to him, but he doesn't know who I am. It won't be long now."

"Is the nurse there?"

Mason Shepherd refused to leave his home. He'd die in familiar surroundings, not in a hospital room with cold, white walls, surrounded by doctors who dealt with tragedy daily. On Thomas's insistence, they'd hired a nurse to care for Mason last month. Since then, his deterioration had quickened.

"She's on the way."

"I'll be right there."

It was almost six when Thomas pulled his truck beside the curb in Poplar Hill Estates. He'd already phoned Aguilar to tell her he'd be late.

"Take as much time as you need, Sheriff," she'd said as he navigated the sleepy village roads. "You should be with your family today."

"Thank you, Aguilar. I'll call you when it's over."

Morning birdsong greeted him as he climbed down from the cab. The morning chill held firm, the fog following him from the lake to the mansion district. He gave the house one look, remembering the first time the training wheels came off his bicycle, the skinned knees, neighborhood friends who kept him grounded when things at home weren't so good. Once, he was young and foolish enough to believe life was forever, that there would always be a tomorrow to repair what lay broken.

Sadness coiled in his throat.

In his heart, he knew this was goodbye.

49

Fall came early to Wolf Lake that year. It rode an Alberta wind and frosted the grass on chilly mornings, painted fiery reds and yellows through the trees, and wilted flowers. The autumn wind rattled the windows on stormy nights, hunted the vacant alleyways in Harmon, and pushed leaves along the village sidewalks until tiny mountains pressed against doorways. Days remained mild, but nights reminded everyone winter was but a breath away.

The Times ran a national story on the Alec Samson case. The boy had a broken employment record after high school, including brief stints at fast-food restaurants and one office temp job for a law firm. His employment record concluded four years ago, and there was no evidence he ever left Wolf Lake and moved to Alaska. His parents were heavy drinkers. Two neighbors told *The Times* the mother and father beat Alec as a child. He'd formed an inseparable bond with his sister, Dawn, who suffered abuse at home and in school. She was Alec's lifeline, his reason for living. When she committed suicide, something broke inside Alec and couldn't be repaired.

Thomas closed the article and scrubbed a hand down his face. There was too much pain and injustice in the world.

Six weeks had passed since his father's death. The loss remained surreal. For thirty-two years, he'd barely known Mason Shepherd, despite growing up under the same roof. How ironic they'd formed a bond days before Mason's body surrendered to cancer. His father had known his time on earth was short. That's why he'd reached out to his son, affirming his love and confidence for the first time in Thomas's life.

Outside the window, the sun painted an intricate pattern of yellows and oranges as it filtered through the trees. Enough leaves covered the ground to justify raking, and more would fall over the coming week. Scout moved down the concrete pathway in her wheel-chair, while Naomi harvested what little remained from her backyard garden. A light shone inside the guest house, and Thomas spied two silhouettes inside. Raven was visiting her brother.

Thomas pushed the chair away from his desk. Jack lay at his feet, panting and grinning. The big dog's eyes kept wandering to the tennis ball in the corner.

"Okay, you convinced me," Thomas said, grabbing the ball.

Jack followed excitedly at his feet, almost slipping on the stairs. Once they reached the lower landing, the dog bounded for the deck door and swung his head back and forth, watching Naomi and her daughter. Thomas slid the door open, and Jack took off running. Then Scout was laughing as the dog set his massive paws on her lap and licked her face. Naomi waved to Thomas, who ordered Jack to get down before tossing the tennis ball across the spacious backyard.

While Jack retrieved the ball, Thomas shuffled to the garden. Naomi clutched an armful of squash.

"Good thing you picked them before the next frost. Let me help you."

She issued a relieved sigh and handed him half the harvest. They carried the squash inside the house and set the bounty on the counter. There was a sign on the wall that read, *What the,* with a fork beneath the words. Sauce simmered on the stove. The kitchen smelled like home.

On their way outside, Naomi said, "The sun feels nice. But it will be an early winter this year."

"We're overdue for a stormy winter," Thomas agreed. "It's hard to believe the lake will be a sheet of ice in a few months."

Jack brought the ball to Scout, who hurled the tennis ball toward the guest house with a giggle. The dog raced after the ball and woofed, tail wagging. Naomi's gaze traveled to Thomas's yard. She wiped her hands on her shirt.

"You have a visitor."

Thomas swung around, expecting Darren or one of his deputies. He caught his breath when he saw Chelsey standing beside the deck with a potted plant under her arm. Fiery streaks of sunlight mingled in her dark, shoulder-length hair. The wind tossed her wavy locks around. There was something in the way the light caught Chelsey's face that stopped his heart. Healthier than she'd appeared in months, Chelsey glanced uncertainly around the yard until her eyes settled on him.

"I'll call you later," Thomas said. "Are we still having dinner?"

"Don't worry about us," Naomi said, setting a hand on his arm. "We'll save you a plate. Go to her before you lose your nerve."

He felt naked after Naomi joined Scout. The wind shoved him around, prodded him to move his feet before he rooted himself to the ground. Stuffing his hands inside his pockets, he crossed the yard.

"Chelsey, I didn't expect you."

"I come bearing gifts," she said, handing over the plant. "It's not much, but I'm told they're quite beautiful once they mature."

"That was kind of you. I have just the place for it. Would you like to come inside and get out of the wind?"

She bit her lip. He was certain she'd decline, and that would be the last he'd see of her for weeks.

"I'd like that."

His mind raced as he walked her into the dining room. She hadn't set foot in his house since the night Jeremy Hyde tried to murder them.

"May I get you something to eat or drink? Maybe a—"

"Thomas, I'm sorry."

He leaned against the table.

"For what?"

"For being a fool. I should have been thrilled when you moved back to Wolf Lake. Instead, I panicked."

He pulled out a chair and sat, motioning for her to do the same. She ran a hand through her hair.

"I wasn't fair with you, Thomas. You always had the best intentions, and I was too stubborn to admit I was scared."

"Why? What were you afraid of?"

She looked at the ceiling and exhaled.

"Seeing you again reminded me of my depression. And that's not fair, because you had nothing to do with my sickness. I couldn't bear another bout. Ironically, pushing you away was the reason my depression returned."

He swallowed. Until now, he'd only suspected Chelsey suffered from depression. Hearing her admit it was a dagger through his stomach.

"I'm sorry this happened to you. I trust you're getting help."

She nodded.

"My doctor started me on an antidepressant and an anti-anxiety medication. And I see a therapist three times a week."

"How's that going?"

A pensive look came over her face. It morphed into a smile.

"It's working."

"I've spoken to a therapist since April. If you ever want to talk, my door is always open."

"I'll take you up on that offer."

He hadn't expected that response. Thomas cleared his throat.

"Thank you for the sympathy cards. My mother was especially pleased you wrote."

"I should have been there for you. Losing your father...it isn't right you went through that alone."

"It was for the best. He's not suffering, and my mother can heal."

"What about you, Thomas? Are you healing?"

His eyes moved to the yard where Raven and LeVar joined Naomi,

Scout, and Darren, who'd arrived to take Raven to lunch. Thomas smiled.

"I am. It's good to have loved ones so close."

She reached across the table and took his hands in hers.

"I've waited too long, and I understand if you're uncomfortable having me around. I've done little to inspire confidence. But I'd like to be part of your life, Thomas, if you'd allow it."

A sob wracked his chest.

"Yes, I'd like that. Very much."

A tear crawled down her cheek. She wiped it away and laughed.

"We're quite the pair, aren't we? Both of us in therapy and figuring out how to make it to the next day."

"It's easier when you have a friend who understands."

"So how do we do this? I'm not sure where to start."

Thomas leaned back in his chair and slid the door open.

"Well, we can't move forward until you meet Jack."

The dog rushed into the dining room as if summoned, his tongue hanging out as he glanced between Thomas and Chelsey.

"Jack, this is my good friend, Chelsey. Chelsey, Jack."

The dog barked and licked Chelsey's hand. She laughed and pet Jack's head.

"I'm already in love. He's perfect."

"He sure seems to like you."

Thomas raised his head as Darren led Raven and LeVar inside.

"Are we interrupting?" Darren asked, cocking an eyebrow when he noticed Chelsey.

"Not at all." Thomas smiled. A completeness he hadn't experienced in over a decade settled over him. "It's great to have the family together again."

～

Thank you for reading!
Ready for the next Wolf Lake thriller?
Read the Killing Moon Now

GET A FREE BOOK!

I'm a pretty nice guy once you look past the grisly images in my head. Most of all, I love connecting with awesome readers like you.

Join my VIP Reader Group and get a FREE serial killer thriller for your Kindle.

Get My Free Book

www.danpadavona.com/thriller-readers-vip-group/

SHOW YOUR SUPPORT FOR INDIE AUTHORS

Did you enjoy this book? If so, please let other thriller fans know by leaving a short review. Positive reviews help spread the word about independent authors and their novels. Thank you.

ABOUT THE AUTHOR

Dan Padavona is the author of The Darkwater Cove series, The Scarlett Bell thriller series, *Her Shallow Grave*, The Logan and Scarlett series, The Dark Vanishings series, *Camp Slasher, Quilt, Crawlspace, The Face of Midnight, Storberry, Shadow Witch*, and the horror anthology, *The Island*. He lives in upstate New York with his beautiful wife, Terri, and their children, Joe, and Julia. Dan is a meteorologist with NOAA's National Weather Service. Besides writing, he enjoys visiting amusement parks, beach vacations, Renaissance fairs, gardening, playing with the family dogs, and eating too much ice cream.

Visit Dan at: www.danpadavona.com

.

Made in United States
Orlando, FL
21 March 2022

15980318R00141